W9-BQS-766

The Marble Mask

ARCHER MAYOR

The Marble Mask

WHEELER
PUBLISHING, INC.
ROCKLAND, MA

★ AN AMERICAN COMPANY ★

√ PENN YAN PUBLIC LIBRARY

Penn

DISCARDED

NOV   2001

Copyright © 2000 by Archer Mayor
All rights reserved.

Published in Large Print by arrangement with Mysterious Press, an
imprint of Warner Books, in the United States and Canada

Wheeler Large Print Book Series.

Set in 16 pt Plantin.

Library of Congress Cataloging-in-Publication Data

Mayor, Archer.
    The marble mask / Archer Mayor.
        p. (large print) cm.(Wheeler large print book series)
    ISBN 1-58724-129-3 (softcover)
    1. Gunther, Joe (Fictitious character)—Fiction. 2. Police—Vermont—
Fiction. 3. Art thefts—Fiction. 4. Smuggling—Fiction. 5. Vermont—
Fiction. 6. Large type books. I Title.

[PS3563.A965 M37   2001]
813'.54—dc21   2001047440
                                                                        CIP

To Castle Freeman, Jr., with many thanks. A kind and thoughtful friend with a keen eye for detail, he is both a graceful, observant writer and a very good shot.

ACKNOWLEDGMENTS

Before I give thanks to the various organizations and individuals who helped me with this book, I feel I ought to explain two somewhat mysterious references that appear in the story that follows:

The first is the Vermont Bureau of Investigation—VBI—for which the hero, Joe Gunther, works. This organization does not exist in fact. It came about as a result of fictional events in an earlier Gunther book, *Occam's Razor,* in which I had the Legislature try to consolidate some of the many, occasionally redundant, law enforcement agencies in Vermont—and end up merely creating one more.

The second elusive reference refers to Michelangelo's *Mask of a Faun,* a sculpture he is purported to have created when he was only fifteen years old and which vanished from its Italian place of safekeeping, perhaps forever, during the turmoil of World War II. It is a true mystery I couldn't resist toying with.

None of which would matter if *The Marble Mask* had never been written, which it wouldn't have been without the help of those listed below, to name just a few. My apologies to anyone I may have inadvertently left out, and my thanks to all.

Hal and Charlotte Bills Annette and Jeff Goyne

Paco Aumand   Jim Walton
Karen Carroll   Dave Stanton
Joe Famolare   Ken Kaplan
Wayne Dengler   Dan Snyder
Marc Robert   Dorothy Wilkins
Bob Lussier   Robert and Diane Marier
Brian and
DeJane Hussey   Neil Van Dyke
Jim Leene   Guy Desmarais
Eric Buel   Alice Angney
Paul Morrow   John Martin

The Vermont State Police
The U.S. Attorney's Office, Vermont
The Stowe Police Department
The Windham County State Attorney's
   Office
The Vermont Forensic Lab
United States Customs
Sûreté Provinciale du Québec
The Brattleboro Police Department
Stowe Mountain Rescue
The Office of the Vermont Attorney General
The Vermont Medical Examiner's Office
The Vermont Department of Public Safety
The Royal Canadian Mounted Police

CHAPTER ONE

J oe. You still there? Talk to me, buddy."

I didn't open my eyes. It was so dark I felt if I did, more light might fall out than enter, sapping what little energy I had left. I remembered having the same sensation once as a kid, when my brother Leo and I had hidden in one of our father's grain boxes in the barn, closed the cover over us, and shut out all light and air. Lack of oxygen hadn't been the issue, though—we were out of there, pale and laughing too loudly, long before suffocation became a threat.

It was darkness that had defeated us—invasive, all-absorbing, reaching in through our wide-open eyes to extract whatever was keeping us alive. Squeezing my lids shut had been like hanging on to a cliff edge with my fingertips.

Which paradoxically made me wonder if suffocation could be a problem here, entombed as I was. Certainly I felt sleepy, which I'd heard was one of the signs, but then that counted for cold, too, and God knows I was cold.

"Joe? We need to know if you're still okay. Give us an indicator at least—hit the transmit button a couple of times if you don't feel like talking."

I really didn't. I was talked out—talking to them, talking to myself. I wasn't even sure where the radio was anymore. I'd shoved it under my coat when I'd pulled my arms out of the sleeves to turn my parka into a thermal straightjacket and better preserve my body heat. Besides, assuming I could find it, I doubted my fingers could operate the damn thing. That was probably why they'd told me to just hit the transmit button—they were guessing I was almost gone.

I thought about that for a moment, which was no mean feat in itself. My mind had been wandering for hours, easily bringing up images of my parents, life on the farm, Leo, times during combat I'd thought were the coldest a man could endure.

Until tonight.

But pondering the here and now was both a challenge and a bore—an impediment to more pleasant things. The vague memory that I hadn't lost the radio at all, but was still holding it in a numb and senseless hand, barely caused a flicker of concern. I was far too busy leafing through my life's album, evoking sunny, hot, open places.

And pictures of Gail.

I saw her above me, straddling my hips as I lay on the floor, her eyes narrowed, her mouth open just slightly. There was a faint shimmer of sweat on her upper lip as she raised her arms slowly, smoothly, and stripped off her T-shirt.

"Joe? It's Willy. Hang in there, pal. You croak, they'll nail me for sure. Don't be so god-damned self-centered."

What a guy, I thought—always the right word at the right time. What must his parents have been like?

I tried retrieving that last image of just seconds ago, remembering only that it had been of something pleasant and warm. I was beginning to feel warm again myself, in fact. At long last.

"Won't be too much longer," Willy resumed. "They say the storm's almost over—at least enough to try another sortie. Give us some kind of signal, though, will you? This playing coy shit is driving me nuts."

He'd always been an impatient man—always in a hurry and with nowhere to go. Not like Sammie, for example, equally driven but headed straight up the professional ladder.

Gail was ambitious, too, although a lot more complicated—one of the reasons we no longer lived together. Not that the love could be diminished—no matter the test.

I furrowed my brow, or thought I did. Sam and Willy and Gail and I were becoming blurred in my mind. Maybe there were similarities I'd never glimpsed before—he and I sort of stuck in our ways, the two women either using us as anchors, or fighting the pull of our inertia.

Surely there had to be more to it than that.

The radio spoke again, sounding like the last man to enter a noisy, crowded room—too far off to be understood. And I had too much to ponder anyway.

Let it go, I thought. Let me be.

CHAPTER TWO

Three Days Earlier

"Vermont Bureau of Investigation—Joe Gunther."

"It's Bill. You're sounding very official."

I looked across my small sunlit living room at the snow-covered trees outside, feeling more unemployed than official. "Try hopeful. This is the first time I've used this phone since you guys put it in last month. Is this a good-news call?"

"Good and bad—we've got a job, but you're going to be flying damn near solo."

Bill Allard was the chief of the newly formed VBI. Purportedly an exclusively major crimes unit with statewide jurisdiction, but as yet nonexistent except on paper, it had become a victim of the Department of Public Safety's face-saving "analysis paralysis."

"What've you got?" I asked him.

"You hear about the hiker who froze to death on Mount Mansfield?"

"Vaguely. There was something about it on the radio yesterday."

"The Stowe PD was trying to keep it under wraps, making it sound like an accident, but the medical examiner just ruled it a homicide. Anyhow, someone must've leaked it, because at the governor's weekly news conference this morning, a reporter asked if VBI was going to be called in. He didn't turn a hair, said, 'They're on it as we speak,' and went on to the next question. I scrambled to have the AG call Stowe's chief and offer him our services before the press told him he'd already accepted."

"The state police'll love that."

"Love it or not, it looks like we're out of the closet."

I was a little less sanguine. "Or Doctor Frankenstein's lab."

Sammie Martens took her eyes off the road to stare at me. "What the hell was he thinking?"

I shrugged and pulled out into the fast lane to pass an eighteen-wheeler slowly grinding its way uphill. We were shouldered in between Vermont's Green Mountains on one side and a serpentine river on the other, heading west on the interstate toward Burlington and the chief medical examiner's office.

"He was being governor," I explained. "Someone popped him a question and he answered accordingly. He didn't have to be thinking of anything so long as someone made it look like he was. Not that I'd complain," I added. "Without this, God knows when we might've been activated."

"What do we know about the dead guy?" Sammie asked.

"Not much that makes sense. He was found

frozen stiff high on the mountain, presumed to be a lost hiker with a Canadian ID, but missing a few body parts and according to Allard not looking at all like your run-of-the-mill tourist—whatever that means. Bill only said there was something about him that had everybody wondering. So now it's up to Vermont's version of the Untouchables to fill in the blanks, with or without resources, manpower, infrastructure, or equipment."

"Untouchables, hell," she said half to herself. "Unheard of is more likely."

I didn't agree with her there. Even if nonfunctional, we were almost as well known as Ben and Jerry's ice cream, at least locally— and as popular as the plague with every cop in the state.

The Vermont Bureau of Investigation had been the Legislature's reaction to a hot-button killing the year before, in which a communications breakdown among several police departments had led to a known criminal's remaining free until after he'd killed two kids. The original pipe dream—pushed by the same man who'd been elected governor on the strength of it—had been to replace the state's sixty-eight separate law enforcement agencies with a single coherent force. Instead, hounded by a lobbyist free-for-all, the Legislature had compromised by creating a face-saving sixty-ninth—a small, elite unit which, unlike the state police's Bureau of Criminal Investigation—BCI—whose ranks were filled only by state troopers, would be staffed by the cream of the crop from all departments.

But only if they supported it.

As with most grand visions, VBI was being seen so far as a device to steal away every department's top people and best cases.

The irony was that initially, I'd been one of those critics. A career veteran of the Brattleboro PD and the lieutenant in charge of its detective squad, I'd watched with disgust as an interesting trial balloon had been deflated by confusion and lack of support. When the time had come to fill VBI's ranks, I hadn't even applied.

Now I was its field force commander—the number-two man. A leap of faith I hadn't quite finished rationalizing.

Sammie seemed to be puzzling along similar lines, as well she might, being another newly anointed VBI special agent who'd been cooling her heels at home ever since. "What're we supposed to do here? Take over the case? None of this is turning out the way I thought it would."

I shook my head sympathetically. "Until I'm told otherwise, I'm looking at us more like the forensic lab, or the arson guys, or the bomb-disposal squad. We deliver manpower, expertise, contacts, and our own prosecutor to whoever asks for us, and we leave them with the collar, the kudos, and the headlines if we're successful."

"The Lone Ranger," she muttered, "making the town sheriff look good."

"Kind of," I agreed. "If we do it right, we'll get all the tough cases, act pretty much autonomously, and let whatever department head requested us handle the reporters, politicians, and the cranks. It's a cop's dream come true."

Hearing it out loud made it sound pretty good.

"If you weren't sure what this was," I asked her, perhaps hoping she wouldn't ask me the same question, "why did you sign up?"

Sammie flushed slightly. I knew she'd applied to VBI early on without telling me, while still on my squad in Brattleboro. She was smart, tough, persistent, and normally loyal, which I knew was embarrassing her now. But she'd always been hard-driving and ambitious, and I'd never expected her to stay with us forever—all of which was moot anyway, since I was once again her boss.

She began hesitantly. "I thought I could maybe learn a few things." She groped for something more meaningful in the face of an obviously different reality. Finally, she gave up. "It looked like an interesting opportunity."

I took her off the hook. "Me, too. Does what I just described help?"

She reflected a moment and then smiled. "It *sounds* great. You think it's realistic?"

I laughed. "Beats the hell out of me. How we perform right now'll probably tell us."

The ME's office in Burlington is tucked into a corner of Vermont's largest medical center, a happy beneficiary of the state's efforts to lock horns with competing hospitals in bordering New York and New Hampshire. Once located above a dentist off campus, Dr. Beverly Hillstrom's office was now extraordinarily well appointed and the source of considerable pride. Which was entirely fitting—over many years, and despite Vermont's small size and tight budgets, she had created one of the most efficient and highly respected medical examiner systems in the Northeast. These modern facilities were a long-overdue reflection of that.

She greeted us as soon as we were announced and escorted us down a gleaming hallway to the autopsy room at the far end, making well-mannered small talk along the way. Tall, slim, and Nordic in appearance, Hillstrom was of indefinable age and unmistakable bearing. Having worked closely together for years, we still referred to one another by title, and not once had she shared a single detail of her personal life. Yet the depth of our friendship was without doubt. She'd proven it many times, extending me courtesies she rarely granted others.

Titles, however, were causing her a problem right now.

"Lieutenant—in point of fact, that's no longer accurate, is it?" she asked as we neared the wide, blank door of her autopsy room.

"Not technically. I don't mind if you want to stick with it."

She shook her head. "No, no. That wouldn't do. How should I address you?"

I was still ambivalent about that. "It sounds a little silly, but we tore a page from the FBI book—officially I'm a Special Agent in Charge, or a SAC. Not that I'm in charge of anything yet. Why don't we just make it 'Mister,' with the understanding that I'd really prefer 'Joe.'"

She swung back the door and ushered us over the threshold, frowning slightly. "No. Mister is fine."

The room before us was broad, deep, bright, and neatly arranged, with a skylight overhead and two operating areas extending from the wall like twin boat slips. Laid out on one of the metal tables was a body so unusual in appearance, it looked more like a lab experiment than an autopsy candidate.

Standing next to it were two men, Hillstrom's longtime lab assistant Henry, and Ed Turner, a state trooper assigned to this office as its law enforcement liaison.

Turner raised his eyebrows as we entered, and greeted us with a reserve I knew we'd better get used to. He was, after all—and until or unless these prejudices were sorted out—a member of a "rival" agency. "Well, look at this—the feds that aren't. What're you doing here?"

I laughed and shook his hand, sensing Sammie tense beside me. "Just helping out the Stowe PD. How've you been keeping?"

Hillstrom, sensitive to matters of turf, quickly took over. "We have an approximately mid-forties male, in good physical condition aside from a few missing parts, who appears to have suffered a single fatal puncture wound to the heart, although we'll have to wait for toxicology to rule out anything additional. The body itself has thawed out," she explained further, "although some of the organs are still a

10

little hard. We're trying to speed things up by flushing them with warm water, but I don't want to move too quickly."

Sammie had been studying the open body with professional interest, staring down at its unusually dark red interior. Hillstrom's finding, however, made her look more carefully at the chest. "He was stabbed?" she asked.

Her confusion was understandable. The ME's patient was anything but traditional—its skin was red fading to a leathery brown, instead of the usual sickly yellow, its eyes were strangely sunken and dry, and its nose, ears, and fingers were dark, as if dipped in soot. It also was missing one arm and both feet, the amputations so clean, they looked cut through by a razor. But there was no sign of any violence aside from some bloodless scratches on the side of his face.

"You're reacting to how he looks," Hillstrom responded. "That's what stumped the Stowe police and the local assistant medical examiner, I'm embarrassed to say. It's also what led them to think that he might have just been a hiker who got lost and died of natural or environmental causes, perhaps scraping his face in the process."

She pulled on a pair of gloves, moved closer to the man's chest, and parted a few strands of his chest hair, revealing a tiny hole in the skin the size of a ruptured pimple. "There's the point of entry."

Sammie leaned so far over that her nose was inches from the wound. "What was it? It almost looks like a small-caliber bullet wound."

"He was run through," Ed Turner answered, "like with a shish kebab skewer."

I could see from Hillstrom's expression that she disagreed with the allusion, but she merely changed the subject. "Another interesting detail can be found with the victim's extremities, including the ears." She lifted his one remaining hand. "Notice the shriveling of the fingertips—its weatherbeaten quality?"

"Almost looks like a mummy," Sammie softly observed.

Hillstrom smiled broadly. "Very good, Agent Martens. That's exactly right."

"Implying he's been around for a while," I suggested.

"Longer than you think, I bet," Turner added, his earlier reserve now gone.

He crossed over to a pile of clothes on a nearby table and spread the top garment out for examination—a curiously constructed wool herringbone jacket with a belt across the back. It was worn, tattered, and faded. "Look at his duds."

Sammie glanced at it from where she was standing. "Looks like something out of a pseudo good-old-days catalogue."

Turner shook his head. "Not pseudo. We're thinking it's the real McCoy. Check out the rest of it."

We gathered around him as he displayed it all—wool pants and shirt, cashmere sweater, silk underwear. It reminded me of an old movie about a debonair city slicker going country for the weekend.

I reached out and fingered the material. It

was coarse and brittle despite its high quality, and much of it was in shreds, especially along the same side as the scratches on the body's face. "How old is it?"

Turner laughed. "Wild guess? Nineteen forty-five, six, or seven—in that range."

"You having a good time?" Sammie asked testily. "How're you so sure?"

He waved a hand in apology. "I'm sorry. This one's just so far off the charts. Here." He extended a small plastic bag to her from a sampling of similarly protected documents. Inside was a single piece of thick paper.

Sammie studied it a moment, turned it over, and finally gave it to me. "It's a Canadian driver's license, expires nineteen forty-seven. Name of Jean Deschamps."

I glanced at it. "That's it?"

Ed passed the other documents around. "No, no. He had all the usual stuff—money, business cards, kids' photos, picture of a guy in uniform, what looks like an ancient credit card for a Sherbrooke oil company, presumably for his car. There's also an identity card with his photograph, birth date, and address. It all looks like it came straight out of a museum."

"Let's see the paper money," I requested.

He handed me another envelope. "There's about five hundred dollars, Canadian," he said. "Good for a short vacation."

I didn't need to check for dates to know the currency predated 1952. Queen Elizabeth's profile was conspicuously absent from any of the bills, in favor of her father, King George VI.

"Not right after the war, it wasn't," I countered. "Adjusting for inflation, that's worth close to three thousand dollars, and even that's misleading, since three thousand back then bought a lot more than it does now." I waved my hand at the pile of clothes. "And those aren't for hiking—they're just dandified countrywear."

"I think so, too," Beverly Hillstrom said from behind me.

I turned to her. "So, what are we looking at? A man dead for fifty years, or something disguised to make us think so?"

"The answer," she said, "might lie in the depth of his refrigeration. Generally in hypothermia cases, we can either see or regain some degree of flaccidity shortly after we take possession of the body, even with the complication of rigor mortis. Here we had a subject frozen through and through at something around twenty degrees below zero, centigrade—a unique situation in my personal experience. And I would say that what Agent Martens identified as mummification is also in part what I would call old-fashioned freezer burn.

"Finally, add that to the equation," she waved her hand at the clothes and documents, "along with the three amputations and the postmortem scrapes on his face, and I would venture that our friend has not only been in this state for a very long time, but that he was brutally handled recently, resulting not in the severing but the breaking off of some of his anatomy. I studied the points of separation carefully, and they show little sign of the weathering the rest of the body's suffered, and no signs whatsoever of slicing, chopping, or sawing."

"Pretty unlikely Mount Mansfield had much to do with any of this," I suggested, mostly to myself.

Beverly Hillstrom smiled slightly. "I would agree."

"What about the amputations?" Sammie asked.

"One hypothesis," Hillstrom answered, "might involve dropping. If the frozen body hit a rocky outcropping or an icy surface at the proper angle, parts of it could break off or even shatter upon impact, as with a marble statue. That would also explain the lacerations and the torn clothes."

I looked over at Ed Turner. "Did the Stowe PD search the area?"

He nodded. "They didn't find anything."

"The body could have been dropped prior to its final delivery on the mountain," Hillstrom suggested. "Mr. Deschamps was not a small man, and in that condition must have been quite difficult to handle."

"So we might find an arm or a foot in a Dumpster somewhere," Sammie ventured.

I glanced around the room, restless with all this abstract musing. Until I recalled a small reaction of Hillstrom's earlier.

"What do *you* think caused that puncture to the heart?" I asked her.

She returned to the side of the presumed Mr. Deschamps and placed her finger gently

15

on his chest. "It may not be possible to prove, but my suspicion is that it looks odd because it's rare—another indicator that all this happened long ago. I think he may have been killed by an old domestic standby, both in fact and in the movies: an ice pick. You don't see many of them nowadays. And certainly not as a lethal weapon."

CHAPTER THREE

The Department of Public Safety is located in the small town of Waterbury, not far from Vermont's capital of Montpelier, in an aging complex of state buildings, which includes the old insane asylum—now partially converted into a women's prison. Like the others on this campus, the red brick home of the DPS is unenlightening to look at—large, plain, and stolid—and as functionally awkward as the average crumbling high school everyone wishes they could afford to demolish.

Bill Allard's office, and the technical heart of the VBI, was a small cubbyhole located on the top floor, just above the second-floor headquarters of the Vermont State Police.

Allard welcomed Sammie and me with a broad smile, handshakes, and the offer of two guest chairs, one of which had obviously been stuffed into the room especially for the occasion. We gained our seats with as much decorum as possible, trying not to make it look as though we were picking through a cluttered closet.

"What did you find out?" he asked once we'd settled down.

He was a thoroughly likable man, once a captain downstairs, a veteran state trooper of almost twenty years who'd done stints in every department from BCI to Internal Affairs to Intelligence, and had proven himself capable at all of them. His being chosen as bureau chief of VBI by the Commissioner of Public Safety had been at once a concession to the slighted state police and a demonstration of keen insight. I knew of no one who didn't think highly of Bill Allard, even while I was sure that his appointment would strike other agencies as ironic proof that the VSP was in control of VBI.

"From what we know right now," I answered him, "this is no slam dunk. It looks like the body was a Canadian named Jean Deschamps who was killed with an ice pick around nineteen forty-six or seven and then frozen solid for fifty-plus years."

Allard pushed out his lower lip and stared at his desk top for a moment. "What's your plan of attack?" he finally asked, avoiding a lot of questions he knew we couldn't answer.

"The address on Deschamps's driver's license is Sherbrooke, Québec. We probably ought to start there, running what we've got by the local cops. I don't know if it's a munic-

17

ipal department, the provincial police, or the Mounties covering that area, but one or all of them might have this guy on a missing persons list. Confirming his identity would be a good start. 'Course that all depends on what Stowe PD's been up to and what they want us to do."

"Sherbrooke has a new joint police department including it and a bunch of its suburbs," Allard said, pointedly ignoring my last comment. "As for the Royal Canadian Mounted Police, I'd check their records but rely on the Sûreté Provinciale du Québec for any help. The Sûreté *is* the RCMP up there— part of that Anglo/Franco battle they're having all the time."

"Who actually has this case right now?" Sammie asked, stranded between the support role I was implying and Bill's proprietary tone.

Allard looked at her curiously, which didn't strike me as a good sign.

His answer confirmed my doubts, and revealed how political expedience had invaded our own organization. "Stowe initiated the case, of course. But the ball's pretty much ours. No way they're going to be committing people to this kind of goose chase."

Sammie glanced at me and raised her eyebrows. I sighed inaudibly and asked, "Exactly how did that conversation go with Stowe's chief? Frank Auerbach? He runs a pretty tight department—well equipped, well organized. A full-service outfit."

The pause in the conversation told me Bill

18

got my point. "You and I have hashed this over before, Joe," he finally said. "Our charter specifies we can initiate investigations where we see fit." He held his hand up as I opened my mouth to respond. "Not that we're doing that here. After the AG paved the way following the ME's initial report this morning, I called Auerbach to introduce myself. I offered him our services in case the need should arise, nice and polite. He thanked me very much."

Allard sat back in his chair and crossed his arms.

"He hasn't officially accepted us?" I asked, trying to keep calm. "I thought we were already on board. That's what I told Ed Turner in Burlington, who by now has probably spread it all over downstairs, maybe even back to Auerbach."

He shrugged. "Look. No one's a virgin here. The Legislature may have created us, but we're already ancient history. It's a brand-new session stuffed with freshmen, and so far they've been happy to let us hang in the wind. Every cop shop in Vermont is hoping we'll vanish without a trace, and if the governor doesn't hear some good news after bragging to the press this morning, that's probably what'll happen. We're going to have to be a little pushy to start with, Joe, or we're not going to survive. Auerbach's going to need help with this. He'll know that as soon as the ME gives him her report. All I and the AG did was make it diplomatic for him to ask for us instead of the state police. Heavy-handed, maybe—underhanded if you want—and maybe you'll have to smooth a few feathers because of it, but at least you'll be in business."

I couldn't argue with him. He was absolutely right about our shelf life. Our co-existence with other units was going to be initially bumpy in any case—either because we were untested or because we were seen as competition. We might as well just get started, show some signs of life, and try to work out the details along the way.

But if that was the plan, I had an additional problem. "Bill, as far as I know, you and I are the only two people on the VBI payroll with assigned responsibilities. Sammie here got a welcome aboard letter, as did a bunch of other people, but none of them have heard a word since. Now I know the Bureau's supposed to have regional offices, and that Stowe and Brattleboro couldn't be much farther apart, but if we're going to play this like a pickup game, I'd like to select my own team—just this once. Given how disorganized things are, I don't think it'll bother anyone, especially if it leads to more cases."

Allard seemed relieved by my acceptance of his backdoor strategy concerning Auerbach. "Sure," he said. "Who do you want?"

"Sam, for one," I told him, "and Willy Kunkle for another."

Allard rubbed his chin with his finger. "Name rings a bell. Doesn't he have a little attitude problem?"

Neither Sammie nor I said a word, but the question alone told me Kunkle's name had come up in at least one context in this building.

After an awkward pause, he added, "I'm not sure what the status is on his application, to be honest. And that's one part of the process I don't want to fool with right now—can't be seen playing favorites."

I seriously doubted Willy Kunkle was anyone's favorite, including mine, and he'd worked on my squad alongside Sammie for years. A recovering alcoholic, he'd beaten his wife before she left him over ten years ago, and he was cynical, sharp-tongued, dismissive of others, and difficult to work with. He was also smart, honest, hard-working, and an excellent cop despite his faults, which made him even harder on himself than he was on others—no small statement. No one aside from Sammie understood what I saw in Willy, or why time after time I'd gone out on a limb to save his career. There was more to it than his simply being good at his job—dozens of others were as capable, and all of them were a hell of a lot more pleasant. But I'd seen value in aiding in his redemption and been rewarded with signs of progress, not the least of which was Willie's discreet, still largely unknown romantic pairing with Sammie. Childless and a widower, perhaps I wanted for Willy what a parent wants for a troubled but promising son. He had fought off the bottle, learned to control his physical outbursts, dealt with a bullet wound that had left him with a withered, useless left arm, and had been caught being sensitive and considerate when he thought nobody was watching.

But my leaving the Brattleboro department had threatened that evolution. My old chief, Tony Brandt, while a supportive and considerate boss, had made it clear that without my protection, Willy was a targeted man. Anticipating that, I'd already made the consideration of his VBI application a condition of my own signing on, something the commissioner had agreed to only reluctantly. I'd stressed then that all I was requesting was that the man get the same fair scrutiny we'd all received.

Allard's reaction made me realize my request might not have been honored.

I wasn't surprised, but I hated to think that all I'd done by helping Kunkle was to perhaps set him up for the hardest fall of all.

"Who does know what his status is?" I asked. "The commissioner?"

"He's head of the selection committee," Allard answered indirectly.

I nodded toward the phone on his desk. "Let's give him a call, then."

Bill Allard frowned. He didn't know Willy Kunkle, as did Commissioner Stanton, but this was not playing ball, as the political vernacular had it. In one stroke, I'd picked a fight and gone over his head before our very first case was a day old—all over a man of dubious pedigree.

He made the call. Next to me, Sammie was looking as if she wanted to melt into the floor.

David Stanton didn't look happy, either, when the three of us filed into his office one flight down five minutes later.

A tall, skinny man with a mop of thick, tangled hair, he was a keen organizational animal—smart, ambitious, and restless to make his mark. In the early blueprints of what VBI was to be but didn't become, Stanton had been slated for a cabinet secretary rating. His failure had dulled his interest in the whole experiment.

"What's up?" he asked without preamble, not bothering to shake hands or greet us by name.

Allard spoke first. "Since the governor caught us flat-footed, we're trying to cobble together a squad with minimal break-in needs."

It was the preferred indirect approach, but I didn't feel like wasting time any more than Stanton did. I might have also been reacting to his perfunctory tone. "I'd like Willy Kunkle."

Bill tried softening the message. "I didn't know the status of his application."

Stanton kept his watchful eyes on me. "He's in the pipeline, Joe, along with several others."

"Maybe so, but since proper procedure's already out the window, let's cut corners," I suggested, matching his stare.

"I don't think that would be a good idea, not right out of the starting gate."

"Why not?" I asked, anger slowly beginning to build in my chest. "When were you going to decide about him?"

Stanton's mouth tightened slightly. "It's not up to me alone. There's a panel—"

"Which you bypassed to hire me," I interrupted.

"You were a special case," he said, giving the comment a clear double meaning. "Kunkle doesn't fit that category."

I turned to the door, resting my hand on the knob. "Maybe you got me wrong."

"Don't be so melodramatic, Joe," he said with an exasperated sigh. "When you signed on, the deal was we consider Kunkle's application along with everyone else's. We're doing that. You can't force us to accept him—it wouldn't be ethical."

I laughed, the frustration of waiting around for weeks coming to a boil. "Ethical? You didn't want him to begin with, and it's starting to look like you've lost interest in VBI. If Willy really is under consideration, and not just being jerked around to keep me quiet, now would be a good time to show some good faith. Let me have him for this case on a provisional basis. Call him a consultant if you want, instead of a special agent, and make his performance a factor in his passing muster, but give the poor bastard a chance, stop treating me like some senile chump, and let the Bureau prove itself in the real world."

Stanton scowled at me. "I made you SAC of the whole outfit, for Christ's sake, and I'm one of the few people who *doesn't* want the Bureau chopped off at the knees. Everyone has the highest respect for you. *You're* the one putting a monkey wrench into the works with your obsession with this guy."

I didn't say a word, but I left my hand on the doorknob.

He finally relented, which ironically highlighted his ambivalence about our fate, since if ever there was a time to call my bluff, it was now. "All right, you can have Kunkle—provisionally. He's not to have VBI credentials, and once this case is over, whether he's accepted or not, I don't want to have this conversation again.

"And," he added, pointing his finger at Bill Allard, "I want at least two more people of *your* choosing assigned to this, regardless of how many break-in problems it might create. They are not to be from Brattleboro or Windham County or even from the southeast corner of the state. If Kunkle's going to be part of the equation, I want him counterbalanced with the best you can get your hands on. In fact," he added after a brief pause, "why don't you pull in someone from BCI as an unofficial intern? That way, Kunkle won't be alone, it'll help show we're not a closed shop, and maybe word'll leak back to the BCI rank-and-file that we're not the threat their brass is making us out to be."

He shifted his glare to me. "That better be acceptable, Joe, or you damn well *can* walk out that door."

I smiled at him instead, amazed I'd gotten away with it. "Don't worry, Dave. This won't bite you in the ass."

He shook his head. "The way I see it, it already has."

Bill Allard laughed as we shoehorned ourselves back into his office. "Christ, that was hardball. What's with this Willy Kunkle guy?"

25

Sammie rolled her eyes. "If you have to ask, you obviously *don't* know the man."

She knew that better than most. Still, I saw the relief in her face and hoped my gambit would benefit both Willy and her.

By conventional wisdom, however, neither chicanery nor time would be kind to them. Opinionated, headstrong, and passionate, they were fated to clash more than they might commingle. Which probably should have concerned me as their boss. But I'd known them for years and had seen their focus on the job, which is no doubt why they'd remained such perennial loners so far.

There was an additional influence working on me, of course, more personal and elusive. My own years-long relationship with Gail was undergoing some adjustment, ever since we'd decided to go back to living apart and she'd taken a job in Montpelier for half of each year. We'd shared a house only briefly— and then only because she'd needed to rebuild herself after a harrowing sexual assault—but I'd grown used to the domesticity and was by nature less driven than she to climb a career ladder.

Which made nurturing Sam and Willy's odd romance all the more instinctive.

"Willy's definitely an acquired taste," I explained to Bill, "but he's a dog with a bone on something like this, and I'm used to working with him."

Allard slid behind his desk. "So who else do you want?"

I watched him carefully. "That's a little

26

risky, isn't it? Given Stanton's marching orders."

He allowed a thin smile, revealing a bit of what had made him so successful within the ranks of the state police. "Stanton's a good guy—savvy at paddling his chosen waters." He paused and then added, "But he's not Bureau chief."

"Nevertheless," I said, "I don't want to be too obvious. He did say to pick someone from outside Windham County. How 'bout Lester Spinney?"

Sammie Martens immediately laughed, reminded of Spinney's famous sense of humor. "I didn't know he'd joined up. I thought he was happy investigating for the Attorney General."

"He was happy working for Kathy Bartlett," I emphasized, "but when the AG made her VBI special prosecutor, he figured he'd tag along."

But Bill shook his head. "Maybe later, if things start heating up, but even I know you've worked with Spinney before. Stanton's bound to smell a rat. We need some relative stranger we think'll fit your style."

I was stumped. I knew quite a few of the approximately one thousand full-time cops in the state, but only a handful had risked joining the Bureau so far. A conservative bunch by nature, police officers were inclined to sit back and watch when politics were in motion.

"You know Paul Spraiger?" Allard asked.

"I know his boss," I answered, "assuming he's the Spraiger from the Burlington PD."

"One and the same. A twelve-year veteran.

He was about to be rotated back into uniform when he decided he'd gotten used to plain-clothes. He's a quiet guy, a good interrogator—has a way of making people feel comfortable. Incredibly smart but keeps it to himself. He also speaks French, which might come in handy."

I nodded. "Sounds good. What about the BCI intern?"

This time, Allard didn't hesitate. "Tom Shanklin. He's in the Middlesex barracks right now—a good people person, easy to get along with, popular with the troops, and a gung-ho Green-and-Gold type, but not obnoxious. If we can turn him around to what we're up to, he'd be a great ambassador."

"He been with BCI long?" Sammie asked, obviously mistrustful of all the strategizing.

Bill tried putting her at ease. "Oh yeah, years. He's worked several major cases on his own. He'll be an asset."

I'd heard only good of Tom Shanklin, although we'd never met. I rose to my feet. "Okay by me, and unless you feel otherwise, we might as well keep it at five total for the moment, till we know what we're facing. You want to meet with us once we're all assembled?"

Allard's smile suggested otherwise. "Give you all a rousing speech? I don't think so. You're the field man, Joe. Run things as you see fit. Just keep me informed and let me know when you need help."

He escorted us four feet to his door and shook us both by the hand. "It looks like a good case to start with—custom-made for what we can offer. Maybe the governor wasn't so crazy, after all."

Sammie merely smiled politely, no doubt wondering what she'd done to her career.

I felt no such constraints. "Well, if he was, we'll probably all be out of a job soon enough."

CHAPTER FOUR

To most people—especially those "from away"—Stowe, Vermont, means downhill skiing. Which, sadly but understandably, counts for a great deal, since Vermont itself has been reduced to skiing, maple sugar, fall foliage, quaint villages, black-and-white cows, taciturn people who make for lousy waiters, and, just maybe, the eccentric top competitor in the luxury ice cream market.

Not surprisingly, the town didn't start as a ski resort. The mountain that has made it such isn't even named Stowe, but Mount Mansfield, and the village can follow its roots back to when skiing was unheard of and lumber its primary cash source. But it is tourist-dependent now, to the point where most of its money actually comes in during the summer months, and many of its key decision-makers are originally from out of state, referred to by disgruntled, dispossessed locals as "flatlanders."

It has become a place gently at odds with itself, where wealth conflicts with poverty, residents with tourists, native-born with newcomer, tradition with the trendy. Even the population has extremes. Resting at 3,500 during the off-season, and swelling to 25,000 within the right couple of days, it supports seventy-two businesses selling liquor and the highest concentration of motels and hotels in the state. Among Vermonters, Stowe has been dubbed a "gold" town—its residents painted as financially above the norm, regardless of their origins or the actual size of their bank accounts. To be "from Stowe" is to be regarded differently, perhaps distrustfully, as if the person being scrutinized might be capable of some immediate capitalist sleight of hand that would play to the observer's disadvantage.

As with all such perceptions, of course, the truth is far more complicated. In the huge mountain looming on the edge of town—the tallest in the state—Stowe had found an asset that could offer it some economic stability through the years. It made concessions to the outsiders and their money, watched how these visitors expressed their needs and desires, and slowly transformed itself from a ski slope's service-oriented road stop to a year-round commercial enterprise, hosting antique car rallies, dog and horse shows, and a broad selection of hiking, biking, tennis, golf, and other outdoor activities. The fortunes of the company owning the actual ski resort have wobbled now and then, to the point where of old the town might have become alarmed, but the breadth of business diversity has reached such an extent by now that the once vital umbilical cord, though still important, isn't what it used to be. Stowe as a whole has become a corporation, and the mountain business, like the parent of an ambitious, precocious family, has had to concede to being one of the crowd.

The police force for such a place faces a challenge, largely because of the population swings. The Stowe PD is in the unusual position of having more part-time officers, at seventeen, than its full-time staff of thirteen, just to handle the seasonal discrepancies. And they are a hard-working crew. On a per-officer, per-complaints-handled, per-day basis, the Stowe cops outwork the hundred-member police force in nearby Burlington, although the Burlington crew would correctly contend that their population contains a rougher mix of humanity. The Stowe PD also works high profile, making frequent vehicle stops, dropping in on bars and nightclubs unannounced and unasked, and generally making itself seen, patrolling the streets in a small fleet of sport utility vehicles.

This visible police presence has largely been because of Frank Auerbach, whose philosophy has long been that the more cops the bad guys see, the less appealing Stowe will appear for easy pickings. And bad guys there have been—every year, drug dealers, thieves, con artists, and sexual predators came to town like camp followers trailing an advancing army. As a result, Auerbach's force was trained to ask for more than just a driver's license and registration at a vehicle stop. His officers could be downright chatty, wanting to know where you were headed and staying, what your plans were while in the area, what you did for a living, and what place you called home. The grumblers complained of harassment. Auerbach countered that if you kept your nose clean, you never had to have such a conversation. And he played no favorites, barring one exception. Selectmen, millionaires, and bums were all handled the same, but his "guys" as he called them—regardless of gender—he pampered as much as he could. He bought them the best shoes he could find, the best vehicles, guns, armored vests, and anything else he could think of, all from money forfeited from convicted drug dealers. The upside to the area's expensive taste in narcotics was that the Stowe PD could reasonably join federally backed drug task forces, from the DEA on down, and thus benefit from the federal rules of booty sharing. To judge from the PD's equipment, business had been good.

All this I researched before heading out to visit Frank Auerbach for the first time, alone and unofficially, hoping to smooth whatever rough water might have been created by the ham-handed way our services had been offered. Happily, I already knew the door was at least half open. Bill Allard had been right—Auerbach had phoned to accept the offer of VBI assistance before Sam and I had left

VSP headquarters—apparently stimulated by Hillstrom's findings. But I had no idea if Auerbach had felt pressured to do so or had merely yielded to need and curiosity. Knowing the truth, I thought, would be crucial to our getting along, so I'd done some fast homework, leaving Sammie to call the team together and write up a quick report.

The police department is located on the west side of Route 100, just below the northernmost—and larger—of Stowe's two villages. It is a modest building, one-and-a-half stories, red brick, and set deeply enough into a hollow by the side of the road, that by the time you notice the fire and rescue station next door, you've already passed it by.

I pulled into the parking lot, hemmed in by stained, craggy walls of piled-up snow, and got out of my car, enjoying the cold on my face after the steady blast from the heater.

I'd passed the PD's driveway once already on this trip—after arranging for lodging at a local motel—to explore the village's small, busy, appealingly plain heart farther on, hoping to put into some perspective all the information I'd just acquired.

It had been a worthwhile detour. Along the twelve-mile drive north of Interstate 89, I'd been struck by a growing commercial momentum on both sides of Route 100. The gas stations, tourist shops, motels, and restaurants had become increasingly serried, creating the visual equivalent of an encroaching critical mass. The village itself was the natural apogee of all this, teeming with a blur of multihued cars and people. But despite the activity and some of the tacky architecture leading up to it, the unpretentious town of a hundred years earlier showed through, clap-boarded, useful, and blandly functional. As background to the colorful Spandex and insulated ski clothes, stalwart behind the endless stream of high-end SUVs, the build-ings held their own against most modern influences, content to look as they had for decades.

And crouching to the west, white-capped and gleaming against a shimmering blue sky, was the stimulus for it all. Mount Mansfield hovered like a multipeaked Olympus, majestic, daunting, both maternal and threatening, its sheer bulk endowing it with indefinable deeper meaning.

Knowing that somewhere high on its slopes, an old, near mummified corpse had myste-riously been deposited made me wonder for whom that meaning boded ill.

I entered the police department lobby, unbuttoned my coat in the sudden warmth, and stepped up to a counter blocked by a sliding glass window.

"Hi. Is the chief in?" I asked a slim, middle-aged woman through the open half of the window.

She looked up from her typing and smiled. "May I have your name?"

"Joe Gunther. Vermont Bureau of Investi-gation."

She stared at me for what felt like a long count. "I'm sorry?"

I extracted my new shield from an inner pocket and showed it to her. "Joe Gunther. I'm a cop."

She rose and approached the window, her face expressing pure wonder. "No... I mean, yeah, but what was the other thing—the Bureau?"

I gave her the badge for closer scrutiny. "The Vermont Bureau of Investigation—new statewide unit."

She returned it cheerfully, seemingly recovered. "Neat. I just never heard of it. The chief expecting you?"

"Not by name, but he knows we're coming."

Looking mystified again, she said, "I'll check," and disappeared.

Moments later, an immensely tall, large, barrel-chested bald man dressed in a white uniform shirt and black cargo pants entered the reception area and stuck out a meaty hand. "Joe Gunther? Frank Auerbach. Glad to meet you at last. You're a famous guy."

"So was Son of Sam."

He laughed and waved me through the inner door. "Oh, oh—wobbly self-image there. People giving you shit about this VBI thing?"

I thought back to the woman at the counter. "Assuming they even know about it."

He led me into an office just off the small dispatch area. It was cramped, unassuming, and had two doors he left wide open, one looking out into the building's central hallway, the other leading to the squad room in back. There was a symbolism here that apparently reflected the man.

"This is your first case, right?" he asked. "For VBI, I mean."

I sat in the chair he offered me. "Yes, and I'm sorry about the way you were approached. Must've seemed a little lacking in subtlety."

He shrugged. "Didn't bother me. You want some coffee?"

"No, thanks."

"The way I figure it," he resumed, pouring himself a cup from a Thermos parked on his windowsill, "you people have resources I don't, and you'll be falling all over yourselves trying to make a good impression. You *are* going to give me the spiel about how I get all the credit afterward, aren't you?"

I gave him a hapless look. So far, I instinctively liked this man, but with that comment I wasn't sure I could distinguish bluntness from irony—I didn't know him well enough yet. "That *is* the spiel. We'll work under your command, talk to the press only by your say-so, and vanish as soon as you don't want us anymore."

He nodded. "Sounds okay. 'Course, BCI already does all that."

"Yes," I agreed, "with the difference that they wouldn't actually work under your command. They would work *with* you. Not that it usually makes any real difference," I added quickly, sensing he might still send us packing. "But it's a point I'm sure you can appreciate. In any case, this isn't a competition. I didn't dream up this unit, and didn't apply for it when it was born. But I ended up joining because I think it's right to have a major

36

crimes squad that's open to all that're qualified. Again, that's not meant to be disrespectful to the VSP—just more democratic. And the best of BCI will end up in VBI anyhow."

Frank Auerbach smiled broadly, obviously enjoying himself. "Okay. That's great. Between you and me, I don't really care. I'm happy where I am, and I'm happy for any help I can get. How you and the state police duke it out is your business. Just so long as you don't make me the kewpie doll," he added, his smile fading.

"That's the deal," I promised.

"Good," he concluded. "How many people are you bringing on board?"

"Five right now, including me. More later if we've got them. And our own special prosecutor to help us through the shoals, especially if we end up in Canada, and since both the governor and the commissioner are cheering us on, money won't be a problem, either."

"Any of you speak French? It's going to be a pain in the ass otherwise."

"Supposedly Paul Spraiger does, late of the Burlington PD. We've never worked together before."

"I know Paul," Auerbach said. "He's good—quiet, real smart. What about Jean Deschamps? You done any digging yet?"

I shook my head. "Despite our pushy manners, I didn't want to presume. We'd like you to take the lead on how to proceed. I should add, though, that my boss, Bill Allard, has a contact with the Sûreté in Sherbrooke—one

of their investigators he met at a conference."
I handed him a slip of paper. "Gilles Lacombe.
Apparently, they hit it off, and Lacombe was
singing the praises of cross-jurisdictional
cooperation."

"Thanks. I already sent faxes to the Mounties, the Sherbrooke police, and the Sûreté,"
Auerbach said, taking the note, "asking them
to check their old files, but given the way
this is looking, we'll need all the inside help
we can get. I'm assuming Hillstrom told you
what she told me, that the guy's probably
been dead fifty years or more."

"She did. What gets me, though, is why he
was frozen in the first place, why's he surfaced
now, and how the hell did he get on the
mountain?"

"Airplane?" Auerbach suggested. "He was
found in a pretty deep hole, and there were
no signs anyone dragged him there."

I was glad to have that suspicion confirmed.
"You have an airport just north of here, don't
you?"

"Morrisville, yeah, like a dozen others all
over Vermont. Morrisville is unmanned at
night and doesn't have a tower, so we'll check
it out. But you gotta wonder: If all you're
going to do with a dead body is dump it
across town, why go to all the trouble of air-
mailing it? We got Dumpsters like everyone
else. Plus, the guy *was* a Canadian," he added
meaningfully.

As far as it went, it did make sense. "I'm
guessing you didn't find any spare body parts
on the mountain."

Frank Auerbach shook his head. "No, but we also haven't done a total site search. It was getting late when he was found, and I wanted to know what Hillstrom would say first. The area's been cordoned off—not that it matters way up there—but it needs a better look. Come to think of it, it's our busy season and I'm pretty shorthanded, so that might be where you and your guys could really be a help. Are they in good enough shape to hit the mountain? It's not much—a gondola ride most of the way up and the Hazardous Terrain Team will be running the show—it would free me up something wicked."

"I'll ask them," I said slowly. "I can probably guarantee at least three of us. How much is 'not much'?"

"You'll have snowshoes and crampons. It's not like a stroll in the park, but it's not too bad, and it's a hell of a view. Basically, if you're even near fit—like you—it's no sweat, and the Hazardous Terrain folks really know their stuff."

"Yeah," I said, wondering if he wasn't over-selling this a bit. "I've heard about them."

"Great." He rose to his feet like a happy used car dealer. "By the way, what do I tell BCI when they come knocking?"

"Indirectly, they already have," I answered, thinking Stanton might've known what he was doing after all. "One of my team is a BCI liaison—Tom Shanklin."

Auerbach glanced at his watch. "I know him, too. Sounds like you got good people."

My mind flashed to Willy Kunkle and I

kept my mouth shut. The chief gathered together the fanned-out contents of a folder from his desk. "It's too late to go up Mansfield today, but we could make it tomorrow morning, if that's not moving too fast."

We returned to the reception/dispatch area. "No. Everyone'll be based at the Commodore Inn, just down the street, 'cept maybe Shanklin and Spraiger, who live close enough to commute. I thought that'd be best till we figured out what's ahead. What time you want to meet?"

"Let's say oh-seven-hundred hours at the fire and rescue building next door. Give us time to run through a few things before heading out." He handed me the folder. "That's what we got so far, by the way—scene photos, initial findings, and Hillstrom's report. A little bedside reading."

We shook hands and I headed back into the cold.

From the outside, the Commodore Inn's most striking aspect is an enormous sloping roof—vast, broad, and gently angled—projecting far out in front of the building's entrance to form a deep carport. In the winter, it is all the more impressive for the thick mantle of snow coating it like icing, making the hotel vaguely resemble a long, low cave sliced into an otherwise frozen landscape. The inn gets its name from a three-acre pond out back, which in the summer plays host to weekly model-boat regattas, a selling point played up by an assortment of life rings, buoys, netting, and other sailing paraphernalia that hangs from the walls and ceiling of the bar and dining room out back.

I didn't head that way, however, choosing instead a long hallway to the left off the lobby and a room about halfway down its length. As arranged earlier, waiting for me there were the first vital signs of the Vermont Bureau of Investigation—Sammie Martens, Willy Kunkle, Paul Spraiger, and Tom Shanklin from the state police—gathered around the room like card players expecting the banker.

I removed my coat and draped it over a chair, crossing the room to shake hands with both Shanklin and Spraiger. "I just left the Stowe PD," I explained to all of them. "Chief Auerbach was very receptive and spoke well of Tom and Paul, which I hope is a good sign. I take it you've all introduced yourselves to each other?"

Everyone either nodded or didn't disagree. It was my experience from working with other special units that conviviality comes slowly, delayed by a professional caution that sometimes borders on suspicion. Cops are a clannish bunch, dependent on one another for understanding, support, and sometimes their lives. It is a strong, long-lasting bond, of necessity forgiving of quirky personalities, but it takes time to form, since its foundation is trust, rather than simple compatibility. I noticed that Willy had parked himself in a far corner, behind a small round table, removed and unapproachable. Sammie, despite her professional and personal ties to him, was perched on the low dresser across the room, next to the silent TV set. She knew the unspoken rules, knew Willy's prickly ways, and knew to protect herself from them in a meeting with new acquaintances.

Shanklin and Spraiger were the unknowns. The first—short-haired, square-jawed, and military in bearing—seemed the most uncomfortable, as if fearing we'd be asking him to pass some rite of initiation. Spraiger was more unusual. Sitting comfortably in a chair with his legs crossed, he exuded an aura of utter stillness, bringing to mind either a shrink or a sage.

"This is obviously not how VBI was designed to come out of the gates," I continued, "with Willy and Tom serving under their own colors. But starting as a mixed bag is kind of fitting. For the most part, we exist to integrate with other departments, so now we're a polyglot ourselves."

"And with zero credibility," Willy added in a low growl from his corner.

Every head in the room turned toward him.

"No problem there," I answered, pretending he'd voiced a pertinent comment. "We have to start somewhere and our role is real enough. Auerbach's so hard up for manpower, he'd like our help in a detailed search of the mountain site at oh-seven-hundred hours tomorrow morning, along with their Hazardous Terrain Team. It'll be a good way to get to know these folks, and might get us some more information. I take it everyone's read the report Sammie prepared on the case so far?"

"What's the theory on the missing feet and arm?" Paul Spraiger asked quietly.

"Right now, we're thinking they broke off, maybe when the body was dropped from an aircraft."

"Implying a possible Canadian departure point that might be a red herring," Tom Shanklin suggested, touching on what Auerbach and I had discussed.

"Possibly," I agreed.

"Is there anything so far linking Jean Deschamps to Stowe, or even the U.S.?" he asked.

"His dead body," Willy said glumly.

Again, there was a slight lull in the conversation, which I quickly filled, wishing Willy would stop acting like Oscar the Grouch: "Sad but true. Possession in this case is *ten-tenths* of the law—unless we can prove Deschamps was killed in Canada, he's ours."

"So, we're going to have work both sides of the border," Spraiger suggested.

"That's how it looks now," I said. "The Sherbrooke police, the Mounties, and the Sûreté du Québec have been contacted for any information, but if Hillstrom's right about the time of death, I don't see them breaking into a big sweat over this."

"Depending on who Deschamps was," Sammie corrected.

"Right—which I hope we'll learn tomorrow."

"So what's the plan?" Shanklin asked.

"That's up to Auerbach," I answered. "My guess is we'll be looking into Deschamps's history, trying to find out if and when he last entered the U.S. legally, interviewing old-timers here and in Canada to see if we can pick up a trail, checking airfields and all air traffic control radars for any mysterious, late-night flights, talking to the Stowe mountain folks to try to pin down when the body might've been put in place, and anything else you can think of. Unless we get some eighty-year-old pilot who shows up at the door and says, 'Book me, Danno,' I think we'll be here for a while. This trail may be about as cold as it can get."

"Great," Willy muttered. "And while we run around looking like nobody can live without us, whoever planted this stiff will make it crystal clear why he did it. Seems to me it'd be smarter to just sit tight and see what happens."

Spraiger, the French-speaker with the thoughtful air, considered Willy's point carefully. "Unless the body wasn't put there for us. Someone else could hear a message through the media coverage that we wouldn't recognize, such as, 'I did this once. I can do it again' or, 'I'm on your tail.'"

To his credit, Willy recognized the potential wisdom of this, and so lapsed into silence.

I stood up from the edge of the bed and checked my watch. "Okay, let's leave it there for now. It's still early—use the evening to explore the town, get something to eat, maybe get better acquainted. Tom and Paul, I know you both have families and'll be commuting, but if you want to hang out a couple of hours, feel free. It might be our last

44

downtime for a while. I'll be here reading the case file in case anyone wants to talk.

"Willy?" I asked as the rest of them headed for the door.

He'd stayed put, still wedged in his corner, looking at me with a sardonic smile. "Yeah, I know—gotta stay after class."

I waited until the others had left before taking Sammie's place on the low dresser, facing him across the room.

"What's the lecture gonna be?" he asked. "Good attitude making for good teamwork?"

I was so used to him after all these years, I actually laughed. "The day you give anyone a good attitude, I'll start watching my back. I figure this bunch'll get used to you just like the old one did."

"I may not be rid of the old one," he reminded me.

I pursed my lips for a moment before telling him, "I wouldn't be so sure. You flunk out here, you might not have anything to fall back on. I don't think Brandt'll take your shit for long—not without a buffer."

He didn't look impressed. "Right—Joe the buffer. Why do you keep doing that? Saving my ass... What d'you get out of it, beside a holiness medal from people like Sam?"

I paused before answering, hoping I understood myself enough to be truthful. "That may be part of it, although everyone else thinks I'm an idiot. I'm not sure—I was thinking just recently it maybe had to do with my not having kids, and your being a good example of why that had been a really smart move."

He laughed and scratched his ear with his good hand. "With that fatherly approach, you may be right."

"You're a bright guy, Willy," I continued more seriously. "And a better man than you admit, especially to yourself. I don't want to see that wasted just because you're a social misfit. Maybe I believe it would make me less of a human being if I let you slide, or maybe it's because I want to be around when you finally wake up and realize what you've got to offer. That would be the ultimate last laugh."

"One you'll never live to enjoy," he said, his grimness turned inward.

"Who knows?" I countered. "You don't drink anymore, I haven't heard of you beating on anyone lately, you work hard and get results, and you didn't turn me down when I suggested joining this crew. Why is that, if you're so convinced you're worthless?"

He scowled at me, unhappy at having the tables turned. "Somebody had to cramp your style."

I ignored the diversion. "Sam seems to think you've got something to offer."

He could have come back with another one-liner—and would have in the old days. But I was right. He was in slow evolution, growing like a thwarted, water-starved plant toward whatever light he could see—including this job.

And he knew it.

He got up abruptly, graceful despite the useless, limp arm, which he kept from flopping around by leaving his left hand shoved into his pants pocket. "We done here?"

I looked at him for a moment. "We may be just beginning."

CHAPTER FIVE

Mount Mansfield isn't much by global standards. While it's the best Vermont has to offer, it still measures only 4,393 feet—a relative shrimp compared to its brethren in New Hampshire and New York, and less than a sixth of Everest. But it has great presence, especially since its western slope sweeps straight out across the Champlain Valley, ending at the lake a mere thirty miles off. And it can be brutal because of that bearing. Over the years, several claims have been made clocking the wind on Manfield's summit in excess of one hundred miles per hour.

That summit is actually a row of blended peaks, running along a north/south axis, the tops of which in profile, specifically from the east, look vaguely like a mile-long human face staring straight up at the sky—a supplicant giant—silent, determined, without hope of response. The Anglo name "Mansfield" has a murky genesis, but the ancient Abnakis showed how appearance can deceive: They called it "Mountain-with-a-Head-like-a-Moose."

The most obvious of its summits is the Nose, but the tallest is the Chin, at the north end, and it was at the bottom of the cliff between the Chin and the Adam's Apple where the frozen body of Jean Deschamps had been discovered by a daredevil skier looking for virgin snow far off the beaten path.

According to Ray Woodman, the head of Stowe's Hazardous Terrain Evacuation Team—locally known as Stowe Mountain Rescue—such off-trail forays are not uncommon once the snow becomes firmly seated on the higher, sometimes cliff-steep slopes. Hunched over a topographical map at the fire department the following morning, he traced with his finger a reverse-curving, horizontal S, up and over the Chin's left side, down around to the throat between the Chin's base and the Adam's Apple, and across the throat to the edge of a deep, steep ravine above Smuggler's Notch, two thousand feet farther down, and the hot dog skier's planned destination.

"We'll be following roughly this path," Woodman explained. "A diagonal climb from the gondola to just under the summit, along this swale here. Then down Profanity Trail above Taft Lodge. Another traverse to catch the top of the saddle between the base of the Chin and the Adam's Apple, and then an easy climb down the saddle's western slope to where the body was. We won't be on skis. I never thought that was particularly sane. We'll have snowshoes or crampons, depending on the surface. And ice axes."

Willy leaned forward and planted his own

finger next to Woodman's. "If the skiers are trying to end up at Smuggler's Notch, what was this guy doing on the western side of the saddle? The Notch is to the north."

"He got disoriented," Woodman explained simply. "Happens all the time. The saddle is almost flat along its crest. You hit a whiteout like he did, you think you're sliding north beside the Apple, heading toward Hell's Brook, but in fact you're just slipping off the saddle's side. It's not particularly dangerous. It just ruins your day 'cause you end up miles from where you want to be. But he didn't get that far. Way I heard it, he actually fell into the hole with the body."

Frank Auerbach, towering above most of us, nodded in confirmation. "Talk about ruining a day. He was a basket case when I talked to him. What's the weather report, Ray?"

Woodman straightened from the broad table we'd been leaning over to see the map. "A little iffy. There's some activity in the area, but no rhyme or reason to it. I wouldn't mind waiting for a better day."

Auerbach shook his head. "I'm already getting enough heat as it is. You saying we can't go?"

Woodman looked unhappy. "I don't know enough to say for sure. That's why I'm suggesting caution."

That seemed to settle it for Auerbach. "Duly noted. We go."

I glanced around the room. Most of the ten people there wore Woodman's stamp of experienced casualness. Wind-tanned, lean, and wearing their outdoor gear with the ease that older cops wear their guns, they all but radiated self-assurance. My crew and I looked like neophyte hikers in borrowed clothes.

Which was in fact the case. Even Sammie, who'd come with her own equipment, had been further complemented with a few extra items. The rest of us had been outfitted virtually from head to toe. We'd also been given a crash course in climbing protocol, rope use, and how to use carabiners and ice axes, some of which harked back to familiar special weapons training, others of which felt foreign and awkward.

"Jesus," Willy muttered as we all prepared to leave, "it's not like we're assaulting K two or anything."

"Maybe not," Woodman told him. "But it's what you don't plan for that'll kill you."

An hour later, I was staring out the gondola window as we were pulled up the mountain's face, wondering if this was what a spider felt climbing a silken filament up the side of a dormant human, knowing that if the host took notice, the end would be fast and brutal.

The bottom hadn't been bad, surrounded by base buildings and a swarm of colorfully clad tourists. It had been entertaining looking down on the broad trail below us, watching skiers trying to strike a balance between self-control and speed. Farther up, though, I'd become aware of the mountain's sheer mass overhead, and of my own comparative insignificance. To challenge such a huge, powerful, prehistoric chunk of the earth's crust felt like tempting fate. I watched the approaching ridgeline, stretching across my entire horizon, with growing dread.

"Impressive, isn't it?" Ray Woodman said beside me. "Most people turn their backs to the mountain and look at the valley to admire the view. I like this better—it's the mountain I have to deal with, whether the view's there or not."

I glanced over my shoulder. What view there was seemed imperiled by a series of ever shifting clouds. But what I could see was spectacular. "You can't blame them, though," I commented.

"Oh, no. I wouldn't do that. Once I'm on top, I always look around. Be crazy not to. Besides, by then I've earned the right. It's just that for me, the view's like the cherry on top, and I always eat the cherry last."

I resisted mentioning that I found it unsettling putting ice cream sundaes and life-threatening excursions into the same sentence, especially when the speaker was the climbing team leader. "I think I'll just be happy when the whole meal's over," I said softly. "This is not my element."

Woodman was sympathetic. "You're in good company. It's just what I like to do. I wouldn't be a cop for all the tea in China. Up here, I only get in trouble if I make a mistake. You guys never know what's going to hit you, no matter how careful you are. I couldn't live like that." He swept his hand across the approaching ridge. "You have to admit it does grab the attention, though. Even if all you want to do is slide down it."

A few clouds were caught on the ridge like translucent ragged cotton, the stark cliffs below them dark and brooding in their shadow. "It is beautiful," I had to agree.

"People have been taking runs at it for a hundred and fifty years," he explained. "Ever since the Civil War, when they actually built a hotel right under the Nose, called the Summit House. That's when the toll road began, too. They ended up having to hold the place down with cables, the wind blew so hard. Even then, they'd lose a roof or a porch every once in a while. It housed fifty people and their horses and carriages. Talk about guts or arrogance or whatever it was—those people were nuts. I never would've done that."

"What happened to it?" I asked, trying to dispel the hint of foreboding that had caught my attention like the sound of something solid sliding under a boat's hull.

"They tore it down and burned it in '64. Lousy profit margin. Ironic when you think of all it went through—to be destroyed by the very dynamic that built it, like an out-of-date filling station on Main Street. We've pretty much treated the mountain that way from the start," he added, his voice dropping with contempt. "Turning it into a ski slope, a place to plant radio antennas and entertain flatlanders who drive to the top for twelve bucks to claim they climbed Mount Mansfield.

Through the years, they've talked about paving the ridge with a parkway, planting a Bomarc missile guidance system on the Chin, and even putting in an airfield."

I glanced at his angular profile, weatherbeaten and hard. Ray Woodman was probably in his fifties. Auerbach had told me he was a high-end building contractor by trade, benefiting from the very excesses he was currently belittling. Had he gotten the contract 150 years ago, I had no doubt he would have built the Summit House, taking pride in beating the elements. Such inconsistency is one of the quirks of our species, and certainly one of the big reasons we're so amazed by our own behavior.

We were nearing the cavelike entrance to the gondola's top station, perched on the slope a couple of hundred feet shy of the ridge, when Woodman abruptly pointed off to the right. "There's the Chin," he said. "That big dome on the end with the cliffs below it. Left of it and much closer to us, angling this way, is the swale I showed you on the map—like a shallow gutter running up the side of a roof. That's our route to the top and back down Profanity."

"Why not just cut straight across to the saddle between the Chin and the Adam's Apple?" Sammie asked from behind us.

Woodman didn't bother turning around. "You'd find out if you tried. It can be done, but it wears you to a stump. Once we reach Profanity, we have gravity on our side. Cuts down on the effort big time." He finally faced her with a smile. "I may not like skiers much, but they do know how to slide downhill."

53

We soon discovered what he'd meant. Snow-shoes strapped to my boots, plodding up the angled slope like a clown dressed in floppy shoes, I could only imagine the effort it would have taken to make a right angle traverse. I also had no doubt that's where I would have ended up had Sammie been team leader.

As it was, I could see her far ahead of me, pressing Woodman from behind like a sports car trying to pass a pickup. Not that he paid her the slightest attention. He was now where he liked to be most, in control and in command, and extremely respectful of all the factors allied to kill him if he erred. No hyperactive cop was going to make him change his ways.

The mountain itself, however, was a different matter. We were still fifty feet shy of the ridge when he turned, raising both hands, and waited until we'd all clustered around him.

His concern spoke for itself. As I reached his position, I found he'd stopped right under the lee of a steady blast of freezing wind coming from the other side. The shredded clouds I'd seen earlier suddenly fell into con-text. We huddled on our hands and knees to hear his voice above the eerie howl.

"Things're kicking up a bit," he shouted. "It's not too bad and we won't be in it for long, but since some of you are new to this, you want to be extra careful. We'll put our crampons on here, stow our snowshoes on our packs, and rope up in single file. Goggles and face masks on, hats secured under your chins. Make sure nothing's loose anywhere. Keep low, use your ice axes, and keep your faces downwind to breathe." He paused, eyeing Sammie, and added, "There's no rush. This is where taking your time will keep you alive."

We did as we were told, Willy allowing Sammie and me to help him switch his gear, before we all started up once more, in defiance of instinct or common sense, straight into the frigid, moaning, lung-searing blast.

And the shock awaiting us wasn't just from the wind. As we topped the crest, the entire mountain fell away, revealing a vast, flat, empty stretch of clouds before us, obscuring the entire Champlain Valley to the west as completely as the Stowe side had been clear. The appearance of this featureless plain was so abrupt and disorienting that while we were being pushed back by the icy gale, the sheer emptiness ahead drew us forward like a magnet, tempting the beginners among us to step onto the vaporous field and proceed outward. Despite gasping for air, even through the protection of my ventilated neoprene face mask, I fought Woodman's instruction to look away and tried to permanently imprint this one instant in my mind. Only the urgent tugging of the rope around my waist brought me back to the task at hand and the need to get under cover. For despite the dramatic feeling of being on an island surrounded by foamy sea, I realized I was precisely where Woodman loved to be most—right on the edge of life itself and in peril of making one of the mistakes he'd warned us against.

The trip to the top of Profanity trail was blessedly short as advertised, and we huddled there as before, just beyond the wind's bite on the clear side of the mountain, awaiting Woodman's orders.

"Okay," he shouted, "that's basically the worst of it. The rest, as they say, is all downhill." He pointed to a narrow gap between two rocky outcroppings below us. "What you can see from here is as bad as it gets. It's steep enough at the top that even the skiers mostly sidestep it, but then things open up a bit, plus we get to move laterally to the north once we reach the bottom of the cliffs surrounding the Chin. We'll stay roped in for safety's sake. All set?"

We headed out, looking, I guessed, like a string of mountaineers retreating from some Himalayan summit, masked, goggled, and groping carefully with axes and crampons. Now wishing for some clouds to obscure the dizzying view, I felt barely connected to the mountain's almost sheer flank, dangling between this epitome of the Earth's dependable solidity and thousands of feet of open space beneath. Aside from the rope linking me to my fellow climbers, there was nothing to stop me from simply tilting my center of gravity a scant few degrees, and vanishing from their company as if I'd fallen through a hole. There was an odd exhilaration to that realization, and no doubt a faulty sense of insight into what drove people to do this recreationally. I sensed that tightrope walkers, stunt pilots, and bungee jumpers alike—while hiding behind the cool technical jargon belonging to each—

shared with mountaineers the same fascination with walking survival's edge, exalting in their lives being dependent on the smallest detail, like a rope, a misstep, or a slight miscalculation.

It was not a thrill I shared, however, nor was I shamed by Willy's casual dexterity in doing everything I was, one-handed. Instead, I was merely delighted when the pitch finally lessened and we began working our way toward the more level plane of the saddle.

The contrast there was considerable. From hanging like pictures on a wall, we ended up standing back in snowshoes on a pasture-sized plot of land beneath the threatening mass of the Chin above and the gentle elevation of the Adam's Apple ahead. This sense of standing in someone's ample backyard was enhanced by the view's having succumbed to the low-lying cloud cover. Where the summit ridge had been just adequate to dam it up from the eastern valley, this saddle served as a kind of overflow outlet, and was therefore socked in with a fast-moving, dense fog.

It wasn't as viciously windy as at the top, where both height and exposure had conspired to create a gale, but strong enough to make the masks and goggles a necessity and to dictate that all conversation be held at a loud pitch.

We traveled to the far side of the saddle, where it began dropping off to the west, sharing—as the mist eddied and swelled—the same disorientation that must have misled Auerbach's distressed skier. And in fact, despite the yellow tape someone had absurdly staked out in the snow, Woodman himself almost suffered the same fate, coming to an abrupt halt right at the edge of the grave-sized hole.

Its depth was confirmation enough for me that the body of Jean Deschamps had fallen from a considerable height, but whether from a plane or the surprisingly nearby cliffs of the Chin was suddenly open to debate.

The chain of command changed at this point, slipping from Ray Woodman as guide and temporarily falling to Gary Smith—the senior of Auerbach's two detectives—as the man he'd put in charge of the entire investigation.

Smith, whom I'd only met that morning, didn't share his boss's ebullient nature nor his ready acceptance of my VBI-as-support-role speech. Though younger in years, Smith was more traditional in outlook and openly viewed us as a threat to his authority.

He was what I feared would be more the rule than the exception in the future.

I approached him clumsily in a moment of sudden visibility, when the proximity of the rock wall overhead revealed itself so abruptly, I felt it was about to fall on us.

"How would you like us deployed?" I yelled at him.

His face turned toward me, his dark goggles blocking his eyes and his mask giving him the warmth of an oversized action figure. He waved a hand around. "Be my guest."

"That's exactly what we are. What would you like us to do?"

He didn't move for several seconds, and then said, "The Chief tells me you think this guy might've been dropped from a plane."

"Could've been, but I didn't realize how close the cliff was."

He looked over his shoulder dubiously. "Somebody climbed all the way up there to chuck the body over? Why?"

I shrugged. "Why drop him from a plane after keeping him in a freezer for half a century? We're not even in the suburbs of normal here. He might've also bounced off the rocks before ending up here. Those body parts broke off somehow."

Another pause. "All right," he finally said. "I'll put the Mountain Rescue people on the cliff. You guys can form a circle around the hole and work outward, using the rods we brought as probes. And take the metal detector in Mike's pack, too. You all have radios?"

"I think so."

He turned away from me and lumbered off to coordinate with his team, solidifying the them-and-us division in physical terms. But the plan was reasonable enough, given the environment, and we outsiders were still playing a useful role. For the moment, that would have to count as a victory.

It didn't feel like one, though, after three hours of struggling in the wind-whipped snow, sometimes working a methodical search pattern, other times simply standing stock still in the fog, all visual and tactile references so removed that to venture in any direction was to invite becoming lost or falling prey to the unpredictable terrain. Gentle saddle or not, the supposed "ground" we were standing on was only a thick mantle of compacted snow covering boulders, pitfalls, small cliffs, and a stunted forest of dwarfed evergreens, any or all of which could suck us in, especially if encountered sight unseen.

Eventually, I discovered I wasn't the only one growing concerned. During one of the few moments when visibility allowed a better view, I saw Ray Woodman about halfway up the Chin, gesturing at his watch to Gary Smith, and then pointing toward the sky. I wasn't sure if it was the weather or the daylight that had caught his eye, since I thought both were deteriorating, but it was obvious the search team was going to metamorphose back into a climbing party soon.

I was just about to confirm that suspicion by radio, when the entire subject was put on hold.

"Gary? It's Mike. I think I got something."

Another blanket of mist was quickly forming, but just before I lost sight of the rocks, I saw one of Smith's men waving his arms from near the top. After that, I had to rely on my ears alone to learn what was happening.

"What is it, Mike?" Gary Smith asked.

"It's sort of wedged in here, but it looks like a hand."

"Leave it where it is. I'm coming up. Did you copy, Gunther?"

"Loud and clear."

I could hear from his labored breathing that Smith was working hard to join his colleague as he spoke. "If it really is jammed in there, I don't want to mess it up by moving too fast. You want to get up here? It's pretty easy. I think you could make it."

I ignored the pointed condescension. "On my way."

Ray Woodman spoke up just as I felt the unrelenting wind both pick up and become noticeably colder. "I'm not sure I'd recommend that. The weather's changing. Might be best to just mark the spot and come back."

Smith tried a sidestep. "How 'bout a compromise? You take the rest of them down. The three of us'll follow either as soon as we get the hand loose, or can't and mark where it is instead. I hate to walk away now."

I didn't back up Woodman as my instincts told me I should. Too concerned with appearing pushy, and privately fearful that Smith would take such caution as weakness, I allowed his intemperance to overwhelm my good judgment.

Surprisingly—or because he felt outnumbered—Woodman apparently thought Gary Smith was enough of a climber to make this choice, although his tone of voice betrayed some doubt. "All right, but I'm lowering the boom on everyone else. And don't take too long— you know how fast things can sour up here."

I made my way over to the Chin's base, passing Sammie on the way, who murmured, "Show him what you got, boss," and found that from the foot of the cliff, the climb didn't look as daunting. During the summer, I remembered, the Long Trail came right down this same face, regularly traveled by people carrying thirty-pound packs. Snow and ice didn't make it any easier, but I was pleasantly surprised at how fast I joined Smith and Mike on their elevated perch.

Once there, I was also rewarded by Smith's more subtly respectful demeanor.

"Take a look," he said, and placed his back against the rock so I could squeeze by to where his colleague Mike was crouching by a crack in the wall.

"It's right in there," he said. "You can see the ring on his finger. That's what caught my eye."

I peered into the gloom of the crack and saw a faint glimmer of gold. Taking Mike's flashlight, I then clearly saw the stump of a human hand, looking as if it had been broken off a discolored marble statue. I straightened and looked around.

Smith pointed overhead into the mist. "I guess the body bounced here hard enough that the hand stuck like an arrow before breaking off. You may be right about the airplane. I don't see that happening if someone just chucked him over the edge. It's too close."

"How do we get it out?" Mike asked, still crouching over his find.

I held up my ice ax. "Use these as crowbars?"

There was only room for the two of us. Mike put his ax in on one side of the small crack, and I applied mine to the other. It took a while, but eventually we loosened it enough that I could reach in and extract the hand.

I gave it to Smith, who examined it closely.

"We can probably get prints from it, and the ring might tell us something."

A sudden whiteout drew our attention. We looked up at a world without any markers whatsoever. Even our precarious perch had disappeared from view, making me feel I was standing on a cloud.

"Damn," Mike muttered.

"It'll pass," Gary reassured us. "It's done it a couple of times already today."

"Not this bad, it hasn't," Mike said.

He was right.

"Let's give it a few minutes," Gary said. "If it doesn't blow over, we'll just have to climb down by feel."

"We can barely see our feet."

Gary Smith was losing patience, perhaps goaded by his lingering against Woodman's advice. "Mike, I've been in this crap before. It's more psychological than anything. You take it slow, it works out fine."

No one spoke for a couple of minutes, until, as if yielding to an inner, heated argument, Smith wrenched his radio from his pocket and addressed it. "Smith to Woodman. Come in, Ray."

Woodman's voice, clear and calm, sounded otherworldly from out of the clouds. "What's up, Gary? You folks okay?"

"Yeah, just socked in by the fog. What're conditions where you are?"

"Bad and getting worse. You still on the wall?"

"Yeah."

"The wind's picking up. You better get off as best you can. It feels like a storm coming.

We'll head back to intercept you. If that fails, make for Taft Lodge instead of going back up Profanity. Things are a little better on the east face."

Smith signed off and looked up at me. "You should be in the middle. You got the least experience."

I was standing behind Mike, who expressed what I was thinking, "Already can't see the ledge, Gary. We start switching places, we could all go off."

Smith nodded unhappily, saying softly, almost apologetically, "Wish we had some rope."

The going was slower than I'd imagined it would be. I'd envisioned the equivalent of climbing backward down a ladder with my eyes shut, but this wasn't close to being that easy. Each move was punctuated by the fear of slipping, each tentative groping for a foothold accompanied by the doubt about what, in fact, was being trusted with my weight.

And in the midst of such uncertainty, the wind grew harder, now pushing snow ahead of it.

And making everything much colder.

When I slipped and fell, I had no real sense of it at first. I merely extended my boot as I'd been doing all along, and felt nothing. For a fraction of a second, still unaware that my hands were no longer holding the cliff, I began to simply look for another perch with my toe. And then my body hit something hard, and I knew I was in freefall.

It didn't last long. A couple of jars, dulled by my heavy clothing, and then a single, stunning smack to the head.

Followed by nothing at all.

CHAPTER SIX

I don't know how long I lay there. It was dark, pitch black, and I was so cold at first, I had trouble moving. My head also hurt, although not as badly as I thought it should, for which I figured I had the frigid temperature to thank.

But useful or not for headaches, the cold was about to kill me. I knew that before I'd even confirmed that all my parts were functional and intact. As soon as I opened my eyes, and heard the screaming of the wind, I realized most of my body was almost totally numb.

I didn't worry about the others. They were either alive or not, either safe or in peril. I also didn't think about how I'd come to be lying in the snow at night alone, seemingly abandoned by people who more than most were trained to work as a team. My only thoughts were about survival and how to attain it. It was the same kind of focus I'd encountered in combat, when the enormity of the threat comes second to the will to live.

I tried standing at first, more to see if I could than to actually start walking anywhere. I had no flashlight, and knew that even if I had, it wouldn't have done much good. But the point was moot in any case—the wind threw me to my knees before I got halfway up.

I felt around me. Like Jean Deschamps, I'd created a hole where I'd landed, although blessedly less deep, and so decided to finish what I'd unwittingly begun by digging not just down but to the side as well, hoping to end up with a cave of sorts.

It wasn't easy going. I couldn't see, couldn't feel with my hands, and I wasn't even sure if I was burrowing in the right direction. It occurred to me that if I'd landed on a slope, and was tunneling downhill, my reward would be to eventually reemerge back into the storm.

But I got lucky. After what felt like hours, I not only began feeling comfortably entombed, sheltered from both the wind and its incessant, biting howl, but I was warmer as well, my exertions having pushed warmer blood if not to my fingers and toes, at least most of the way there.

It was only then that I thought beyond the immediate and remembered the radio.

I pulled it awkwardly from my pocket, fumbling with hands that felt like senseless claws, and finally succeeded in depressing the transmit button, the small red light on top of the radio giving me a curious, instant comfort.

"Gunther to Mountain Rescue. Anyone out there?"

The response was instantaneous. "Jesus, Joe. That you?" Ray Woodman's voice betrayed a relief he'd obviously all but abandoned.

"One and the same."

His next question was more hesitant. "How're you doing?"

It was a professional's concern. In his place, I might have asked where I was. Knowing the futility of that, he was more interested in how long I might last.

"Okay so far. I hit my head, but I don't think there's any damage. I've dug a snow cave, so I'm out of the elements. Can't feel my hands or feet."

There was a telling pause.

"Where are you guys?" I asked, more to quell my own anxiety than out of any curiosity.

"Taft Lodge. The weather totally shut down the mountain. After you fell, Mike injured his ankle. Gary tried to find you, but I ordered him to take care of Mike. As it was, we had to go back and get them—they were already lost in the storm. Dumb luck they even made it." There was another long hesitation. "I'm sorry, Joe. I had to save who I could."

I understood what he was going through, and could only imagine the efforts he'd expended. Good news that it was, my returning from the dead was also like the resurgence of a guilt-evoking ghost. "Don't worry about it. I would've done the same thing."

"Well, we're in good shape now," Woodman came back with forced optimism. "The storm shouldn't last too much longer. You just stay hunkered down there, and we'll come get you as soon as we can. I got someone who'd like to talk to you. After that, we better conserve our batteries. And put the radio next to your body if you can," he added.

I waited for a moment and then heard Sammie's voice—small, worn, and worried. "Hi, boss. How're you doin'?"

"Not bad—kind of making like a bear."

Again, there was a long silence. I knew she'd already been dealing with my death, and now was groping with my resurrection. If I'd correctly judged Woodman's false nonchalance about the storm's length and ferocity, she was also contemplating losing me all over again. Stowe Mountain Rescue was famous throughout the state for braving weather other people called lethal, especially if the lost person was a colleague. But they were buttoned down now.

Things were really bad out there.

I tried to ease her distress a little. "Sam, thanks for asking, but we'd better follow Ray's advice for now. Keep warm and I'll see you in a bit."

I took my finger off the transmit button and watched the red light die, wondering how long it would take me to do the same.

CHAPTER SEVEN

It was snowing—the kind of fat, lazy flakes kids love to catch on their tongues. It came down gently, incessantly, softening the view of the hospital parking lot and crossing the window with a soothing, lulling monotony. It was all I could do to turn away at the sound of the door opening.

Gail stood on the threshold, watching me, her expression a mixture of concern and irritation.

I tried stacking the deck by giving her a big smile. "Hey, there."

It had the opposite effect. She frowned and said, "Why's it always you who gets banged up? Couldn't you let someone else go first, just once in a while?"

"I was last in line this time, and someone else did get hurt."

She shook her head. "I heard—a twisted ankle."

Still, she came across the room to the bed and kissed me long and tenderly.

"You're a pain in the neck, Joe Gunther," she added after straightening up. She dragged a chair over to where she could sit within reach.

I hit the control button by my head and moved the bed to a more upright position. "You didn't ask how I was feeling."

She smiled grudgingly. "God, just like a kid. I know how you're feeling. I just spent fifteen minutes with your doc getting the lowdown, and half an hour before that being briefed by Sammie Martens on the phone. It's a miracle all you got was hypothermia—you should've at least lost some toes or fingers. You need to do something about that girl, by the way. She's a walking grenade—steel on the outside and a wreck inside. If you ever do get your-self killed, she'll go to pieces."

I waved a hand dismissively, understanding from her rapid patter that Sammie wasn't the only one wound up. Self-serving as it sounds, I found comfort in that. "She's not that fragile."

"Don't bet on it."

I knew not to. When it came to judging character, Gail, hyper or not, was rarely wrong. We'd known each other a long time, had been lovers almost from the start, and, whether living together or not, were as inter-twined as any long-married couple.

An odd couple, of course—a lifelong rural cop with a hodgepodge education and an affluent, city-born, liberal lawyer, currently staff counsel for the state's most powerful environmental lobbyist group. Over the years, Gail had fought for women's causes, the pro-tection of children, to help the downtrodden, and to keep the planet healthy, working var-iously as a chronic volunteer, a selectman, a political advocate, and even briefly as a deputy state's attorney. She'd made it her business to know what made people tick and how to win them over.

I therefore conceded her take on Sammie. "How is she?"

"Fine, now—in total denial. Ready for combat."

"That's a little harsh, isn't it?"

Gail's face softened. "Joe, she wasn't the only one who thought you'd died."

I reached over and took her hand in mine. "I'm sorry. When did you hear about this?"

"Kunkle called me on a cell phone when you were all still on the mountain. He didn't want me to find out listening to the news. He also wanted me to know there was a chance. Good thing, too, because later the press had you all but buried."

"You've been here a while, then."

Her expression cooled once more. "Yet again, yeah."

I didn't respond. Our life together hadn't been overly peaceful in that respect. This wasn't the first time she'd come to see me in a hospital, or the first time she'd had to keep her own company for hours or days, wondering if I'd pull through. The toll had cost us both.

"Are we okay?" I suddenly blurted.

Gail looked at me, visibly startled, and then laughed, leaned forward, and kissed me again. "I'm sorry—yes, we're okay. If I didn't love you so much, I wouldn't be so angry. I'm just a little frazzled—and being a hard-ass."

She looked out the window at the snow. "I don't tell you often enough what you mean to me, Joe," she said softly.

"I don't expect you to," I told her. "I was just making sure, that's all."

But she was shaking her head. "No, it's

the least I could do. You give me freedom when I need it and support when I crash and burn. Sometimes I feel all I give you back is a hard time."

"That's not true. You tell me the truth. That's why I asked what I did."

She squeezed my hand. "You don't have to worry—not from my end. I'm bugged about this job keeping me in Montpelier for so long, though. It's tougher than I thought it would be. I miss you a lot."

There was a discreet knock at the door and Gary Smith stuck his head into the room. "Oh, I'm sorry," he said, and began to retreat.

Gail stood quickly to stop him. "I have to get a cup of coffee. You can have him till then."

Gary watched her pass him without comment, but then raised his eyebrows. "I didn't mean to interrupt."

"Gail Zigman," I explained. "My unofficial better half. How's Mike?"

Smith took a few steps into the room and stopped, looking awkward. "Fine. Barely limping, already."

The conversation stalled.

"Well, then," I tried, "I guess it wasn't such a bad deal after all. You get anything from that severed hand yet?"

He seemed lost in thought and looked up at me suddenly, as if dragged from some reverie. "What? No. The lab's still working on it. Your contact at the Sûreté in Sherbrooke came through, though—Gilles Lacombe. Asked to meet with us." He finished walking to the foot of my bed, grabbing the rail as if

72

it separated him from a great fall. "I wanted to thank you for covering my butt."

"I did?" I asked, momentarily lost.

"From what I heard, you told the inquiry team this morning you were the one who held us up on the ledge—till we were caught in the whiteout. You implied you didn't follow my recommendation to leave when the leaving was good."

"I did slow us up," I countered. "Using the ice axes as crowbars took too long."

He compressed his lips a moment, pondering whether to accept my gift or not. Being the oldest, the novice climber, and the injured party all in one, I'd known shouldering most of the blame wasn't likely to result in any reprimand from the inquiry team, and in fact they'd been gracious to a fault. It hadn't been a great sacrifice on my part—I'd been as aware as everyone of the closing weather, and I knew that both Woodman and Smith were judging themselves far more harshly for this near miss than any disciplinary board could.

Smith's appreciation showed in his response. "Still. I wanted to thank you. I should've had ropes—should've gotten us off in one piece. It was my responsibility."

"Which is why you got Mike to safety instead of risking all three of us looking for me," I said. "I know what those kinds of situations are like, Gary. I wish I didn't, but they tend to crop up."

"How long you been a cop?" he asked unexpectedly.

"Over thirty-five years."

He nodded, as if coming to terms with the argument in his head. "You have a good reputation. I'm sorry I was a jerk before."

"You didn't know what I was up to."

He smiled then. "I still don't—not really. This VBI thing doesn't make much sense to me."

"It will," I said, sympathizing with his confusion. "And I'll try to make you like the end result."

Gail reappeared at the door, a Styrofoam cup in her hand. "Too early?" she asked.

Gary looked back at me, responding to my last comment. "Well, so far, so good. Thanks again." He then turned to Gail and gestured in my direction. "He's all yours."

She shook her head, smiling. "Not hardly, but I'll take what I can get."

There were three of us in the car, heading northeast on Route 100 toward Newport and Derby Line, Vermont, and Canada beyond, to meet with Gilles Lacombe of the Sûreté du Québec in Sherbrooke—known in cop shorthand as the "SQ"—Gary Smith, Paul Spraiger, and myself. Sammie Martens had lobbied to join us, but the meeting was to be an icebreaker only, and I didn't want to load the deck with VBI personnel. Also, Spraiger spoke French, although I'd asked him not to advertise the fact until it proved absolutely necessary.

"What did Lacombe sound like on the phone?" I asked Smith, who'd made the arrangements.

He slowed to a stop to let a small herd of cows cross from a barn to the pasture on the other side, their nostrils enveloped in periodic bursts of vapor as they plodded along. We waited until the farmer had latched the gate behind the last of them before resuming our trip. Route 100 meandered up the spine of Vermont, broad-shouldered and well maintained—a pleasure to travel at any time of year, but particularly right after a fresh snow had made everything from mountaintops to old trailers look like pictures from an art book.

"Real friendly," Smith answered. "And he spoke decent English, too. I think we hit a nerve with Deschamps. Our Popsicle's first name—Jean—that didn't mean much to him, but he said the family was well known. To use his words," and here Smith affected a thick accent, "'We 'ave a very big file on dem.'"

"A criminal file?" Spraiger asked from in back.

I'd already been briefed on that when Smith had updated Frank Auerbach and me earlier. "Apparently," I said. "It sounds like the Deschamps have been in business for a while."

Spraiger looked out the side window reflectively, "Huh."

"What?" I asked him. "That mean something to you?"

"Maybe not. Sherbrooke's a pretty interesting town, though—a little lost between Montreal and Québec City. Magog is nearby, and a big hangout for the megarich, but people drive by Sherbrooke barely looking out the window. It's actually pretty big. Seventy-five thousand in the city itself, maybe double that if you throw in the suburbs. A lot of industry."

His voice trailed off. I'd come to appreciate Paul Spraiger over the short time I'd known him. He mulled things over before shooting his mouth off, and was generally worth listening to.

"Which ties into Deschamps how?" I prodded him.

He took his eyes off the scenery and looked at me from the back seat. "Oh, I don't know—not in any specific way. But I'd heard Sherbrooke was a Hell's Angels stronghold—one of their biggest and most secure. I was just surprised another group was working the same turf."

"Hell's Angels?" Smith asked, surprised. "I thought they were mostly in Montreal."

"They're there, too," Spraiger explained, "and a bunch more places. But so are a lot of others. Sherbrooke was like a haven—at least I thought so—a place to call their own."

"The local cops must love that," Smith laughed.

"They don't complain too much," Spraiger told him. "Sherbrooke's got one of the lowest crime rates in Canada, in part because the Angels have done a number like the Mob in Boston's North End—they've made it safer. The cops wish they weren't there, of course, but they keep to themselves, run a tight operation, and make pretty sure everyone else stays out."

"Doesn't sound like the Hell's Angels I know," I murmured.

"They still have the guys with the Nazi helmets riding hogs," Spraiger continued. "They've got an image to protect. But they've also got members who're lawyers and accountants, wearing suits and driving Beemers. They're big-time nowadays."

"How do you know so much about them?" Smith asked.

"From my days at the Burlington PD. We used to bump into them coming down from Canada, selling drugs or moving weapons or money. They liked what Burlington had to offer. That got me started doing research—one thing led to another... I like digging into stuff like that."

I returned to the topic at hand. "What do you make of there being a rival organization in Sherbrooke?"

Spraiger shrugged. "I guess we'll find out, but I'd assume the word 'rival' doesn't apply. If the Deschamps clan is a separate entity, then it probably means there's a working arrangement of some kind. That's the only thing the Angels would tolerate, especially there and especially now."

"How so, 'there and now'?" I asked.

"The Angels are in a squeeze. For years, they were pretty much kings of the hill. Then, several smaller competitor gangs formed an association called the Rock Machine. They're hungry, big, and act like they've watched too many gangster movies. Rumors are a major power struggle is brewing, so it's no time for the Angels to be skirmishing on their flanks. That's what I meant about Sherbrooke—it's behind the front lines. They're going to be protective of that. If the Deschamps have been around awhile, like Gary was told, I'd bet their relations with the Angels are very cordial."

As Gary worked his way through downtown Newport, there was a prolonged silence in the car while we pondered what all that might mean for us. Periodically visible between the buildings to our left, the huge, pale, frozen slab of Lake Memphremagog extended off between the mountains into Canada like a scarred cement airfield, long abandoned.

Reaching the far end of town and I-91 toward Derby Line and the border, Gary finally asked, "Why would Sherbrooke attract the Hell's Angels?"

"Lots of reasons," Spraiger answered him. "It's big enough to give them something to do—strip joints, bars, discos, whatever—but not so big as to allow for much competition. It's close to the border, but not on the priority list of the RCMP or Canadian Customs. It's a low-profile town—working class, industrial—not a place where too many tourists will raise a fuss about a motorcycle gang. And I suppose it doesn't hurt that some very ritzy places, like Magog and Lake Massawipi and Mount Orford, are right nearby.

"Actually," he added, leaning forward in his seat, his enthusiasm growing, "there's historical precedent, too. The developers of the Sherbrooke area were American Loyalists who migrated after the Revolution turned against them—a Vermonter named Hyatt being the primary one. I suppose you could say that's what the Angels did, too. The ones in Sherbrooke are Canadian now, but the first of them crossed the border thirty years ago or so because they thought the pickings would be easier—not to mention they wanted out of the draft during the Vietnam War."

Gary Smith looked back over his shoulder at him. "Jesus, Paul, you're *full* of bullshit, aren't you?"

Spraiger smiled apologetically. "History major in college—made me chronically curious. Also drives my wife nuts."

It no longer had anything to do with crime families and why we were on the road, but by now he'd caught my interest. "So if American Loyalists started Sherbrooke," I asked, "why's it totally French now?"

"The simple answer," he said, "is railroads. Before eighteen-fifty, the town had a few hundred Anglos in it, running sawmills, tanneries, furniture factories, foundries—things that ran well with the hydro dams on the Magog River. But after the trains came in, the market exploded. Industry took off, workers were needed, and where the French had at first avoided the area, they now found themselves both crowded in their previous stomping grounds, and attracted by the cash flow. They went from fifteen percent of the population to fifty in twenty years.

"Not that it *is* totally French now," he added. "People think that, but there're still small English pockets all over Québec. Lennoxville is one of them, and it's Sherbrooke's oldest suburb."

"Fascinating," Smith muttered, sounding bored. "Border's coming up."

The interstate ahead widened as we approached the customs check, which spanned the roadway like a line of toll booths, one of which housed a thin man with an oversized mustache.

"Good day, gentlemen," he said in careful English. "What is your purpose in visiting Canada?"

"We're police officers," Gary answered for us. "Going to a meeting with the Sûreté in Sherbrooke."

"Are any of you carrying weapons?" the man asked without further comment.

"Nope. Left 'em at home."

He finally allowed a small smile. "Then welcome to Canada. Have a good meeting."

Smith picked up speed, now traveling the Canadian version of I-91, Route 55. "I thought we'd have to show our badges, at least."

"You never been over here?" I asked him.

"Nope. Never saw the need," he said, as if to counteract Spraiger's exuberance.

"Good place for a cheap vacation," Paul said from the back seat, undaunted. "The U.S. dollar's worth a bundle."

Silence returned as we all three watched the countryside slowly change to something markedly foreign. Québec is where the Appalachians peter out in altitude, becoming a plateau that gently tilts back down toward the St. Lawrence River farther north. The sky, restricted in Vermont to whatever mountain stands nearest, here opens up, leaving the impression that you're traveling not at the bottom of a series of geological cereal bowls, but instead across an enormous plate, bordered only in the far distance by a fringe of low hills.

And the occasional mountain.

As we drew abreast of Magog to our west, and took the right fork where Route 55 hooks up with Route 10, we were struck by the enormity of Mount Orford, the area's largest ski resort, made all the more impressive by its uniqueness amid the relatively flat terrain. Hulking like a sleeping monster, it was a reminder of the earth's travails, and of the fire and ice that had made our planet habitable, if perhaps only briefly.

The final approach to Sherbrooke, by contrast, was subtlety itself. Apart from the snow-covered forested terrain's being occasionally scored by high tension lines, there was no hint of the city until after Gary had turned off onto Route 410 and was just a few miles shy of downtown. Even then we only saw a vast, largely vacant industrial park to our right, with clusters of apartment buildings and shopping malls across from it. If the history lesson Paul Spraiger had given us was accurate, this introduction to Sherbrooke held true to its roots. It spoke of industry, of a worker's town, of the interest of erstwhile pioneers to transform themselves into modern merchants.

And the final unveiling didn't disappoint. As we topped the last hill and descended into the shallow valley that held the Magog River and the city in its crease, these values became clear.

King Street Ouest, Sherbrooke's major commercial east-west boulevard, was a string of fast food restaurants, low-cost housing, motels, and—across the water slightly below and paralleling the road—a long, low vista of factory buildings, railroad lines, and petrochemical holding tanks, some of which loomed so large as to appear faintly menacing. As far as I could see, there was not a single building that didn't speak of practical function. It all reminded me of what can happen after a flash flood sometimes, when the flotsam and debris is washed up on shore and then left behind by the receding water to dry, helter-skelter, in the sun.

Still, despite its lack of graceful architecture or picturesque antiquity, the city had a comfortable, lived-in feel to it. A place without pretension or misguided sense of purpose.

Gary Smith obviously didn't agree. "Jesus—shades of New Jersey."

Spraiger laughed. "It gets better downstream. All this is new—kind of a miracle mile. Downtown's prettier. Twenty-five years ago, there wasn't much here. Better pull into the right lane. Don Bosco Street is up ahead."

"What'd you do?" Gary asked. "Memorize the map?"

"Kind of," Paul answered without guile. "I used to live near here when I was a kid. That's how I learned the language."

We slowed at a traffic light just beyond a half-abandoned Days Inn parking lot.

"There it is," Spraiger said, pointing through the windshield.

We turned into Don Bosco, which dead-ended at some railroad tracks at the bottom of a steep incline, right at the river's edge, and saw a large, flat-topped cement building, surrounded by a white spiked fence, identified only by a small highway sign announcing, "Sûreté du Québec—Police."

Gary Smith was sounding more depressed by the minute. "I thought these guys were supposed to be the Mounties of Québec. This doesn't look like much."

We drove through the open gates and pulled into a parking area directly opposite the building's front door.

"You only wish we were rigged out like these guys," I told him. "They're provincial police, not the feds—but they damn near cover the earth. About four thousand officers. They do everything from bomb disposal to scuba work to helicopter surveillance to hostage negotiation, plus a lot more. They just don't put on a flashy cover."

We crossed the parking lot, climbed the stairs, and entered the lobby—a cold glass enclosure with two opposing windows revealing office workers going about their business. Before us was a locked door leading into the rest of the building.

Gary glanced around, hoping to catch the eye of one of the people behind glass. Paul crossed to a phone hanging on the wall with a sign beside it. "Here we go," he said, picking it up and speaking with someone.

"Nice personal touch," Gary muttered, a stranger in a strange place, feeling increasingly alienated.

Which was quickly alleviated by the rapid appearance of a small man in a dapper suit, wearing an infectious smile and the thick accent Gary had mimicked earlier. "You are the American police?" he asked, shaking hands all around. "I am Gilles Lacombe. Welcome to Québec."

We followed him up several flights of cement stairs and down a corridor of cluttered offices. The room he ushered us into had narrow windows facing the river, but didn't actually have a view of it. Predictably in this town, I was beginning to learn, a metal warehouse stood in the way.

"Please. You should sit down. Would you like to have coffee?"

We all declined, and Lacombe joined us at a small round table across the room from what I assumed was his desk.

There was a folder before him which he opened. He extracted a photograph from it and held it up. It was obviously old, in black-and-white, and it showed a man dressed as if he'd stepped out of a vintage movie. "Is this the man you call Jean Deschamps?"

I nodded. "That's certainly the man I saw at the autopsy."

Lacombe smiled, something he did frequently. "It is Jean Deschamps. You are right. This is the latest photograph we have of him." He checked the back. "It says June, nineteen forty-six. Afterwards, we hear nothing more about him."

"What did you think happened to him?" Gary Smith asked.

Lacombe's eyes widened. "Ah. I cannot say. I was not even born then, but I have asked the questions, and we will talk soon with a man who will tell you. This," he indicated the file, "is the first thing I did after you telephone me and say the name Deschamps. Right now, I can tell you about the Deschamps and what they are doing today, and maybe you can tell me about the body of Jean. Then later, we can talk to the retired man who knew Jean Deschamps."

He suddenly got to his feet, looking down at us affably. "But first, I would like to invite you to have lunch, no? You are hungry?"

I could see Gary getting ready to reject the invitation. "Wonderful," I said quickly, grabbing Paul's elbow and rising. "That's very kind of you."

Gary shut his mouth and joined us. "Yeah. Thanks."

We all filed back downstairs to a rear door leading to a closed garage with only a few cars in it. Lacombe headed toward a new minivan.

As we followed him, I murmured to Smith, "Sorry. I figured it would help break the ice."

He nodded several times, looking relieved. "No, no. That's fine. Keep him happy. I'm a little out of my depth here."

We piled into Lacombe's van and he backed us out into the parking area behind the building, confirming his status, to me at least, as one of the organization's higher-ups. In fact, no formal introductions had been made, as they would've been back in the

U.S., so I actually didn't know our host's rank or responsibilities.

Lacombe returned us to King Street, crossed it, and headed uphill toward the town's modern northwest quadrant.

"You know Sherbrooke?" he asked.

I was once again riding shotgun in the front seat, watching buildings slide by that made me think they'd been collected at some American architectural lawn sale. "Paul does. He was giving us a history lesson a while ago, plus a bit about the Hell's Angels."

Lacombe laughed. "Yes, the Hell's Angels. Very big. They are not actually in Sherbrooke, but in Lennoxville. They have a house I should show you. It is like a fortress—cameras, barbed wire, dogs, bulletproof glass."

"I thought things were calm around here," Paul said, surprised.

Lacombe looked back at him. "You are right. But the Rock Machine—you know them? The Rock Machine has made them very nervous. They have been shooting and bombing the houses of the Angels in Montreal. Very bad people."

As we topped the hill, I glanced back and got a more panoramic view than before. For the first time, I noticed, beyond the river, a tall hill with a huge metal, Erector set–looking cross planted on top. And I could just make out to the left the tops of what seemed to be some much older buildings—the part of town Paul had mentioned earlier, and the first visible signs of a distinctly foreign influence.

I, too, had glanced at a map before we'd left.

Sherbrooke was like a capital letter T lying on its right side, with the Magog River being the center leg and the cross being the north/south St. François River, connected to the Magog via a steep and narrow gorge—the source of the town's hydro-electric power and the site of the original settlement. Unlike other communities, whose roots become less visible over time, Sherbrooke showed its origins as openly as the timeworn lines on a factory worker's face.

Eventually, Lacombe brought us to a restaurant at the back of a sprawling, nearly empty shopping mall parking lot—a visual paradox I was to discover fit Sherbrooke like a glove. "I eat here always. Very cheap, but good."

"Which part of town do the Angels control?" I asked him as we entered its doors.

"There is a street downtown called Wellington South. It is where are the bars, discos, cheap hotels, tattoo places, *et tout le reste*. That is where the Angels and the Deschamps work."

In contrast to the outside, the restaurant was dark and friendly, with gentle piped-in music and booths and tables placed on various high and low platforms, breaking up the enormity of the place and injecting a sense of intimacy. We were shown a table high and toward the back, with fewer people, less noise, and an almost treehouse view of the floor below. The waitress and Lacombe were obviously old acquaintances.

For the next several minutes, Gilles Lacombe played host, translating our requests into a Québecois patois called *Joual,* which bore no resemblance I could detect to the French taught in our schools. For drinks, Paul, Gary, and I had water or Cokes. Lacombe had a beer, which I noticed caught Gary's disapproval. Despite the short, forty-minute drive from the border to here, I was beginning to feel like we'd just landed in Europe—an unsettling but pleasant sensation.

No doubt harking back to our theorizing during the trip, Gary asked Lacombe, "Have the Deschamps and the Angels shared this area for long?"

The Sûreté man looked at him meditatively. "I would say the Angels are here about twenty-five years. The Deschamps, much longer. I don't know about Jean, but he was a big shot already when he disappeared. At first, there was trouble. The Deschamps had everything and they didn't like the competition. I was just a patrolman back then, but I remember. We would find bodies outside of the town. But I think that with time, like two boxers, they finally realized no one body could win, and the Angels, they are not going to go away. So there was a peace, and it has been there for many years."

"What about you guys?" Gary asked as sandwiches arrived for the three of us—fat things made of French bread, which Gary eyed with suspicion—and soup and an odd bread, cheese, and pâté assortment for Lacombe, which looked to me like dollops of cat food. "You didn't just watch this happen, did you?"

Lacombe shrugged away the bluntness of

the question. "It was not as it is now. Sherbrooke had its police, we had a station here—only an outpost—Rock Forest and Lennoxville/Ascot had police, too. And the RCMP was there." He hesitated, then smiled thinly. "Now, we are big happy family. The Sûreté has a headquarters here, the Sherbrooke police joined the other two. We work well together."

He was obviously being diplomatic. "We went through the same growing pains back home," I said, hoping to soften Gary's implied criticism. "Still are, here and there. People like to defend their territories, and the bad guys take advantage of it."

The smile widened again and he relaxed. "Yes, that is it. Also, it is not so easy to fight them." He looked at Paul Spraiger, who unlike Gary was utterly at home negotiating his food. "You study history, yes? Did you study the Algerian War in the 1950s and '60s?"

Paul nodded enthusiastically. "Sure—what a mess."

"Yes, yes. The French paratroopers would search the Muslim Kasbah for rebels. If they could catch one, they would torture him, but mostly they could only get two names from him. The Algerians, they keep information in triangles of three people, so that one could only betray two more. You understand?"

"And that's what they did here?" Gary asked. "Both Angels and the Deschamps?"

Lacombe wiped his mouth on his napkin after taking another bite. "The Angels have become very big—about twenty-five people. The

Deschamps, they are smaller, but they have deeper roots. They are about ten."

"That's all?" Gary blurted.

"No, no," Lacombe continued, frustrated by his linguistic limitations. "That is what I was saying. Each one of them is like a *capitaine,* with his own people. All the *capitaines* know each other, but they do not know each other's people. So for each Angel or Deschamps, maybe you have ten others working for them, maybe more. It is difficult for us to know."

We all paused, contemplating the potential of what he'd just said. "And the Rock Machine is threatening to bust that wide open," I finally commented.

"You see why we are interested in your old, frozen Jean Deschamps," Gilles Lacombe said softly.

CHAPTER EIGHT

Jacques Chauvin was small, wrinkled, slight, and as agile as a monkey. He looked at us warily from under bushy white eyebrows as he muttered a few quiet, rapid-fire questions at Gilles Lacombe in *Joual,* standing in the doorway as if choosing between fight and flight.

Lacombe made the introductions, followed

90

by, "Jacques is the Sherbrooke policeman I spoke to you about. He knew Jean Deschamps and the others in the family back then."

We resumed our places around Lacombe's round table, Chauvin sitting so close to Lacombe their legs were almost touching.

"Jacques does not speak English," Gilles explained, "so I'm afraid you have to listen to me. It will be very slow. I have tried this before. But is that okay?"

I glanced at Paul and nodded. He cleared his throat. "I could give it a shot, if you'd like. I speak a little French."

Lacombe smiled broadly and winked at us. "Ah. You were keeping a secret on us."

"I doubt that," I answered, "given how well you speak English. But if you ever get stumped or would like to speak in French to us, I'm sure Paul wouldn't mind helping out."

Lacombe waved his hand dismissively, as I'd thought he would. "No, no. It is no problem. I need to have practice. So," he then added with emphasis, "let us go into Jacques's brain. I think it would be good if I translate into French for him and Paul can then translate into English for you. Okay?"

I glanced at Gary Smith, who was in fact our team leader, but he merely nodded at me to continue. "Mr. Chauvin," I began, "we really need as much information as possible at this point. Could you start by giving us a little history about the Deschamps family?"

Chauvin listened carefully to Lacombe and responded through Paul. "They go way back.

91

I don't know where they come from originally, but it was Jean who made them what they are today. As a young man, he smuggled booze into the U.S. during Prohibition. It was a big business all over Canada, of course, but it was particularly good just south of here, since the RCMP didn't cover this part of the border too well. I don't know why—maybe because this area was pretty wild and far from places like Montreal, given the bad roads. But Jean had a knack for it, too. He was ambitious, clever, and very, very nasty. Most people in that business just did it to make ends meet. Jean was out to create an empire. He started by carrying bottles across on his back, all by himself, then moved on to cars, then trucks. He even had some of them rigged with smoke pots, to blind whoever was giving chase. Very soon, he had almost every member of his family involved, and he was expanding from pure smuggling into warehousing, importing illegal goods, loan sharking, murder. As the twenties got wilder, he began supplying drugs through contacts he established in the Orient— the South American supply line didn't exist back then and Canada was still considered part of the British Empire, as was Hong Kong. One big tribe where contraband was concerned.

"Anyway, by the Depression, Deschamps was sitting on a pot of money, but with nowhere to hide it. If he ever had any, those might be called his tough years, since not only was the economy bad, but the authorities had finally taken an interest in him and were making things difficult. But he made up for it with a vengeance during the Second World War. That's when he became respectable, producing goods for the war effort, sacrificing all for king and country, including putting two sons into uniform, one of whom was killed. In fact, he turned a big pile of illegal cash into a really big fortune, buying up factories and controlling the flow of materials. By the end, he was one of the region's heroes and would have qualified for a knighthood if he hadn't been a crook—and hadn't created a new rebel image as an independent, damn-the-British, free Québecois.

"None of which mattered in the long run, anyway, because shortly after the war ended, he disappeared."

I leaned forward, opened the file Lacombe had left on the tabletop, and extracted the old photograph of Jean Deschamps. "Is this him?" I asked.

The old man's face creased into a thoughtful smile. "Yes, at the top of his form."

Gary Smith had been taking notes throughout Chauvin's long discourse and now looked up to ask, "What was the thinking at the time he disappeared?"

Chauvin replaced the picture and sat back. "We didn't know what to make of it. It wasn't a here today, gone tomorrow type of thing. We only gradually became aware of his absence and of Marcel's being the one calling the shots."

"Marcel?" Gary asked.

"His son. His younger son, actually. Antoine had been killed in Italy around 1943 or '44.

He was the one we thought would inherit the business, although I don't know how he could have improved on Marcel. There's a cold-hearted son-of-a-bitch."

I returned to Gary's question. "Surely you asked around once you noticed Jean hadn't been seen in a while?"

"Of course," Chauvin answered through Paul. "But we got different stories from everyone we asked. He'd become a recluse, enjoying the second half of his life in religious contemplation; he'd been killed by the opposition or by his own people in an unsuccessful power struggle; he'd been executed by Marcel in a *very* successful power struggle. You pick a theory, we heard it at least five times. But we had no body, no proof of a crime. So we did all we could—we dealt with reality and stopped chasing ghosts."

"You asked Marcel?"

"Yes. He said the Old Man had retreated to a religious life." Chauvin smiled. "Maybe he knew more than all of us about that."

"You think he murdered his father?"

The smile faded as he gave that serious thought. "At the time, it didn't make any more sense than the retreat story. Marcel and Antoine were close to their father. It was one of the reasons the gang worked so well, because the family did, too. Antoine was the eldest and the heir apparent, but we never thought Marcel had a problem with that. He had his own responsibilities. It wasn't like he'd been relegated to washing cars out back. The feeling was that the operation would be so big after the war that the two sons would work together as equals with their father."

"So how did Marcel manage?" Gary asked.

"He had Pierre Guidry to help him," Chauvin said simply, "and Gaston Picard."

"Guidry is the family second-in-command," Lacombe explained. "Apparently he helped guide Marcel in the early days, teaching him the ropes. Picard's the family lawyer—pretty old now."

Chauvin looked confused and asked for a translation. Then he shook his head vehemently. "No, no. Guidry and Marcel helped each other out. After all, they're about the same age now. Guidry was never the Old Man's advisor. That was Picard. Guidry was a chauffeur and a bodyguard—a kid from the streets who Jean Deschamps virtually adopted as his own. Guidry was almost as much part of the family as the two boys, and he filled a gap for Marcel after Antoine died, only as a slightly younger brother, which suited Marcel better. It was a good fit, too."

"But until Jean died," I said, "Marcel may not have been washing cars, but it sounds like Pierre was."

Again, Chauvin disagreed. "You had to have known them back then. To call Pierre Guidry a chauffeur/bodyguard misses what he meant to the others. That was his job, sure, but he was family."

I had no choice but to grant him his insider's knowledge, although I found his comments raised more questions than answers.

Gary moved on. "How 'bout the opposition you mentioned? What did that consist of?"

"They're the ones we finally concluded killed Jean," our guest admitted. "At least the majority did. And it does make sense. Deschamps wasn't the only one to come out of the war rich, or the only one to see big potential in the postwar crime business. The U.S. was suddenly top dog in the world, hungry and ambitious, and we were right next door. There were criminal power struggles happening all over Canada. The Deschamps had some real problems keeping control—everybody was scrapping for a piece of it, from little guys to the more organized types."

"So who made your top-five list of suspects?" Gary persisted.

Chauvin laughed. "Suspects for what? We didn't have a body, and the family hadn't reported a death. What I'm telling you never left the bull-session stage."

And wasn't treated too seriously in any case, I thought. Whether it was because they were overworked, undertrained, apathetic, or corrupt, the cops back then apparently thought the death of any crook—for any reason—was simple good riddance. Not a reason to launch a major investigation.

I retreated a couple of steps. "You said Deschamps's business was very dependent on the United States. Do you know if he ever traveled or owned property there? In Stowe, for example?"

"We know he used to go there, especially in the early days when he was smuggling. As

96

for owning property..." Chauvin shrugged. "We didn't keep track of that, but it's likely. It makes sense to keep money outside the country. But he probably would have used fake names anyhow."

There was a long pause while we considered what we'd learned.

"Mr. Chauvin," I finally asked, "when did you retire?"

"Nineteen sixty-two."

"In the years following Jean's disappearance, as you and your colleagues worked against the Deschamps family, did you notice any cracks developing in their structure? Any indications that things weren't quite as tightly run as they had been under Jean?"

"No. Like I said, Marcel was a natural. Maybe he was twenty-one when he took over—really young—but his Old Man would've been proud. He kept things running, he changed with the times, he made deals with people like the Angels. The operation should have died with the founder. Instead, it only got bigger."

"Which made you personally suspect, with hindsight, that Marcel killed his father instead of the competition," I suggested. "Do you think he was helped by Guidry and/or Picard?"

Chauvin shook his head. "Guidry rode Marcel's coattails. He wasn't smart enough to do more. And Picard's position never changed, so for him, there was no advantage in killing Jean."

I still couldn't shake the idea that two second fiddles had gained top ranking with Jean's sudden disappearance.

"How about some of the old-timers, retired like yourself?" I asked. "Could you recommend someone in or near the family who might be willing to talk to us?"

I'd expected him to say no. Instead, he reflected a moment, and then said, "Lucien Pelletier. He's about my age. That would take you to a few years before the war. He's not related by blood, but he worked pretty closely with Jean."

"Why would he talk to us?"

"He's been out of the business for forty-five years. I don't think Marcel liked him much, and moved him out. There haven't been any connections since, I don't think. He's just an old man with memories now." Jacques Chauvin smiled and added, "Like me."

I got up from the table after Chauvin left and crossed to the window to admire the view of the metal warehouse.

"Well, gentlemen," Lacombe said, closing the door on our guest. "Was that of help?"

"Not much," Gary admitted. "Thanks for setting it up, though."

"I don't know," I said. "We learned a bit about the family dynamics. It's a start, anyhow. Maybe we ought to ask you, Gilles, what if anything you want to do about this?"

Lacombe sat back down thoughtfully as Gary Smith shot me a quick hard look. "The Deschamps family is a very big deal for us," he said. "Especially if the conflict between the Angels and the Rock Machine takes place. It would be nice to have a..." he glanced at Paul Spraiger. *"Pince-à-levier?"*

"Crowbar," Spraiger explained.

"Yes. A crowbar we could use to get more inside. I would like to explore the situation. In fact, I would like to make a task force, since we are several jurisdictions. This way, we would all know what is happening."

Gary was visibly in need of getting something off his chest. "Can I ask a question?"

We all looked at him silently.

"I know I'm the odd guy out here—the small-town cop who's never been across the border. But this is my department's case," he looked straight at me, "unless that support role pitch you gave us was a crock."

I shook my head. "Nope—that was straight."

Lacombe smiled broadly, leaned forward, and patted Smith on the knee, catching him off guard. "I understand your worries," he assured him. "You are feeling on the bottom of the totem. It is why I proposed the task force. You have a dead body, we have a crime family we are wanting to open up. I hope this way we all get a reward. I would like to invite everyone—someone from the Sherbrooke police, all of us here, and a *procureur de la couronne* to work with yours—a prosecutor. Also, if you are agreeable, a member of the RCMP. They would be interested in the federal offenses, like narcotics and smuggling. But only," he repeated, "if that is no bother to you."

Lacombe paused to reflect and then added, "I am saying this because I do not wish the

99

Deschamps to slip away. It is a very old murder that seems the most weak link, and I do not think we should place all the eggs in that one basket. A task force will approach from all angles. Am I saying this wrong?"

Gary shook his head slowly. "No, I get the point."

I considered Gary's seemingly small-minded objection in a wider context, and said in part to help him out, "Rumor is the SQ and the RCMP don't get along very well."

"There was a time, perhaps," Lacombe conceded. "New attitudes are making it easier. But you are right—there is still some rubbing."

"What happens if we shut them out?" I asked for argument's sake.

"They will bang on the door. The name Deschamps is in their computers, too."

I looked at Gary Smith and raised my eyebrows inquiringly.

"The more the merrier," he said with a weak smile.

Lacombe nodded, apparently satisfied. "Very good. Now, I would like to ask you more about what you found that brought you here."

Gary picked that up. "Not much—basically his driver's license, his clothes, a ring from his finger, a few odds and ends from his wallet, and an autopsy report. I called my office to see if anything else had come up from the computer search we ordered, but so far, there's nothing to indicate he was ever in the United States, at least not legally."

"Which brings up an interesting point," Paul Spraiger said. "Jacques Chauvin listed all the people who might've had it in for Jean, including some unnamed competitor. Who's to say that competitor wasn't an American? We've been assuming the body was dropped from a plane that flew in from Canada, but there's nothing to prove that."

"Nothing is right," added Gary. "The office also said that an analysis from the various radars covering the Stowe area over the last two months came up empty, meaning either there was no plane or it flew into the drop zone at under two thousand feet."

"Okay," Paul said. "If we're playing 'what if,' I was struck by the fact that Marcel reached the top over two conveniently dead people."

Lacombe looked startled. "You mean he had his brother killed in the war?"

Gary merely shrugged, but I was impressed. It upped the ante on my own ruminations.

"Chauvin said the two brothers got along—were slated to share the business," Paul protested.

"Maybe," I said, "maybe not. Gary might have something—not necessarily that Antoine was murdered, but that his death changed what the Old Man had in mind. If something happened between Marcel and Jean after Antoine's death that Marcel felt threatened his ascension, he might have had his father killed. It wouldn't be the first time ambition was thicker than blood."

Paul voiced the obvious next step, easing away from too much hypothesizing: "Sounds like we ought to have a little walk down memory lane with Lucien Pelletier."

CHAPTER NINE

We were back in Gilles Lacombe's minivan, joined this time by Rick Labatt—one of his intelligence officers. The Deschamps family's current activities were one of Labatt's pet projects, so while he couldn't add much to Jacques Chauvin's history lesson, he was eager to be part of Lacombe's new task force and heading off to visit an old Deschamps associate like Lucien Pelletier.

His English syntax was better and less accented than his boss's. "I wish I could tell you that finding Jean Deschamps fits a change in the family's operations," he said from the back seat. "But as far as we can tell, everything is running as usual."

"How good is your information?" I asked him.

Labatt was young, wiry, and energetic, very expressive with his hands, but to that question, he gave but a rueful look. "You are right, of course," he admitted. "It is not very good. The Deschamps are careful that way. We have never put anyone inside their organization. We watch, we listen when we can, we look at surveillance photos, but we don't know very much. It is why I am excited about this happening with Jean."

"Do the Deschamps compete head-on with the Angels?" Paul asked.

Labatt shook his head. "No, no. Well, maybe a little in the places where there is more room, like smuggling drugs. But locally, the

Deschamps, for example, control all the auto theft. The Angels don't do that. Also, there are bars that are run by one, where the members of the other do not go. It is very strictly followed."

"And you've never gotten close to nailing Marcel," Gary stated.

"That is correct. He is very protected. We nibble at the edges. We take down a chop shop here or there, capture a runner along the border, arrest a few prostitutes. But we can only go so far up the line. Then we run out of what the judge wants to see. We know who's responsible, but we cannot prove it."

We had driven in the same general direction of the restaurant, but then veered off into a neighborhood of upscale, tastefully appointed modern homes, each planted in the middle of a three-quarter lot, facing a sinewy street and looking new and artificial enough to have been made of plastic parts. Even the snow resembled powdered sugar.

"There it is." Lacombe pointed ahead to a house on a corner. "Chauvin told me Pelletier lives with his daughter, who doesn't know his history. I will make up a story for her."

We got out of the van after Lacombe parked it on the street, looking like a hit squad ourselves, but I left it to Lacombe to spin his tall tale to the sixty-something woman who answered the door, and tried to appear as innocent as I could.

Eventually, after some fussing from the daughter about coffee and cookies, and a bit of chicanery from Lacombe about the need for privacy, we found ourselves in an upstairs bedroom with a large old man who sat in his oversized chair like a walrus in a cave opening.

He spoke no English, so we repeated the routine we'd followed in Lacombe's office. But no playacting was necessary. Immediately following his daughter's departure from the room, Lucien Pelletier shot Lacombe one quick, hard question.

Lacombe laughed while Paul translated. "He wants to know what he's done to deserve so many lousy cops."

"Tell him he's lived too long," I said.

Pelletier let out a wet, gurgly chuckle that ended in a prolonged coughing fit.

"Then it's a good thing you dropped by," Paul said on his behalf, "'Cause I'm about to get that over with."

Gary Smith sat on a chair just off to Pelletier's side. "We're here for a history lesson," he said. "About the early days of the Deschamps family."

The old man studied him a moment. "Why?"

"It's an American case. We think we have something that goes back to World War Two."

Pelletier smiled and nodded. "Ah—when Jean ran things."

"Yes. What was he like?"

"Very tough. A man of his word."

"You got to know him when?" I asked.

"Nineteen thirty-one. Back during Prohibition. I was still a teenager. Deschamps was a big cheese in the business, with lots of trucks and warehouses. He was moving thousands of bottles a week by then. I broke into one of his depots to steal a few cases. I didn't see why he should have all the fun and profit. And he caught me—personally. The Old Man himself. He'd seen me casing the place earlier and kept an eye out for me. He let me break in, waited till I had my arms full, and then stuck a gun in my ear."

Pelletier laughed again with the same wet, racking results. We all waited until he'd regained his breath and wiped his mouth with a handkerchief. "It was lucky for me," he resumed. "If it had been one of his boys, I would have died that night. People disappeared all the time when they ran foul of the Deschamps. But the Old Man took a shine to me. I don't know why. He said he liked people with balls, and who planned before they acted. I didn't think I'd done too well in that department, but I wasn't going to argue. So he hired me instead of killing me."

"Just like that?" Gary asked incredulously.

Pelletier smiled ruefully. "He did say he'd kill me if I crossed him. I guess he knew I'd never do that."

"What did you do for him?"

"Not much at first. I worked in the warehouse I'd tried to rob. Eventually, I moved up to driving trucks—"

"Across the border?" Gary asked.

"Not at first. It was pretty legitimate to start with. I'd drive to just shy of the border and leave the truck. When I came back, it would be empty. Later, I found out what happened to the stuff."

"Which was?"

"It depended. Sometimes it went onto the backs of men or horses or horse-drawn sleighs; other times, it was switched over to an American truck. About a year after Jean Deschamps didn't kill me, I was doing work like that, going across the border."

"What about after Prohibition?"

"Things were changing even before then. The Mounties were feeling the heat from the Americans. A lot of our men were getting caught. The Old Man had almost gotten out of the liquor business by 1933. By the Depression, we were moving other things—anything that had a market value."

"But you were doing more than smuggling by then, no?" Labatt asked.

"Of course," Pelletier admitted, but then fell silent. "It's more than a history lesson you want," he said after a pause. "What is this American case?"

Lacombe cleared his throat and tried to address his problem. "Monsieur Pelletier, this conversation is just that. It is not being taken down as evidence. Whatever you might have done will not come back to haunt you through us."

But the loyalty born all those years ago was unaffected by either threats of reprisal or promises of anonymity. This man's feelings for Jean Deschamps clearly mirrored a son's for his father.

I tried a different approach. "You must have gotten to know his two sons pretty well."

"Jean had them doing other things," he said. "But we saw them around. Antoine made it a point to get to know us. He was a nice kid. Jean was a broken man after he died."

"In Italy, during the war?"

"Yes."

I thought I'd try exploiting the prejudice that had influenced our coming here. "Still, he had Marcel to lean on. That must've been a comfort."

Lucien Pelletier didn't answer at first.

"Marcel was next in line," he finally said, blatantly restraining himself. "He's done a good job."

"Actually," I added, pretending not to have noticed his reluctance, "it's kind of ironic when you think of it. First Antoine dies, breaking his father's heart, then Jean disappears, which must've been equally hard on Marcel. Tragic, in a way. He was pretty young then, wasn't he?"

"I never saw Marcel feel anything about anybody," he said bitterly.

"But his own father," I exclaimed, feigning surprise.

Pelletier finally opened up. "He didn't care. He took over the family like he'd been born to the job. Didn't give a shit about a damn thing except his own ambition."

"What happened to Jean?" I asked suddenly.

There was dead silence in the room. Pelletier had been staring at the floor through most of the conversation. This time, he looked straight at me, his eyes moist. "I don't know."

"He just vanished?"

"Yes."

"How?"

"We think he went for a drive. He took the car. We never saw him or it again."

"I thought he had a chauffeur."

"He did, but he didn't use him all the time. Sometimes, when he wanted to be alone, he'd drive himself."

"So he was feeling reflective the day he disappeared?"

"I didn't think so. I thought he was acting like he did when a deal was about to go down—energized. Restless and distracted. I'd seen it before. Like before a big job."

"You must have had some ideas about what happened. What did you all think?"

"We knew he'd been killed. He'd been so close to it so many times before—robbing banks, muscling the competition, fighting off the law..." He suddenly straightened with pride, and added, "On both sides of the border."

"What was done to find out?" I asked.

"We put pressure on people like never before. But quietly, without noise. That was Marcel's doing, and at first I was impressed. I thought, 'Just like the Old Man—strong and tough. Get the job done right without fanfare.' Only later did I think he only did it that way to make things easier for himself afterward."

"So no one else would know?"

"Right."

"But none of you knew, either," I protested. "You just *thought* he'd been killed. If he had been, wouldn't someone have bragged about it?"

"That's what we were waiting for. It never happened."

"And so things kept going as if nothing had changed?"

"Yes, to the outside world. People asked after a while, when they noticed the Old Man wasn't around anymore. First, we were told to play dumb, then to say he'd retreated to a life of contemplation. What a laugh. Before anyone put two and two together, Marcel was fully in command. The time to exploit any weakness had passed."

"Mr. Pelletier," I said, leaning closer to him, "I hate to circle the same point, but didn't it seem odd that no one took claim of killing the legendary Jean Deschamps?"

"Not in the long run," he said.

I let a long pause follow and then said softly, "Because you all assumed he'd been killed by his own son."

"Yes."

"Had you ever sensed Marcel had that in him?"

He surprised me then, giving me a look of utter bewilderment. "Never. He was a cold boy and a heartless man, with none of his father's knowledge of human nature. He hadn't had to carve his way up from the bottom, so he didn't know how to lose as well as to win. But I never saw him disagree with his father, never caught him looking at him angrily when his back was turned. He was like a machine, before and after his father's death. That's one reason the transition was so smooth."

"But we're missing two people in all this,

aren't we?" I asked. "What about Pierre Guidry and Gaston Picard, Jean's right-hand boys? We heard Guidry especially moved up the ladder after Jean died."

Like Chauvin before him, Pelletier shook his head. "Guidry was more like the Old Man's substitute for Antoine, and Marcel adopted him like he adopted the business. It was a good move, too. Guidry had what Marcel lacked—he liked people and they liked him. Marcel could use him to smooth things out."

"That must've been handy when everyone thought Marcel had killed his own father," I said, almost as an aside.

"We weren't killed ourselves," Pelletier conceded simply. "We took that as a plus."

"That why you parted company with the Deschamps?"

"I shot my mouth off. Guidry was very nice about it, but I knew what would happen if I refused. It didn't matter. I didn't want to stay anyway, and I couldn't have left if they hadn't let me. It was a one-time offer, and it suited me. I did all right afterward. It was a privilege to work with Jean Deschamps. It was a pleasure to leave his son to fend for himself. Not that he suffered any."

"Nor did Guidry, from what we were told."

"Pierre was justly recompensed, and I'm sure Michel will continue the tradition. If it weren't for the blood connection, in fact, Pierre would probably run things. Not that he wants to—he likes being behind the throne."

Once again, Lucien Pelletier had been

staring into space as he spoke—an old man addressing the ghosts of his past. But at the surprised silence greeting his last words, he looked up and took us all in. "What's the matter?"

Lacombe spoke directly to him, letting Paul translate for both sides. "You said Michel—did you mean Marcel's son?"

"Yes."

"Implying he's about to take over?"

I noticed Rick Labatt sitting forward, his expression keen.

"Well, if not him, I don't know who. God knows Marcel's been doing his damnedest to train the little brat behind the scenes. Big mistake, if you ask me, not that I care anymore."

"But why now?" I asked. "With the Angels and the Rock Machine about to rumble, Marcel should want to keep his hand on the tiller."

Pelletier's eyes widened and he let out another long, wet chuckle. "Boy, you do need help. Don't you know? Marcel's dying of cancer—has a few months to live, depending on who you believe. Fitting end to that bastard, rotting from the inside out."

CHAPTER TEN

Lacombe left the cookie-cutter neighborhood where Lucien Pelletier was living out his life and headed east toward downtown on Portland Boulevard—a broad new avenue north of and parallel to King Street, as fast, sterile, and empty as King was stop-and-go, cluttered, and tacky. Not for the first time, I wondered if Sherbrooke might be jamming the American city center-to-strip mall-to-suburbs phenomenon into too small an area—with Alice-in-Wonderland jarring results.

"So, Rick," Lacombe asked in a mocking voice from the front. "Did Intelligence know about Marcel's medical condition?"

Labatt was obviously embarrassed. "We knew he hadn't been seen in public much lately."

"I guess not." Lacombe was smiling, in fact not very concerned.

"It's an interesting piece of timing," I said. "Marcel's father, long dead, is brought out of the freezer just as it's revealed Marcel's living on borrowed time."

"You think there is a connection?" Labatt asked.

Paul Spraiger answered for me. "Jean's body appeared for some reason—must've been a big one, since he'd been kept on ice for so long. Sounds reasonable this might be it."

"But it is to the advantage of who?" Lacombe asked.

No one had an answer for him.

Reinforcing my earlier musing, Portland Boulevard ended abruptly in the town's oldest section, called Le Vieux Nord, or the Old North End. Originally home of the high and mighty, it was a hilly, tree-shaded cluster of elegant, graceful homes harking back to Victorian times and earlier. Unlike Pelletier's nearby neighborhood, this area reflected a passage of years without any town planner's influence. The streets were meandering and narrow, and lined by everything from schools to churches to museums to regal homes. In the center of it all was the gorge connecting the two large rivers, blocked by several dams and lined by factories both functioning and gutted, as impressive in their solidarity and antiquity as the squat, huge, and ponderous cathedral that sat like a sleeping hippopotamus on the hill overlooking it all. It was an industrial tableau of the nostalgic values of church, home, and business—all three equally worn down and neglected by time.

Lacombe pulled over on a side street next to a thick row of trees and killed the engine. "Let me show you something," he said, swinging out into the cold, ebbing light.

He led us through a hole in the trees and out onto a cantilevered platform jutting fifty feet above a misty, boiling, ice-choked tumult of water. Below us and to the right were a dam and a hydro station. Beyond the dam in the distance, the flat expanse of the Magog River was visible under the Montcalm Bridge. But what made the scene remarkable was the *absence* of humanity's touch. Despite the industrial accessories, the gorge itself was primarily wild—a deep cut through sheer rock, bordered by thick stands of trees. Looking downstream, and ignoring the cityscape peering through the denuded branches, I felt I was out in the mountainous wilds, at a secret, never-visited natural aquatic enclave. It was as startling and impressive as the cathedral just one block away. Once again, this town had taken me by surprise, throwing open yet another curtain—mere feet from its predecessor—to reveal a whole other face.

"This is the source of Sherbrooke's existence," Gilles Lacombe explained. "From here came everything. The first Abnaki visitors three hundred years ago and the Deschamps and the Hell's Angels. It is not all the time you can point to one thing and say that."

It was a curiously philosophical comment, especially in the context of our current conundrum. I sensed a yearning inside Lacombe to locate some similar touchstone in the case we were investigating, with which he could restore order where only confusion was now apparent.

We stood there awhile, shivering as much from the sight of such frozen chaos as from the actual cold, and then Lacombe led us back to the van's warm embrace.

"I now take you on a different tourist trip," he said, starting up the engine and heading back into the Vieux Nord.

Five minutes later, he slowed opposite a large, old, dark brown house with a steep slate roof and heavy wooden beams crowning the doors and windows. It looked like what Hansel and Gretel's witch might have called home had she suddenly hit the Lotto.

"This is the house of Marcel Deschamps," Lacombe said. "It has ten bathrooms and two kitchens and all of that."

I studied the house with renewed interest. There was no one in sight, no movement from behind any of the curtained windows. The snowy lawn was large but not vast, the house itself unremarkable from its equally accessible neighbors. In short, it looked utterly normal—for the average eccentric rich guy.

"Okay," Lacombe announced. "Now to the place of business of Monsieur Deschamps."

We left the Vieux Nord for Wellington Street North, proceeded down its respectable corridor of boutiques, restaurants, businesses, and banks, and crossed King to Wellington South, discovering at the intersection, with a suddenness I was becoming used to, King's San Francisco–style plunge toward the Aylmer Bridge across the St. François River below us.

Wellington South was instantly totally different. In a minor key, it reminded me of Boston's old Combat Zone—gritty, gap-toothed, and cluttered with bars, discos, flophouses, cabarets, and a Salvation Army chapel. Craning through the window, I looked up at the apartments overhead, and the tattered shades and greasy panes of human misery and hopelessness.

It made for a fitting contrast with the house we'd left just minutes before, purchased with the proceeds generated from the appetites this neighborhood fed all too well.

Lacombe continued south, to where Wellington became Queen, and then drove a very short distance past a sign announcing our entrance into Lennoxville. "Look to the right," he said, slowing down.

Around a gentle corner, we slowed before a driveway cutting above us into an embankment, and blocked by a reinforced steel gate topped by gleaming razor wire. Behind it was a large, new, red-roofed house festooned with security cameras and a bouquet of oversized searchlights. It was difficult to see clearly, blocked off as it was by the wire, a row of tall hedges, and a cinderblock wall. But it looked like an armed outpost in the middle of enemy territory.

"Hell's Angels headquarters," Lacombe told us, "with bulletproof glass in all the windows. They are the other lords of Wellington Street."

We continued into Lennoxville village, a pleasant cluster of old red brick buildings reminiscent of what we'd left in Vermont, and pulled over in front of a small restaurant/bar. Lacombe led the way to a corner table near the back. He and Labatt ordered wine. Spraiger, Smith, and I chose coffee.

"I thought you might find that of help," Lacombe said. "It gives an idea of how both parties see the world. While they share the dark culture of Sherbrooke, you can see they are very different. One is old, traditional, built like the Mafia. The other is angry, violent, paranoid, and quick for the action. I showed you that because I think you should see how their peace is fragile, even though it has lasted for many years. It is like the two legs on a ladder."

He nodded toward his younger colleague. "Rick is telling me the Rock Machine is now wanting to kick one of the legs. I am worried that what you have brought me with the news of Jean Deschamps is the destruction of the other."

I remembered how Paul had said earlier that one of the virtues of the Angels was that they policed their own—implying the local cops had learned to live with that arrangement, however reluctantly. It underscored Lacombe's remark about having all the crooks suddenly thrown into a competitive free-for-all.

Gary Smith had obviously come to the same realization.

"We can't do anything about the guys in the bunker," he said, his enthusiasm at contrast with his earlier reserve. "But we can research the hell out of the Deschamps family. If we move fast enough and get lucky, maybe we can take that one leg down piece by piece without too much bloodshed. Then you can concentrate on the Angels."

Lacombe shook his head. "I think time will not be enough. Have the American press spoken of Jean Deschamps?"

"They haven't identified him yet," I said. "But it won't be long before word leaks out."

"That is what I thought. I would like to tell Marcel and his lieutenants of the news face-to-face, to see their reaction. We would not be prepared as with your research, Gary, but we might learn more in exchange. Is this acceptable?"

Smith raised his coffee cup to him. "Works for me."

I felt uncomfortable walking up to the home of an unknown man whom I suspected of patricide. It was not the standard—or the smart—way to go. The trick to interviewing potential suspects was to know in advance what they might say. Yet I couldn't fault Lacombe for his reasoning. I, too, wanted to see what Marcel would say about his father's sudden reappearance. And I recognized that time was against us.

We were met at the door by the first indicator that this wasn't just another millionaire's mansion: a very large man with the face of an ax-murderer. He and Lacombe exchanged a few guttural comments in rapid *Joual,* during which Lacombe produced his shield, before the door was unceremoniously closed in our faces.

"Trouble?" Gary asked, angered by the lack of respect.

Lacombe's expression was benign as he turned up his collar against the cold. "No. He is just asking his boss about us."

I was struck once more by the difference in law enforcement styles on either side of the border. Not only was it wine for meals, dapper clothes on the job, and a lack of body builder types around the station house up here, but there was an attitudinal contrast as well. In our conversation with Pelletier, our discussions about crooks, and even in the way Lacombe accepted having a door slammed in his face, there was a lack of the kind of pseudo-military rigidity that so often stamped American cops. Not only had we yet to know our host's official rank, but I'd noticed as well that he didn't bother carrying a gun.

The butler/bodyguard returned several minutes later, accompanied by a slighter, much older man with little hair, thick glasses, and impressively expensive clothing. Lacombe and he obviously knew one another, shaking hands and exchanging pleasantries. Thanks to Paul's quietly translating for Gary and me, we gathered that he was the family's longtime lawyer, Gaston Picard.

As we were escorted down a long, high-ceilinged hallway, cluttered with antique knickknacks and a couple of chandeliers, Gary leaned toward me and whispered, "They know we were coming, or d'you think they keep the lawyer upstairs?"

We ended up in an oversized, high-ceilinged library, wood-paneled, filled with leather furniture, and girdled by a balcony running around three of the walls, the fourth being occupied by an enormous stone fireplace, complete with burning logs, and surmounted by a regal oil portrait of the man I'd seen as still as a marble statue on the medical examiner's table.

Gaston Picard waved us toward a selection of armchairs and sofas, and said in perfect, slightly British-tinged English, "Please, gentlemen, make yourselves comfortable." He then stared at me, his eyes magnified by his glasses, and extended a hand in greeting. "I understand you are from Vermont's new Bureau of Investigation."

The hand was manicured, soft, and slightly moist, like a young girl's. "Yes, that's right. Joe Gunther." I introduced Paul and Gary, whom he also greeted with old-world formality. I noticed that wherever possible, he'd accented his appearance with daubs of gold jewelry—ring, watch, key chain, and tie pin.

"I am Gaston Picard, Mr. Deschamps's attorney. I gather you have something you wish to discuss with him."

I glanced around, waiting for either Lacombe or Gary to fill in, but both of them had obviously decided, as they had with Pelletier earlier, to let me carry the ball.

I was not, however, going to play with Picard. "That's right," I said without further explanation.

In the slight pause that followed, the dandified lawyer smiled humorlessly. "I see. Is this request of an official nature?" He held his hand out. "Accompanied by a warrant, for example?"

I'd expected that. "No. But if you choose to throw us out, I think you'll discover later that your boss will be royally pissed off at you."

His eyebrows rose, as much at my choice of words as at their meaning, the first of which I'd used in reaction to his oily manners. "Then you are offering something of use perhaps? Or of value?"

"Information of value, yes—something he'd like to know as quickly as possible."

Picard nodded officiously. "Excellent. Then I will tell his secretary to put you on the very top of the appointment calendar. I take it I can reach you through le Capitaine Lacombe?"

I smiled at this first use of Lacombe's title, realizing now how he'd rated that exclusive parking spot in the Sûreté's basement. But I didn't move from my comfortable seat, nor did any of my colleagues, despite Picard's taking several steps toward the door.

"You can reach us that way if you choose to in the future. Right now, you better get Deschamps and tell him we're here. I would guess that in his present condition, he's come to appreciate the high cost of wasted time."

Picard was obviously taken off guard. I decided to try to nudge him a little harder.

"Especially," I added, pointing to the portrait above the mantel, "when what we have to say directly involves old ghosts."

He hesitated a moment, ducked his head slightly, and said, "Very well. I shall return in a moment."

He wasn't gone thirty seconds before the silent giant of before appeared through a different door, pushing ahead of him a cart filled with coffee cups and a silver urn, which he abandoned in our midst like a sacrifice.

Lacombe didn't hesitate, rubbing his hands and examining some cake slices he found under a silver dome. "Would any of you like this?"

Gary and I passed. Paul, after a pause,

took him up on the offer, and joined Labatt and his boss in coffee and cake both.

They'd just finished snacking when the double cherry doors swung back and Gaston Picard reappeared, pushing an old man in a wheelchair before him, and accompanied by another—tall, dark, broad-shouldered, and watchful—who struck me as something more than a bodyguard.

We all rose to our feet. Marcel Deschamps sat like a pampered scarecrow dressed in fine clothing, his skin stretched and pale to translucence, his few remaining strands of white hair sticking like cotton candy to his skull. The only sign of vitality—strong and unyielding—were his eyes. Black-rimmed and hollow, they gleamed with intelligent ferocity. Despite the overall frailty of the package, those eyes confirmed the ruthlessness Lucien Pelletier had described.

Picard made the introductions, remembering all our names perfectly, and identified the dark newcomer as Pierre Guidry. We stood in a circle respectfully, not shaking hands, since Deschamps kept his under the blanket draping his knees, and Guidry made no move to be conversational. It occurred to me as we finally broke ranks and settled back into our seats that neither Marcel nor Pierre was that much older than I. Yet while the former looked ancient enough to be somebody's great-grandfather, the latter had the appearance of a man in his early forties.

Marcel's voice, when he finally spoke, mirrored the strength in his eyes, however, and the fact that he chose French—not *Joual*—showed his tactical abilities were fully alive as well, for I was sure his command of English was as good as my own—either that or half the library's contents were unreadable to him.

Paul Spraiger nevertheless took up his assigned role as translator.

"I've been led to believe," Deschamps told Lacombe, "that you have something important to say to me—something that justifies this invasion of my privacy."

Lacombe responded in English. "That is true, and in courtesy to our guests, I think we should speak their language."

Deschamps indicated Guidry with a slight toss of his head, keeping to French. "My colleague and business partner would have a hard time with that, and I'd like him to be a part of this."

I was about to suggest it didn't matter either way, when Lacombe rose to his feet and calmly announced the meeting concluded.

I quickly stood to back him up, the others joining in ragged suit.

Deschamps's expression turned to disgust, but his reaction proved that we'd adequately baited the hook. "Sit down," he said in perfect English. "This is childish—it doesn't become you."

We all sat back down.

"Let's do this quickly," Deschamps added. "Since you have tumbled to my condition, you can appreciate why."

"Mr. Deschamps," Gary Smith asked, "when was the last time you saw your father?"

Marcel looked at him stolidly for a moment, as if wondering how he'd come to appear in the room. "Nineteen forty-seven," he finally said.

"When in nineteen forty-seven?"

"Winter. He came to bid us all good-bye in this very house. He was dedicating the rest of his life to the contemplation of God. I never saw him again."

"That story's due for a revision."

"Why? It's the truth."

"Is your father still alive?"

A thin smile crossed the cadaverous face. "Of course not. He died years ago."

"How and when?"

Gaston Picard interrupted. "Gentlemen, you must know that this entire conversation is being conducted out of our good grace alone. You have no right to be here, and you certainly have no right to badger my client. If you have something to say, please say it."

"We will," I said, "but we want it placed in context."

Again, Deschamps scowled. "He died at the Abbey de St. Benoit, twenty years ago, of a heart attack."

Picard looked at him sharply, the disapproval clear on his face.

Gary extracted a picture from his inside coat pocket, crossed over to Deschamps's wheelchair, and dropped it on the other man's lap. "Is this your father?"

Deschamps hesitated glancing down at it, and when he did, he became so still it almost seemed as if he'd stopped breathing.

"Where did you get this?" he finally asked, glancing back up, even paler than before.

"We took it at his autopsy a couple of days ago," I said. "He'd been stabbed with an ice pick, or something just like it."

Marcel looked confused, staring at the picture again. "I don't understand. He looks younger than me. What do you mean he was stabbed? When?"

"A long time ago," Gary explained. "Back when you claim he went to the abbey."

"Mr. Deschamps," I said. "We know the religious story was so your competitors wouldn't sense a weakness and put you out of business. But your father was murdered. I think even your lawyer will tell you that keeping to the old story wouldn't be smart. It might make us wonder why you were being so evasive."

Deschamps was very still for a moment, still holding the photograph in one bony, blue-veined hand. "Explain what this means," he finally said in a soft voice. I was struck by his overall reaction. Either he still had reserves enough to be a very effective actor, or his apparent grief was real.

"We found your father last week on top of a mountain in Vermont," Gary explained. "He'd been frozen stiff since the time of his death—approximately fifty years."

This time Picard was the one who looked baffled. "It's not that cold in Ver—"

Deschamps interrupted him with a quick command, his emotional stability fully restored. "Enough."

He then stared at me. "How was he kept frozen so long?"

I was impressed at his immediate grasp of the situation. I could almost see his brain whirring behind those penetrating eyes. "No doubt a commercial freezer," I answered. "Are you more inclined now to tell us how and why he disappeared?"

Picard suddenly bent over at the waist and whispered something in Marcel's ear. The ailing man smiled slightly and said, "I will admit to fabricating the story of his religious conversion. If you had known my father, you would have been amused by that invention. Unfortunately, the truth is no more revealing. He simply vanished—took the car, supposedly for a drive, and never came back."

"But that was rare, wasn't it?" I asked. "Didn't Mr. Guidry there usually drive him? And wasn't he more concerned for his own safety to be so casual?"

"Yes and no. He was a strong-willed man, not given to showing weakness. It wasn't his nature to hide from his enemies."

"Meaning he'd gone to meet with one of them?"

"Meaning nothing of the kind. We have no idea what happened to him. One day he was here. The next he was not. It is that simple or that complex. We don't know. There was even talk that he'd died of a heart attack while driving in the country. But every time we thought of an explanation, something cropped up to undermine it. Such as, what happened to the car? If a competitor killed him, why did no one brag about it? If he simply ran away, why no letters or bank withdrawals or early indications that he was unhappy with his present life? In the end, we were left with a mystery, which," and he waved the photo in his hand, "has apparently officially become your property." He extended the picture back to Gary, who rose once more to receive it. "I wish you luck."

"That's it?" I asked. "We tell you we finally found your father and that he was stabbed to death, and you wash your hands of it? Hardly a response to make us think you innocent."

Deschamps's almost hairless eyebrows shot up. "Innocent? You are thinking I killed my own father? Despite all your obvious homework, you've got much more to do. Why would I kill a man I loved? More important from your perspective, why would I kill a man whose position I was slated to inherit soon in any case? He was my tutor and I was his heir, especially after my brother died in the war. What you are suggesting is ludicrous." His breathing had turned raspy and I noticed a damp sheen covering his forehead.

"We wouldn't expect you to say otherwise," Gary told him.

Deschamps lost patience, waving a hand in the air. "Enough. This conversation is concluded. Please leave. Pierre will show you out."

Picard grabbed the handles of Marcel's wheelchair and turned him around to face the door. But my attention was on Pierre Guidry.

He'd been behaving like a palace guard

throughout the conversation, his hands clasped behind him, standing at parade rest, his expression impassive. At Marcel's dismissive order, however, I thought I saw his lips compress slightly and his jaw tense, although when he stepped forward to escort us out, he merely looked like a faithful colleague sharing his boss's outrage.

It had come and gone in the flicker of an instant, and I couldn't be sure of what I'd seen in his eyes. Only the suspicion remained.

CHAPTER ELEVEN

What's it like up there?" Sammie asked on the phone.

I was sitting on my motel bed, my shoes off, leaning back against a pile of pillows, the TV on but muted before me. It was almost midnight. "Pretty nice. Middle-class industrial town with no pollution and no pretensions. So far, that fits the cops, too. Nice, laid-back bunch. Turns out Lacombe's the head Sûreté guy. He set up a task force right off the bat. We had our first meeting an hour ago—Sherbrooke police, us, the Sûreté people, and some guy from RCMP intelligence. Went well. We visited Marcel Deschamps at his home earlier and suggested he killed his old man, just to see what

128

would happen. He threw us out. Lacombe's put surveillance teams on him and a bunch of his top people. We'll keep track of all contacts made for the next week and run them through the computer up here. If we did stir them up, maybe we can make sense of the flurry. Marcel's dying of cancer, so time's against him. He already looks like death warmed over."

Willy Kunkle's voice came over the speaker phone as if filtered through an empty can. "You think he did it?"

I paused a moment, remembering Marcel's reaction. "I'm not so sure. He denied it, of course, but he looked pretty surprised. You two find out anything new?"

"We got jack," Willy said bluntly. "This cancer thing got anything to do with our finding the Popsicle?"

"It's got to," I agreed. "I just don't know how." I then filled them in on all we'd learned, including Marcel's comment that he'd had no reason to kill a father who was shortly planning to put him in charge, and Pelletier's saying that in the long run everyone had just assumed patricide.

"Anyhow," I finished, "it looks like the Deschamps family's made a fortune illegally peddling across the border. I know you got nowhere running Jean's name through the system, but try Pierre Guidry, Lucien Pelletier, and Gaston Picard." I gave them spellings and dates of birth. "They're all old-timers, so maybe one of them got nailed for something in the U.S. during their younger years. Give 'em a shot and see if we get lucky."

"Will do," Sammie said. "By the way, we got the final autopsy report. Stomach contents were the only unusual thing: a combination of venison, raccoon, and bear meat."

I whistled. "Jesus. What the hell was he doing? Living in the woods?"

"If he was," Willy put in, "he wasn't going hungry."

The red light on the side of the phone began flashing. "Someone just called in with a message. I better get off and find out what's up. Let me know if you hit anything with those names."

"You got it."

"Oh, hey, Sammie?" I suddenly asked.

"Yeah?"

"How're you two getting along with Tom Shanklin? Any friction?"

"I try to keep him away from Willy so he won't quit law enforcement altogether," she said. "But he seems pretty mellow. We haven't done a whole lot as a team, though."

"Right. Just being a mother hen. I'll talk to you later."

I hung up, dialed the operator, and got a message to call Lacombe. He answered on the first ring.

"I was wondering if you would like to see how we in Québec work a crime scene. We just have a report of a murder on La Rue Galt Oueste—one of the Deschamps family."

"There's a coincidence. Sure, I'd love to be included."

"A car will pick you up in five minutes."

Galt Street West was another of Sherbrooke's major arteries, but on the older, poorer south side of town. There were no malls or motels or American greasy spoons here. Where I was deposited by a Sûreté squad car fifteen minutes later was working class residential—rows of plain brick apartment buildings, stained by time and neglect, the layers of stacked balconies, typical of virtually every Québec city, sagging and in need of paint.

A pleasant young man in a parka greeted me as I stepped into the slush piled on the sidewalk. "Mr. Gunther? Le Capitaine Lacombe asked me to escort you to him."

I followed him into the nearest building, noticing that while the majority of uniforms belonged to the Sherbrooke police, the Sûreté was clearly represented. Lacombe had briefed us earlier that in a town this size, the Sûreté played mostly a support role, appearing only when requested. I assumed the exception here meant the task force's mission was playing front and center.

In fact, when I reached a dingy apartment two flights up, Lacombe was accompanied by Rick Labatt and André Rousseau, the intelligence officer from the RCMP.

Lacombe turned at my entrance and motioned to me to join them in the kitchen across the living room. "Joe. I am sorry it is so late, but as I said on the telephone, I thought you would find this interesting."

On the kitchen floor, spread-eagled like a butterfly pinned down for display, was a large, barefoot man resting in blood extending like wings to either side of him. A good portion of his skull was missing. Surrounding him like carefully moving ghosts, a forensics team clad in protective clothing went through the motions I knew all too drearily by heart.

Lacombe made the introductions. "This is Monsieur Jean-Luc Tessier. He was a Deschamps enforcer—a big cheese, correct? It looks like he was shot in the head, from behind with one bullet."

I glanced back at the living room. "No obvious struggle. Was the door forced?"

"No. We are thinking that he knew who killed him."

"And trusted him," Labatt added, pointing at the corpse. "He turned his back on the man, maybe to make some coffee."

"He live alone?" I asked, noticing the coffee maker on the counter ahead of the corpse, still half full and with its red indicator light on.

Lacombe smiled. "Yes. You are wondering how we found him so fast. The neighbor became angry at the television sound. When the Sherbrooke police got here, it was very, very big." He put his fingers in his ears.

"But the noise came suddenly, just before the neighbor complained?"

Lacombe nodded.

"Meaning whoever killed him cranked up the volume to attract attention afterward," I surmised. "It couldn't have been that loud when he knocked on the door and Tessier went to

132

pour coffee—it wouldn't make sense. No gunshot heard?"

All three of them shook their heads. The comfortably bilingual Mountie—Rousseau—said, "Tessier was one of Marcel's chosen men. He'd been with him twenty years, and in the last eight or ten handled all the key dealings with rival operators. A hard man—loyal and savvy."

"A big loss to Marcel," I murmured.

"On top of others, yes," Lacombe agreed.

I turned to both Labatt and Rousseau. "You two read tea leaves for a living. Who'd be putting this kind of pressure on Marcel?"

"It might not be so simple," Labatt answered. "We were just discussing that before you came."

Rousseau added, "It's likely Jean Deschamps's reappearance and this murder were orchestrated by the same people, but with Marcel near death and the Rock Machine gearing up against the Angels, Jean-Luc Tessier would have been a perfect target for either one of them—the Angels so they can solidify their grip on Sherbrooke before war breaks out; the Rock Machine so they can attack the Angels through the backdoor by destroying the Deschamps and grabbing their territory."

"Are the Rock Machine that subtle?" I asked. "I would've thought if that was their plan, they'd have knocked off five guys like Tessier tonight. Not just one."

Lacombe laughed softly, escorting us back into the hallway to get out of the way of the crew carrying a stretcher. "It is very American. It would be not so messy to just kill one and then suggest a meeting to avoid more bloodshed. Monsieur Tessier may be something like a calling card. Right now, somewhere, maybe Marcel and Picard and Guidry and the others are negotiating with the people who did this."

"Can't we get wiretaps to find out?" I asked.

The Canadians all shook their heads. "The good old days," Lacombe said. "We could have, twenty years ago. Now, it is very difficult. Taps are for after everything else has been tried and has failed. We are far from that right now."

"We'll have to use the old-fashioned tools first," Rousseau suggested. "Informants, surveillance, intelligence, and patience. If this is leading somewhere, we'll find out about it sooner or later. In the meantime, if they want to kill each other and break down the walls that have kept us out, maybe that's not so bad."

It was an interesting take, and not surprising from a federal man who had no investment in maintaining an unofficial compromise with the local crooks to keep the peace. But if Rousseau was going to mention selfishly practical matters, then I had one of my own. VBI was supposed to be a fast and efficient way to cut red tape and get results—waiting around for crooks to take action wasn't part of the sales pitch. And I had politicians watching me like bookies timing a fledgling racehorse.

I therefore cast my vote for a more energized option—as diplomatically as possible. "Assuming whoever did this wants us to act

134

on it, though," I said, "then they've probably left us some bread crumbs to follow."

Lacombe glanced around at the people streaming in and out of the apartment. "You are probably right. By tomorrow, we should know that."

In Lacombe's office the following morning, however, the killing of Jean-Luc Tessier was not the first topic of discussion. As the task force members gathered around his round conference table, we found several newspapers spread out, all sporting a photograph of Jean Deschamps, alive and well sometime in the late 1930s, wearing a snap-brim fedora and smoking a cigarette. I didn't need a translator to read the headlines.

I remained standing and asked, "I take it this didn't come from any of your people?"

Lacombe shook his head, looking unhappy.

"May I use your phone?"

I called Sammie from Lacombe's desk. "You seen the morning papers?" I asked her.

"Yeah. The leak come from up there?"

"Not that we know of. Phone around and see if you can find out—Stowe Mountain Rescue, Frank Auerbach's crew... I know there was some buzz about who the stiff was when they found him. Maybe a reporter got lucky somewhere. But if it was a leak, I'd like to talk to whoever's behind it. There was a murder here last night that suggests a major move in the making. Call my pager if you hit pay dirt."

I hung up and joined the others at the table. "Had to come out sooner or later," I said philosophically. "Be interesting to know if our visit to Marcel was the stimulus."

André Rousseau, the Mountie, looked at me carefully. "How's that?"

"When we spoke to Pelletier, he had no idea why we were there. Marcel and company might've spilled the beans to the press to guarantee we wouldn't have that kind of anonymity again."

"Does sound like a lawyer's move," Gary Smith grumbled.

"Then again," I said, "it might've been leaked to show there was something rotten in the house of Deschamps."

"Which brings us back to Jean-Luc Tessier," Rick Labatt stated, laying a pile of crime scene photographs on the table. "I spent several hours last night with André and Étienne," Labatt indicated the quietest member of our small group, the Sherbrooke police liaison, "digging through everything we had on Tessier and the Deschamps. It turns out Tessier was more than just the chief enforcer for Marcel, he was Marcel's private man—used not only to take care of business outside the family, but inside also."

"Marcel must be feeling pretty isolated around now," Paul Spraiger commented.

"Why is it nobody talks about Michel Deschamps?" I asked. "According to Lucien Pelletier, he's the heir apparent on the verge of taking over. He must be knee-deep in all this—or he better be."

Rick raised his eyebrows and tapped a folder he'd placed next to the photographs. "That is something I also wondered." He flipped open the folder to a full-face photograph of a young, soft-featured man sporting an immature mustache. "Michel Deschamps, twenty-eight, economics graduate of McGill with barely passing grades, employed by his father ever since as a quote-unquote bookkeeper, and making a salary any real bookkeeper would kill for. He drives a BMW sports car, several motorcycles, has many girlfriends, and is not thought by our sources to be of much use to his father's organization."

Rousseau added, "We have a file on him, too. Seems to be a classic case of generational dissipation."

"So was Pelletier wrong?" I wondered aloud. "Given what we know of Marcel's character, it seems he shouldn't trust his son farther than he could spit him."

Rick shook his head. "I don't know about Pelletier, but I have heard Marcel is crazy about Michel. Father and mother were divorced many years ago, and Marcel has spoiled the boy rotten. André may be right from our view, but not from Marcel's. Michel can do no wrong."

"What do Picard and Pierre Guidry think about that?" I asked, wondering privately how they had viewed Tessier's elite role within the organization.

Lacombe, whom I'd come to see as a bit of a philosopher, merely suggested, "How would you feel, knowing the heir would be totally dependent on you for running the kingdom? It sounds not so bad."

There was a knock at the door and a uniformed policewoman entered, handed Rick a slip of paper, and retired without a word. Labatt read the message's contents quickly and said, "Good thing we put tails on everybody yesterday. A man watching Tessier's place last night just filed this report—he saw someone enter the apartment, stay about five minutes, and then leave rapidly, putting something into his pocket as he went. He followed this man around town for several hours, until he entered the Hell's Angels headquarters at almost dawn. Surveillance photos matched him with somebody named Christophe Bossard."

"We know him," Étienne said softly. "He is...*un apprenti.*"

"An apprentice," Paul translated.

"A Hell's Angels wannabe," Rousseau explained further. "They use them a lot for their dirty work—usually it's carrying drugs, though. Not for a hit job."

"And we know where Monsieur Bossard resides?" Lacombe asked Labatt.

"Oh, yes."

A couple of hours later, I was sitting on the transparent side of a one-way mirror, watching a fat, hairy man in stained biker clothes sitting at a table next door, before a video camera and two police officers, one of them Rick Labatt.

Lacombe, Paul Spraiger, and I were lined up on folding chairs like spectators at a private viewing, Paul's shoulder almost touching mine as he translated throughout the conversation.

"You are Christophe Alphonse Bossard," recited Labatt, "born on January fifth, 1973, in Compton, Québec?"

Bossard stared at them both, hesitated, and finally nodded.

"Speak up for the record, please."

"Yes."

"Mr. Bossard, you have already been explained your rights under the law and have agreed to this conversation. Is that correct?"

"Yes."

"Very well. Let's start with last night, around eleven-thirty. You were seen entering the apartment of Jean-Luc Tessier on Galt Street—"

"That's a lie," Bossard interrupted.

Labatt wordlessly slid a photograph across to him. He stared at it a moment.

Labatt resumed, "You were seen entering the apartment, as it shows in that photo. You stayed there about five minutes and then left in a hurry. The next people to visit Mr. Tessier were the police, and they found him dead with a bullet in the head—a bullet which came from the gun we found this morning in your apartment, in the pocket of the coat you are wearing in that picture. Would you like to tell us what happened in that apartment?"

Bossard swallowed hard. "He was already dead."

Another long silence filled the room. Over the speaker above the one-way mirror, I could just hear Bossard's labored breathing. I imagined the two cops facing him were also smelling his sweat.

"The apartment was under surveillance, Christophe," Labatt said almost gently. "Had been for hours."

But Bossard remained adamant. "He was dead. The blood was still running out of him."

"Your fingerprints were found in every room."

The fat man scowled, wiped his forehead with the back of his hand. "I looked around a little. He wasn't going to miss anything."

"You ransacked the place while he was bleeding to death? Looking for what?"

He shrugged. "Whatever."

"When you left, you were shoving something into your pocket."

"That was the gun. It was the only thing worth a shit."

"You should know. You used it to kill him."

Bossard's face reddened. "I did not," he shouted. "I found the goddamned thing. It was lying on the floor next to him. You think I'm going to leave something like that behind? You stupid or what?"

Labatt declined debating who was most stupid in the room. "Why'd you go there in the first place, Christophe, if it wasn't to kill him?"

"He called me. Said he wanted to talk."

"What about?"

Bossard looked scornful. "If I knew that, I wouldn't have had to visit him, right?"

We all heard the incredulity in Labatt's voice. "So you just wandered over to visit Jean-Luc Tessier for a casual chat—with his reputation?"

Now the fat man moved his shoulders back, swelling the stained Harley logo across his chest. "I wasn't scared of Tessier. Besides, we'd worked together before. He knew I was honorable."

"Why did you work together?"

Again, Bossard looked like he was talking to the village idiot. "I represent the Hell's Angels. He represented the Deschamps. Of course we would meet—iron out the wrinkles that competitors sometimes run into."

Labatt maintained his composure, even sounding solicitous. "Important job. Had the Angels been having trouble with Deschamps?"

Bossard scratched his neck thoughtfully— the consultant hard at work. "Nothing that couldn't be sorted out. You have to keep on top of the situation, of course. Not let things slide."

"Of course," Rick echoed. "Nevertheless, all this has put you in an awkward spot."

The other man's face closed up. "I didn't kill him."

"You better help us prove that, because you're the best candidate we've got. Was the television on when you got there?"

"Yeah."

"Loud?"

"No. It was normal."

"You turn it up to hide the gunshot?"

Bossard's voice rose. "There was no god-damned gunshot—not from me."

"It was loud when we got there, Christophe."

Bossard worked his mouth soundlessly a couple of times, and then admitted, "I heard it as I was leaving—going down the hall... I mean, I heard it *somewhere*. I didn't know it was his." He paused, looking troubled for the first time. "You saying it was turned up after I left? By who?"

"What did you do afterward, Christophe? You must've been concerned, going to a meeting with a Deschamps bigwig and finding him dead. Weren't you worried you'd be pegged with the killing?"

"I didn't do it. Why should I worry?"

"Did you call anyone? Meet anyone?"

"I wandered around a bit, like usual. Saw a few people, but not about Tessier. I ended up at the Lennoxville house to sleep a little. Then I went home. That was it. That's where you assholes busted me."

"Were the guys at the Lennoxville house happy with what you'd done?"

He scowled. "I told you, they didn't know nothing about it."

"Christophe, didn't it cross your mind to tell them? They would've liked to have known that a major Deschamps player had been executed, don't you think? It might've even earned you some brownie points."

Bossard began shifting in his seat, as if feeling it heat up. "Maybe I didn't think it was a good idea," he murmured.

"What? Speak up."

He seemed stung by Labatt's harsh tone. "I said I was thinking it maybe wasn't such a great idea."

"Because you might be blamed. Because the Angels would think you'd taken the law into your own hands and upset the applecart. Maybe, Christophe, you started to think that your grand plan of killing the Deschamps negotiator for extra credit wasn't such a great idea after all, eh?"

This time, he yelled so loudly his neck veins bulged. "I didn't kill him."

We were in a small room lined with vending machines, extracting coffee from one of them—Gilles Lacombe, Labatt, Paul, and I.

"I double-checked with the surveillance team," Labatt was saying. "They'd stepped back a little to avoid being seen directly from Tessier's door. They heard the TV suddenly blare, and then they saw Bossard. But they can't swear he was still inside when the volume went up."

"Meaning that if you believe Bossard," Paul said, "someone was watching and waiting the whole time—maybe even inside the apartment."

"Or out on the balcony," I suggested. "Bossard said he tossed the place looking for loot. Do the crime scene photos show the door leading out there?"

Rick Labatt still had them with him in a manila envelope. He poured them out onto a nearby table and began pawing through them. "Yes—here."

We all leaned in to study what he'd found. Not only was the balcony door deadbolt snapped open, but there appeared to be a damp spot on the rug before it, like a faint, slushy footprint.

Lacombe straightened first. "It has possibilities. But the best murderer looks like Christophe Bossard."

"And that'll be what's told to the press?" I asked.

Lacombe looked faintly apologetic. "I have bosses, also, and they like to show the people we are hard at work."

It wasn't my place to argue. Not only did I have no viable alternatives, but my political position was exactly the same.

CHAPTER TWELVE

Sammie Martens was waiting for me in the lobby of the Commodore Inn when I arrived from Sherbrooke the next day. It had been snowing the whole way down—not much wind, but fat, heavy flakes that turned the view beyond the windshield into a constant mesmerizing vortex of white static. I was tired and my eyes felt like they'd been turned inside out.

"Joe," she said, poorly suppressing her

excitement. "Thanks for coming down. You won't be disappointed."

"That's good. I'm not up for that right now."

I walked stiffly down the hallway, groping for my key. "You said on the phone you'd hit a gold mine. Mind telling me about it now?"

I could tell I'd dampened her spirits slightly. "I guess that was a little childish."

"Not if it's true." I turned the lock and opened the door.

Her enthusiasm returned unabated. "I got a hit on one of those names you gave us. Gaston Picard got a parking ticket in Stowe three days before the Popsicle man turned up."

I stopped halfway across the threshold. "No shit."

She smiled broadly. "And that ain't all. Willy hit a homer, too. Remember that autopsy finding—the venison/coon/bear meat cocktail? On a hunch, Willy started interviewing some of the old-timers in town—checking out the retirement homes, the barber shop, the historical society, the library. You name it. He found out that back in the forties, there was a restaurant named Mickey's Best that had a weekly 'Game Night'—kind of a funky rural pitch to tourists and locals both. It was a big hit while it lasted."

"And Willy found the owner?"

"No. He's long dead, but it puts Jean Deschamps here, right? Makes Stowe not just a dumping ground, but maybe the place he got whacked."

I dropped my overnight case onto the bed. "I hope so. Where's Willy now?"

She checked her watch. "He should be in the bar. I told him you'd like to see him."

I'd really wanted to see the inside of my eyelids for a while, but I couldn't deny that Sammie's information had revived me. As pleasant and cooperative as my Canadian hosts were, and as interestingly as things were evolving up there—for them—I had been empathizing with Gary's concern about our case being left at the back of the pack. Sam's and Willy's discoveries had the potential of putting us more on an even footing with Lacombe and company, and of making our ancient homicide a worthy and unique first outing for the Bureau.

We found Willy slouched over a bar stool, cupping a ginger ale in his hand, staring dreamily at the multicolored rows of bottles lining the wall opposite him.

"Reminiscing?" I asked as Sam and I sat on either side of him.

He didn't bristle, as I expected, but smiled instead. "I guess so. When I was drinking, I used to love to just sit here, watch the colors, listen to the buzz in the air..." He blinked a couple of times, as if clearing his head. "Not 'here' here, of course," he added, sounding more familiar, "all this ship-shape, yachting crap would've made me throw up. There was a bar in Bratt—closed now—had it down perfect."

"Yeah, right," Sammie said, "closed 'cause of health code violations—couldn't tell the customers from the rodents."

He turned toward her. "How would you know? I never saw you there."

"You never saw anything when you were there."

I was about to intervene, but he surprised me again by just laughing.

"I hear you've been hanging out with the Geritol crowd," I said instead.

"Yeah—met a lot of guys that look just like you. God, what a bunch of talkers. Some of them don't even know what century they're in."

"But one of them told you about Mickey's Best?" I prodded him.

"'Game Night'—right. Talk about health code problems. Love to see 'em try that today. It lasted maybe ten years—give or take nine the way this guy was working—but he swears they dished up the exact same roadkill the ME found in the Popsicle."

"But the owner's long buried and the restaurant's ancient history?"

"Yeah." He took a long swig from his drink. "Dead end."

But I knew Willy better than that—dead ends were unacceptable, and pulling my chain a full-time recreation.

"So who did you find to lead you toward the light?"

He smiled and put his glass back down on the bar. "Damn—maybe we been doin' this too long. I haven't actually found him. Only just heard about him. But there's a guy who supposedly worked at the place. A teenager back then, so maybe in his late sixties, early seventies now. Named Arvin Brown. My old geezer said the kid was a real go-getter—

knew the customers, worked the handshake like a water pump. Lives in Richford."

Richford was about forty miles due north of Stowe, so close to the Canadian border some of its roads wobbled back and forth across it. Despite my fatigue of fifteen minutes ago, I suddenly felt the urge to go on a field trip.

"Where's Tom Shanklin?"

"Waterbury," Sammie answered. "He's working the computer from down there, going after the names you gave me, plus anything else he can think of, like the Canadian Hell's Angels and the Rock Machine."

"You two want to go to Richford?" I asked.

Richford is one of those towns you can find in the middle of nowhere that initially defy all rhyme or reason. A glance at a map tells you nothing—there are no major roads running through it or prosperous neighbors next door to justify its existence. There's a single railroad track that seems to wander off unattended. And yet, a drive through the middle of town, down a gentle slope toward the narrow Missisquoi River, tells of a place once teeming with culture and good fortune. On either side of the street, one jewel-like Victorian residence after another, dripping gingerbread and elaborate wrought iron, stands witness to when Richford was a lumber center to be reckoned with, filled with successful entrepreneurs and their many employees.

Now, of course, things are different. Rolling into downtown, we saw a largely secondhand

148

community, still alive and viable, but a shadow of its past, like the single survivor of a once large and bustling family. The heavy brick buildings on the river's shore are empty and hollowed out, many of the homes, certainly on the north end, are begging for occupants, and the whole town has been left—despite its best efforts—looking vaguely abandoned.

I'd asked Sammie to drive—I'd had enough of onrushing snowflakes for a while—and she parked us facing a large-windowed café named Brenda's Kitchen, its panes fogged over by the warmth and humidity within, backlit to make them glisten like ice. The three of us stepped out into the dreamlike silence and fading light of a heavy snowfall, our feet utterly silent on the crystalline white carpet, and we paused to take in the soft contours and generosity that only such weather can grant a hard-luck town.

Willy, always the poet, put the mood to rest, looking around and shaking his head. "Why would anyone live in a hole like this?"

Brenda's was surprisingly full. It was five in the afternoon, a reasonable time for rural folk to dig into their suppers, but we were initially taken aback by the noise and activity in contrast to the empty street right outside.

It was an unusual place, tall-ceilinged and rambling, rough wooden floors and tables scattered about, and the kitchen in plain view beyond a long, curving counter. Brenda's gave off the feeling of a familial social club, like a Bingo hall where the equipment had been pushed out of sight for a special meal.

A young woman approached us. "Would you like a table?"

I was about to simply ask if she knew Arvin Brown, when Willy spoke up from behind me, "Yeah—three."

"Right this way."

I glanced back at him and he raised his eyebrows. "Smell the air, for Christ's sake. Arvin Brown's not going to die in the next twenty minutes."

Our waitress laughed as she introduced us to our table at the back of the room. "Not unless he chokes on his chicken fried steak," she said. "You know him?"

"No," I told her. "Actually, we came here to meet him."

She pointed to a large man with a white beard sitting alone near the window. "You walked right by him."

"I'll be damned," Willy said. "Best eating on the job we'll ever do," and he headed that way.

I turned to Sammie. "Guess we're taking the direct approach."

Brown looked up as we stopped by his table. "I help you?" he asked through a full mouth.

"You used to work at Mickey's Best in Stowe in the forties?" Willy asked him.

Brown's eyes widened and he swallowed hard, half rising to his feet and waving us to the other chairs gathered around the table. "Yeah. I never thought that would ever come back to haunt me."

"Any reason it should?" Sammie asked

150

with a big smile, sitting opposite him. "You have a skeleton in the closet?"

He wiped his mouth and shook his head. "Oh, God no—just that it was so long ago. Who are you, anyway?"

I made the formal introductions, which deepened his astonishment. "My Lord. The Vermont Bureau of Investigation. I'm not sure I've ever heard of that. Is it part of the state police?"

Willy rolled his eyes, but I simply answered, "No—different agency."

"But have I done something wrong?"

I tried putting him at ease by waving to the waitress. "No, no. We're more on a fact-finding mission than anything. Do you mind if we join you for dinner? I notice you just started."

He shook his head. "Be my guest."

We placed our orders, Willy taking the most time. "Mr. Brown," I began, "we heard Mickey's Best had a special night when they served wild game."

He laughed at that. "Yeah—well. It was advertised as wild, and when we could get it, it really was. Mickey would try anything to turn a buck, and back then there weren't so many regulations that could trip you up. It was a harmless trick, really, and it wasn't like he was cheating folks. The tourists were paying for the ethnic charm." He said the last two words with a fake upper-class lilt. "And the locals didn't seem to know the difference, bragging aside."

"We heard it didn't last long," Willy commented.

"No. Mickey was ahead of his time. The tourist trade was a coming thing, but not even close to what it is now. The trains weren't much, the interstate wasn't there yet, and the roads were pretty bad. There was money around, but not in Stowe—not yet. Not like it would be."

He paused to take a small bite, politely slowing down on his consumption until our meals arrived. "Plus Mickey was a restless man. Good at selling, not so good at following through. He got bored fast."

"Rumor has it you were pretty good at selling yourself," Sammie observed.

Arvin Brown ducked his head modestly. "I was just a kid on the make. I thought Mickey had the world by the tail—that he'd take me places. Wasn't till after the restaurant closed that I realized his limitations. I didn't dislike him for it, though. He was a dreamer, and we all need those. But we parted ways."

"What did you end up doing?" I asked.

He smiled. "Selling—no surprise there. I sold darn near everything—appliances, machinery, bulk goods, lumber, property—anything that would take me out on the road. I like people and I liked to travel till I finally got too old for it. Ended up here 'cause it's peaceful, small, and the people are nice, and," he added with a laugh, "it's too far off the beaten path to attract any salesmen."

The waitress arrived with our food, and Brown watched us settle in, especially Willy with his one-handed dexterity. "I don't see why any of that would interest you," he finally admitted. "Did Mickey finally get himself in a jam?"

I decided to stay shy of the real issue for the moment. "We heard he was long dead. But it's an interesting question. Ahead of his time or not, wasn't it a weird place for a hustler to ply his trade?"

Brown finished chewing. "Stowe? Maybe. He wasn't alone, though, and even the ski bums eventually became businessmen. Like I said, it didn't get really big till about the seventies, but the roots went down when I was there. I mean, hell, look at the biggest name of them all. The Singing von Trapp Family, or whatever they called themselves. They weren't hustlers, but they had to hustle to make a go of it, and made a tidy profit, too, and bought up a hell of a lot of real estate. That mood was in the air. Mickey's main problem was that he thought too small."

"Was there any criminal activity back then?"

That froze his fork halfway to his mouth. "Criminal activity? My God, there weren't enough people, not if you mean what I think you do. There wasn't even a police department. I was talking about people looking to make money. Not mobsters."

I waved my hand dismissively. "Sure. I know. I was just curious. There's so much money there now—makes you wonder. Was Mickey's Best pretty popular?"

"It depended on the time of year, of course, but when it was hot, the place really jumped—big ski weekends, fall foliage, hunting season—times like that. And Mickey tried to keep it interesting, like with Game Night. How'd you hear about that, anyway?"

I reached into my pocket for the old photograph of Jean Deschamps wearing a fedora and smoking a cigarette. "Do you ever remember seeing this man at the restaurant? I know it's a long shot—so many years ago—but we heard you were really attentive to the customers."

Arvin Brown took the picture in both hands and fondly regarded the old crook. "Wow. Isn't that amazing. After all this time. Sure, I remember him. He was like a movie star when he came in—his coat draped over his shoulders, dark glasses. Not many people wore those back then, least not the locals." He laughed, "And not at night. He tipped me the same as the bill—one hundred percent. Told me I reminded him of himself when he was a kid. If Spencer Tracy had walked in that night, I wouldn't have been more impressed. He was amazing—just what I wanted to be."

"Did you know who he was?" Sammie asked.

Brown shook his head. "Nope. A rich French-Canadian was all I knew. Never saw him before, never saw him again. You know what happened to him?"

"Yeah." I didn't elaborate. "Any idea why he was there that night? Did he ask directions to anyplace, or mention anyone local?"

"Nope. He seemed real at home, like he knew what he was up to. But then I figure he looked like that wherever he went." He handed the picture back to me. "But I'll never forget that face."

Sammie pulled a pad from her pocket. "Mr. Brown, assuming this man was staying somewhere in the Stowe area that night—not a private residence—where might that've been? Especially for a high roller?"

He chewed thoughtfully for a while, staring at his plate. Finally, he looked up and answered, "Well, the Green Mountain Inn was in business. That's a possibility. And the Summit House was still operating on top of Mount Mansfield. A lot of folks went there for the adventure of it. But it was kind of rustic, and I don't see this guy doing that." He hesitated and then said, "Truth be told, the place I'd bet on doesn't exist anymore—the Snow Dancer Hotel. Funny name, but a classy joint. That's why it went under—owner spent too much pampering the guests, and they ended up not wanting to pay the price. He was from Spain, I think. Always dressed to the nines, complete with a walking stick. We kids used to make fun of him—thought he was a sissy. Anyway, I could see this gent hanging his hat there for a night. Be a perfect fit."

Willy didn't look impressed. "But the place and the Spaniard are ten feet under, right?"

Brown wasn't put off by Willy's tone. "True," he admitted. "The building's still there, though. Last I knew, it was a B-and-B. Very pretty, with a barn out back. It used to have all the original Victorian fixtures—carpets, furniture, chandeliers, the works—and I heard most of that's still there. It's called the Summit View now—must be a thousand with that name—but you could give it a look. That and the Green Mountain Inn, of course. They might even have records going back that far."

He'd finished his meal by now, and half pushed his chair away from the table, his tone hardening just a shade. "So I'm guessing I told you pretty much what you came for, and you've been careful about not showing your cards, which is what I guess you people do for some reason. But how 'bout a little even-Steven? What the hell're you after?"

The three of us exchanged glances. Willy and Sammie both shrugged. Arvin Brown had been forthcoming with us. It wasn't going to hurt to return the compliment.

"It's going to be a letdown," I warned him. "Your big tipper was murdered shortly after he left Mickey's. We figured out he'd been there 'cause his stomach contents matched your menu on Game Night."

Brown's mouth fell open. "His stomach contents? But that was more than fifty years ago..." He paused and then murmured, "My God, the frozen man in the paper..."

"Yeah. I'm sorry."

He stood up, bracing himself on the back of the chair, suddenly looking much older, and absentmindedly reached for his wallet. "I am, too."

I reached out and grabbed his forearm. "The meal's on us, Mr. Brown. Least we can do."

He blinked a couple of times and looked at me. "Oh...thanks. It's funny, but it's not like that photograph brought back old memories. I mean, it did, but I'll never forget that man. I saw that picture and it was like seeing my own father or something." He paused and shook his head. "My father wasn't much to write home about—I guess maybe that's why. At that age, boys like to find someone to look up to, you know? What was his name?"

I didn't hesitate. "Jean Deschamps."

Arvin Brown nodded. "Thanks," he said vaguely, and wandered out into the snow.

We watched him through the window standing motionless for a minute or so, letting a dusting of flakes settle onto his white hair. Then he walked carefully over to a large, new, fully equipped Suburban and climbed inside.

"I guess he took Deschamps's example to heart," Sammie said softly, as he soundlessly drove away.

CHAPTER THIRTEEN

The next morning was enough to make a skier's heart swell. The storm had left behind a thick mantle of snow on the mountains and a sky of cobalt blue. It was calm, giving the illusion of warmth, and aside from a glare off the earth's sparkling blanket that made dark glasses a medical necessity, it was embracingly beautiful—offering a rare moment in which the world feels safe and serene, and one's mental state as sharp as the surrounding frozen air.

Unfortunately, the magic of such glimpses of perfection is that they rarely last for long. I hadn't been standing in the Commodore's rear parking lot for more than three minutes, watching the frozen white geometry of the large pond and distant hills beyond, before Willy Kunkle walked up behind me, heading for the car, and growled, "It's just you and me—Sammie got yanked to do something for Auerbach. Christ, I hate days like today. You think you'll go blind."

I turned away from the scenery and followed him without a word.

The reasonable first stop on our list was the Green Mountain Inn, in the middle of Stowe village. Directly across the street from where a slow-moving and quirky trolley service had once delivered skiers from Waterbury in the 1930s—covering ten miles in an hour—the inn had become as much an institution as the church and the town hall down the street. It had also grown with the town, and now was so large that the word "inn" seemed as disingenuous as an elephant hiding behind a fire hydrant. Nevertheless, it was inviting and carefully appointed, filled with small luxuries designed to win a frazzled traveler's gratitude. Willy and I were brought back to some considerably less appealing offices, and wasted an hour talking to people who had no idea how to help us.

I had higher expectations during our drive

out of town to the Summit View bed-and-breakfast. Ever since meeting Arvin Brown—and all through a dream-filled, restless night, populated by dapper old gangsters and eager, bright-eyed urchins—I couldn't shake the notion of some odd momentum growing, as if Deschamps and Mickey and Brown and the elegant, nameless Spaniard were all links in a chain designed to lead us to the truth.

Many times I'd looked into the inert faces of dead people, wishful that beyond what forensic science might interpret, there'd be something less tangible but more revealing that would make everything clear. It reminded me of the beliefs of early scientists who experimented with the eyeballs of murder victims, hoping to see the imprinted images of their killers.

Nevertheless, watching Jean Deschamps's relatively young face, literally frozen in time, and now knowing he'd swept a white-haired, wrinkled Arvin Brown off his feet as a child, I was imbued with a sense of loosening a knot in time, and thereby altering the future, if only by a fraction.

It never occurred to me to tell any of this to Willy, but as we approached the Summit View, I wished there was a way I could share my optimism.

As Brown had foretold, it was a jewel box of a building—an excess of architectural flourishes that no one in his right mind could afford nowadays. It was a miracle, in fact, that it hadn't been whittled down like so many of its brethren, streamlined by a practical generation driven by time and money concerns to judge half a wooden Victorian wedding cake as better than none at all.

Not that my appreciation wasn't heightened by the fresh icing of snow, the shimmering blue dome overhead, and the clear-cut backdrop of Mount Mansfield's strangely haunting supine profile.

A round-faced, middle-aged woman came out onto the porch as we extricated ourselves from the car, and waved to us cheerfully. "Good morning. Welcome."

"God," Willy murmured as I waved back with a smile.

"Are you here for a meal?" she asked as we drew nearer. "If so, we'd be delighted to have you. But if you're looking for a room, I'm afraid we're all booked at the moment." She kept her eyes firmly fixed on Willy, whose appearance didn't seem to pass her private muster.

As he often did, he picked up on this immediately. "We're cops," he said shortly. "And we already ate."

I felt obligated then to haul out my overly resplendent shield. "Vermont Bureau of Investigation, ma'am. Sorry to bother you. We just wanted to borrow a moment of your time to ask you a couple of quick questions. Would that be all right?"

Disgusted, Willy split off around the right side of the house to better see the barn out back.

"What's the matter?" the woman asked, watching him go.

"It's purely informational. Concerns something that happened many years ago—long before your time."

That brought her attention back to me. "What?"

"Could we go inside?" I asked.

Her eyes widened a bit, as if she'd just dozed off. "Oh, I'm sorry. I should have thought to offer." She hesitated before adding, "Would your companion like to join us?"

"Probably not."

"Good... I mean, that's fine. You're sure?"

"Absolutely." I gestured for her to precede me back into the building.

"I'm Donna Robin, by the way. My husband and I are the innkeepers. I'm afraid he's not here at the moment, though."

"Glad to meet you. Joe Gunther."

We entered a traditionally formal entrance hall—as decked out as Arvin Brown had said it would be—from which Mrs. Robin led us into a front parlor overlooking the driveway and the street beyond.

She took my coat and offered me a seat next to an elaborate fireplace, whose logs were already half consumed by a picture-perfect fire. "Would you at least like some coffee or tea? Some pastries?"

I shook my head, looking around. "No, I'm fine, thanks. It's a beautiful place."

"We love it. We bought it twelve years ago and have never regretted it." She paused to sit down and then added, "Well, maybe a couple of times when the power's gone out or one of the guests gets upset, but mostly it's been wonderful."

"That's great," I answered. "I understand the man who started it was from Spain or somewhere."

Her face lit up. "Is that what you wanted to talk about? Federico Alvarez." She rose eagerly to her feet. "Would you like to see a picture of him? It's in the hallway."

I reluctantly left the fire and joined her alongside the central staircase. Hanging on the wall was a tinted photograph of a stiff and formal man, dressed to the hilt, with a cane and a waxed mustache, which floated away from his nose like two wisps of black smoke.

"Doesn't look like a barrel of laughs."

She smiled and nodded in agreement. "I think you're right, but back then I guess formality went over better than it does now. Everyone expects you to be their best friend and perfect servant both. But from what I heard, he was definitely the latter. That's one of the reasons I hung this here—to remind me to be the best hostess I can be. Mr. Alvarez supposedly set the standard."

"And went out of business."

She led us back to the front parlor and the fire. "Yes, I suppose even he was behind the times. Too bad, in a way. There's something to be said for what he stood for." She waved her hand around. "At least we can thank him for all this. He never let it slide."

"Did he keep any records, do you know? Guest registrations, maybe? Or was all that gone by the time you moved in?"

"Oh no. They're still here. In fact, they're almost like part of a museum—in the barn.

I guess toward the end, this inn became kind of an obsession for Mr. Alvarez. He couldn't afford to operate it anymore, but he had enough to pay for certain 'items of upkeep,' as his will put it. It's like a trust fund. We thought it was very odd when we moved in, and Dick—that's my husband—tried to get us out of it, so we could gut the barn and turn it into a health club or something, but apparently we can't do that. Basically, the barn doesn't belong to us."

She laughed and made a self-deprecating gesture. "You'll have to forgive me. Finances and legal stuff make my head spin. I take care of the cooking, the decorating, and the guests. Dick does the books. Did you want to look at some of that junk?"

"Could we?" I asked, this time far more enthusiastically.

"Oh, absolutely. It's all in a closed-off storage area. There's a lot of it, though, and it's a real mess. The lawyers managing the Alvarez estate didn't say we had to maintain it—just house it in perpetuity."

We returned to the front hall, where she handed me my coat and donned one herself before leading me through the rest of the building and out the rear kitchen door.

Willy was still standing outside, but just barely, his toes on the threshold of the barn's large double doors, which were open just wide enough to allow a single person to slip through. He stepped aside as we joined him, and nodded toward the inside, looking at Donna Robin. "Nice barn."

She gave a startled glance, as if hoping she'd been invisible, said, "Thanks" barely audibly, and disappeared into the gloom beyond.

Willy shook his head and followed her.

There were windows high above us, so the barn's interior wasn't pitch-black, but given the glare outside, it still took us a few moments to adjust, during which Mrs. Robin found the switch to a row of overhead lights.

I saw what Willy had been complimenting. The barn consisted of a wide central feed passage built of broad old planks, lined on either side with rows of horse stalls, all lovingly appointed with brass and wrought iron fixtures. Above us, the roof arched a good thirty feet overhead, with the hay loft tucked along the edges like a deep balcony. The whole place was spotless, obviously not used for its intended purpose, and yet still pungent with the lingering odors of leather, manure, and dry hay. I walked down the length of the floor, admiring the extent of the restoration.

"Mr. Alvarez?" I asked when I reached the far end, encompassing it all with a sweep of my hand.

Donna Robin laughed despite Willy's proximity. "Once again. He had horses for sleigh rides and hay wagon excursions, but you'd hardly know, it looks so nice."

"And your husband wanted to convert this?"

She looked slightly embarrassed. "I know. It does seem a shame. But we couldn't do anything with horses, what with the expense and all, and the space was being wasted otherwise... Well, it doesn't matter, anyway."

"The barn's got a usage restriction on it," I explained to Willy, "maintained by the old Spaniard's estate—name was Federico Alvarez."

He furrowed his brow. "Why? I thought he was dead."

"He was pretty eccentric," Mrs. Robin said quietly, walking quickly toward me. "What you want to see is back here."

She went to a door on the far wall, worked its lock with a key she'd pulled from her pocket, and opened it with some effort.

What faced us resembled the old attic straight out of *Little Women*—a helter-skelter piling of ancient furniture, dress forms, trunks, moth-eaten stuffed animals, and a few turn-of-the-century kitchen and laundry appliances.

"Jesus Christ," Willy said.

Donna Robin didn't take offense. "I know. I'm sorry it's such a mess. We were never told to do anything with it—just to make sure it stayed put. I did poke around a little when we first moved in. I thought maybe I could bend the rules and bring some of the nicer items into the house. But there really wasn't anything to work with. It's old, but it's also all pretty ordinary."

She stayed by the door as Willy and I ventured forward, picking our way gingerly through a few narrow, haphazard aisles.

"It seems so strange," she added, "given the rest of the place is so immaculate. I always wondered why he put such value on this."

I couldn't argue with her. It was strange.

"But the records we discussed," I began. "The registration books...?"

"Oh, they're there," she said quickly, adding vaguely, "although I'm not so sure where anymore. They might've been in a trunk or suitcase or something. I remember opening a lid or a top and just seeing them there—leather books with 'Register' printed in gold on them."

I could tell she was getting restless, lingering by the opening, her hand still on the latch.

"This is going to take some doing," Willy said.

I couldn't disagree. We would need time and more people to even make a dent.

"Okay, Mrs. Robin, I guess we'll take it from here. We'll try to be as fast and discreet as we can, but I'm going to have to bring in some help. I hope that's okay. I'll make sure there are no police cars."

She hesitated a moment. "I don't suppose I could ask what this is all about, in case the guests ask."

Willy ended as he'd begun. "You got that right," he said, and sent her on her way.

I found the registers two hours later, not in a trunk or suitcase, but in a wooden box labeled "Toys." There were six of them, one for each year, starting in 1944.

"Eureka," I said tiredly, holding one of them over my head for the others to see, cold and bored enough by now to barely feel elated.

I was not alone in that. Tom Shanklin and Sammie, who made up our reinforcements, were as covered with dust and cobwebs as were Willy and I, and made their way to my side like miners at the end of a shift.

I handed them each a book and kept the remaining three for myself. "Let's see if we can muscle our way into Mrs. Robin's good graces for some coffee and a warm spot to read this stuff."

I led the way across to the bed-and-breakfast, making sure Willy brought up the rear, knocked on the kitchen door, and entered. Donna Robin was standing at the sink, running water into a plastic bucket. While the others huddled on the porch waiting, I made my pitch and was granted access to the large wooden table by the stove, complete with coffee all around.

For the next hour, we combed through the old leather books, page by page, often pausing to confer about the nearly illegible handwriting. We were further slowed down by the need to go beyond merely looking for Deschamps's name, and search for anything that might seem unusual.

Tom Shanklin, however, hit exactly what we were after. "Jean Deschamps," he said quietly. "January sixteenth, 1947. One night only." He shoved the book over to me. "There's a note next to it—different handwriting. I can't make it out."

I looked at it, Sammie leaving her chair to bend over my shoulder. "It's not English," she commented.

"Oh, for Christ sake." Willy got up abruptly and crossed over to the oversized steel fridge, yanking open its door. Mrs. Robin had long since left us.

"Spanish," I said. "At least I think it is. Close the door, Willy. Who knows what *'efectos personales en maleta en guardarropa'* means?"

Willy slammed the fridge shut. "Doubt *anyone* would know with that accent. This is bullshit."

He marched out through the swinging door leading to the front of the building, leaving us all staring after him.

"Where's he going?" Shanklin asked, still new to Willy's volatility.

Sammie smiled, her expression betraying more than friendship. "To get a solution."

Like kids eavesdropping on their parents, we quietly moved to the door and held it partially open, hearing voices several rooms down.

"Mrs. Robin," we heard Willy say with disarming friendliness.

Her voice, in contrast, sounded almost alarmed. "What?"

"We're in kind of a jam back there, and I suddenly thought you might be the perfect person to help us out. Wonderful coffee, by the way— a lifesaver, today especially. Really appreciated it."

She was obviously taken off guard. "Oh... You're welcome," she said warily. "Did you find what you were after?"

"Well, that's the problem. We're not sure. We've got something written in what we think is Spanish. I thought maybe in a high-class place like this you might have a guest who knows enough Spanish to translate it for us."

"Spanish," she repeated. "Of course. That would have been Mr. Alvarez, probably writing a note to himself. We found several scraps tucked away like that when we moved in, mostly in the kitchen."

"That must've been fascinating," Willy commented, almost convulsing Sammie with suppressed laughter.

"Well, they weren't really," Donna Robin admitted. "Mostly just one- or two-word reminders. Actually, all the guests are gone right now—skiing or shopping or whatever—but I might be able to help. I speak some Spanish."

"Great," we heard Willy say, before retreating to the table and pretending to be hard at work.

Footsteps approached and then Willy ushered in Mrs. Robin like a favorite aunt. "I think I found our translator," he announced.

She blushed and quickly added, "I'm not making any promises. It's not like I'm fluent or anything."

I stood up and made room for her before the open register. "Right there," I said, tapping the phrase with my finger.

She took my place, removed a pair of reading glasses from her cardigan pocket, and sat silently for a moment, studying. "Let's see," she said to herself, " *'maleta'...that's 'suitcase.' And* 'guardarropa' I think is 'wardrobe' or 'closet.' I wonder what that means?"

None of us had any doubts. Half the contents of the barn's back room was luggage of one sort or another, and most of it was full. All the boredom and tedium of the past several hours vaporized. As a single unit, we headed back outside, Willy first, having dropped his charm like a hot rock.

"Thanks, Donna," I said, last in line. "You're a godsend."

It didn't take us long after that, although Federico Alvarez would not have been pleased with our methods. We went through trunks, suitcases, packs, and boxes like a herd of thieves, not quite throwing the contents of each piece over our shoulders, but close enough. Finally, fittingly, Willy said, "I think I got it," and stood back from an open pigskin valise filled with neatly folded, slightly moldy, expensive clothing, on top of which was a leather toilet kit with the initials JMD stamped on it.

"Deschamps's middle name was Marie, right?" Willy asked.

"Right," I said, standing beside him, slightly amazed at our luck. Looking down at the same clothes that had so impressed Arvin Brown, packed by the man I'd met in the autopsy room, I was left revisiting the historical ambiguities that had haunted my dreams the night before—and wondering if they hadn't been prescient after all.

"Better wrap it up," I said. "We're going to want to take our time with this."

CHAPTER FOURTEEN

Later that night, the smell of pizza still in the air, Sam, Willy, Tom, and I sat around the conference table at the Stowe PD with Frank Auerbach and a woman named Carrie Salt, a French teacher from the local high school.

She had just joined us, Frank having called her at home, and was now taking us all in, her face a mixture of amusement and concern, each struggling for the upper hand.

"What's this all about, Frank? You said I might be able to help you with your French?"

"I was pulling your chain a bit, Carrie," he said lightly. "You know how well I speak French."

She laughed shortly. "Yeah—not a word. So what's the real reason?"

"We found a letter. A real old letter. I made a copy of it and was wondering if you could translate it. It's that simple." He slid a single sheet of paper across the table to her.

She resisted picking it up at first, still watching us. "Is this in relation to some crime?"

"We're not sure," I answered, mostly to break the wall of silence the rest of us had unconsciously created. "We found it in an old abandoned suitcase, and we have no idea what it says."

That wasn't actually true. We had a pretty good idea it had been written by Marcel Deschamps.

It obviously wasn't as full an explanation

as she wanted, but it was enough. She picked up the letter and read it.

A minute later, visibly relieved, she put it back down and smiled. "No smoking gun here, I'm afraid. Couldn't be friendlier. It's basically a son writing his father to join him for a little time off."

"Could you give us a word-for-word?" Auerbach requested.

She took up the letter again. "Sure. 'Dear Dad. I don't have much time, but I wanted to tell you what a wonderful time we're having down here. Stowe is up and coming—good food and a few nice inns—and the skiing is excellent. A nice change of pace. It would do you good to join us, if only for a couple of days. I'll be here the rest of the week. Come.' That last word is followed by an exclamation point. The signature is 'Marcel.' That's all there is to it."

"He definitely says, 'we' and 'us'?" Tom Shanklin asked.

"Yup."

"Is there anything in the syntax or word usage that strikes you as unusual?" I asked.

She shook her head. "I can tell it was written a long time ago. Some of the phrasing would be considered quaint today, and you can tell from the way the letters are slightly jumpy that whoever typed it used a manual typewriter. But that's about it."

Frank stood up, encouraging Carrie to do the same. "You've been a big help. We really appreciate it. I'll walk you out."

We waited until they'd left. "Don't know

about the Canucks, but in this country, that would be enough for a warrant," Willy said. "You got the dead guy in town, you got him eating a meal that's still in his stomach, you got his luggage abandoned in a hotel room, and you got a letter from a son who directly benefited from his death inviting him down for a little reunion."

"You also have the same son's lawyer showing up in town three days before the old man's body pops up," Sammie added.

Auerbach reappeared in the doorway. "Joe. You've got a call. Someone named Lacombe." He pointed to a phone on a side table. "You can take it there if you want—in my office if you want privacy."

I leaned over in my chair and grabbed the nearby phone. "Gilles? It's Joe."

"Hello, Joe. How are you doing back in the U.S.A.?"

"Interesting stuff. Can I put you on the speaker? Spare me repeating everything to the others."

"By all means. Of course."

I hit the button next to the dial pad and replaced the handset. "Okay. What's on your mind?"

"Ah. We have found something I thought you should know about. It is a letter confirming a reservation for Jean Deschamps at a place called the Snow Dancer Hotel. It is signed by someone called Federico Alvarez, who calls himself the proprietor. What is really interesting is that the date for this reservation—"

"Is January sixteenth, 1947," I interrupted, unable to stop myself.

There was stunned silence at the other end, followed by "How do you know this?"

"We came at it another way, at least I think we did," I answered. "We got an educated guess from a local old-timer about where a fancy guy like Deschamps might spend the night. It was the Snow Dancer. We not only found the place, but the old register and Deschamps's abandoned suitcase, complete with a letter from Marcel inviting his father down for the weekend. It's looking more likely that Jean was killed down here."

"This is extraordinary," Lacombe blurted. "After all this time?"

"Willy was wondering if it was enough for a search warrant."

I could almost hear Lacombe's brain turning that over. "It might be. We would have to discuss the specifics. I would like to know that Marcel was either in Stowe then or at least not in Sherbrooke, but that is not likely information to get. I will talk to our *procureur.*"

"I'll bring you everything we collected from down here for a show-and-tell. Gilles, we also found out that Gaston Picard was in Stowe a few days before Deschamps appeared on the mountain. He got a parking ticket. You might want to lean on him and find out what he was doing here."

Lacombe's voice betrayed his interest. "I will do that."

"By the way," I asked him, "how did you get hold of that confirmation letter?"

"It was from all the newspaper stories about Deschamps. From being a bad thing we feared, it became a good one. An old woman who worked for Jean Deschamps called us after the news. She never believed what they were telling about a religious retreat, so when she stopped working for the family—after Marcel came in—she stole the letter because she thought it might be a hot item, but she didn't do anything with it because she was frightened, and then she forgot. The publicity made her remember and call us."

"Was there anything besides the letter?"

"I am sorry, no. Nothing that she gave us."

"Okay, thanks. I'll see you soon."

I hung up and watched the others silently, waiting for someone to voice my own misgivings.

Tom Shanklin spoke first. "I've had cases a week old that didn't fall together this fast."

"Me, too," Willy said.

"It's the belt-and-suspenders aspect to it that bugs me," Sammie added. "I could buy the stomach contents leading to the waiter and then to the old hotel and the suitcase, but it's a little weird having a little old lady pop out of nowhere with the same information just in case we screwed up."

"None of what we found was bogus, though," I countered, more for argument's sake. "Not as far as we can tell. We all dug through the contents of that barn—it was real dirt, real cobwebs, real mildew coating the suitcase. Does anyone here think any or all of that was recently planted?"

No one responded.

"It feels wrong," Willy finally said.

"No argument," I told him. "But I can't see what choice we've got—not yet. It *looks* like Marcel knocked off his father. We've heard two different stories so far: that he was wet behind the ears but set to inherit the throne, and that he was blindly ambitious and didn't trust his father's intentions after his brother died. Whatever the truth, he did take over, did prove himself a good manager, and did make a bundle over the next five decades. In retrospect, all good, old-fashioned motives for murder. What bugs me is what's happening now. If we are being used to frame him for a piece of ancient history, why now?"

"Same reason he actually might've killed his own father," Auerbach suggested. "Only now it's someone else wanting access to the throne."

"I'd agree with you if he didn't have terminal cancer. Jean Deschamps might've lived for years, which could've made a young heir impatient. But Marcel is counting the days. Why an elaborate frame when Mother Nature's almost done all the dirty work?"

Sammie suddenly leaned forward in her chair. "Because it's a different script this time," she suggested. "We've been thinking it's somebody inside the Deschamps camp doing this, just like it was fifty years ago. What if the pressure's coming from outside? Could be the Hell's Angels or the Rock Machine *are* behind it all, trying to destabilize the passing of the torch by using us to bust Marcel and destroy his inner circle, killing

Tessier as extra insurance in the meantime. I know they weren't around when Marcel's dad was murdered, but it's not impossible they got in cahoots with whoever's been keeping Jean Deschamps on ice."

"Too fancy," Willy said shortly. With anyone else, he would have driven the point home more sarcastically. I was struck by his delicacy.

I also agreed with him. "It makes more sense that somebody inside is pulling the strings," I said. "I don't know how, why, or if Tessier's death ties in, but I'm inclined to keep that separate for the time being. Both Picard and Guidry are old enough to have played as big a role in Jean's disappearance as Marcel. How 'bout pinning this on one of them?"

But Shanklin shook his head. "That puts you right back where you started. Marcel's about to die. Assuming his son Michel does wind up in his seat, he'll need both those guys to learn the ropes—they're guaranteed jobs for life. Why mess that up? Plus, Tessier was killed by an Angel after years of peaceful co-existence—just before the Angels are slated to go to war. That can't be a coincidence."

I ran my fingers through my hair and stretched. "Okay. So we have no idea what's going on. But we have leads, evidence, and a trail to follow. Let's at least follow it and see where it goes. Could be we're making ourselves nuts here for no reason."

But I didn't believe that for a minute. Nor, I thought, did anyone else. Something wasn't right about all this.

Gilles Lacombe was on the phone when I was escorted into his office the following day. He smiled and waved me to a seat, still rapidly talking in *Joual* to whoever was at the other end.

Then he hung up, leaned back, and locked his fingers behind his head. "Joe. It is good to see you again. I have been talking to the *procureur* and it looks okay for the warrant. We made a list of enough specific items that we should be able to search the whole house. Thank you for faxing me what you found in Stowe. It is incredible that we both were told about the *valise* of Jean Deschamps, no?"

"Incredible might be the right word. We could be being led around by the nose."

Lacombe was unperturbed. "Perhaps. But do we care? It cannot be so bad to put a spoon in the soup and move it around a little. It might be a good time to invite your own *procureur* up here to meet ours. I think we will put the fire under Marcel Deschamps and see what happens."

Surveillance reports had told us what to expect. For days, the comings and goings at Marcel's home had been recorded on tape and logged. When we finally had all the paperwork and people we needed, including Kathy Bartlett and her Canadian counterpart, we waited until the middle of the night and then hit the house without fanfare, surrounding it before politely ringing the doorbell.

It was a Sûreté operation. Paul Spraiger, Gary Smith, Kathy, and I all stood back while the initial contact was made, and only entered the building after the all clear had been given.

There'd been no reason to expect violence or resistance, as there might have been at the Angels' compound, but as I walked down the familiar hallway, heading toward the library, I could tell we hadn't been admitted with grace—several Deschamps bodyguards were being pinned facedown on the carpeting, at least two of them exhibiting bruised or bloody faces.

The scene in the library was similarly ruffled. In place of the icy charm we'd been exposed to before, there was now turmoil and rage. Shouting at Gilles Lacombe were Pierre Guidry and a young man whose resemblance to Marcel stamped him as Michel, the family's heir apparent. Lacombe stood looking like a man suffering the mildest of discomforts, a polite smile on his face.

Paul Spraiger didn't bother translating word-for-word, but merely said, "According to them, Marcel's at death's door upstairs and can't be disturbed, this search is illegal, and we should wait for Picard so we can all be told that our jobs are history."

I acknowledged the familiar refrain and took advantage of being a mere spectator to study Michel Deschamps. I'd expected someone soft and pliable, given the rumors, and was surprised by the real article. Lean and muscular—now lacking the wimpy mustache I'd seen in the picture of him—he was certainly attractive enough to fit a playboy image, but watching his aggressive body language, I had my doubts he was anyone's pushover. In fact, the degree of anger he was venting made me wonder how downright violent he could be. It suggested the lineage we'd assumed was rotting away might be made of hardier stuff.

Or maybe it went beyond simple hardiness. The more I watched him, the more his body language made me think of someone on the edge, although of what I wasn't sure. But his eyes seemed slightly wider than they ought to be, his movements a little jerky, as if held under tight constraints, and his tone of voice, although I couldn't understand a word right now, bordered on the hysterical.

Lacombe eventually saw Paul and me standing there and disengaged himself, transferring the argument to the two prosecutors. He led us back into the hallway and shut the door. "They are not so well mannered when they are surprised. I am guessing we will get no coffee this time. Would you like a tour of the house? Maybe we can talk with Marcel before those two know what we are doing."

The hallway led to a sweeping staircase—ornate, curved, and hung with gilt-framed oil paintings. Upstairs, the luxury was maintained by a second passageway, lower ceilinged and lacking chandeliers, but flaunting more paintings, antique furniture, and a row of elaborately carved closed doors.

Uniformed police officers were milling about, going in and out of various rooms in search of the items specified in the search warrant. Lacombe asked one of them a question and then motioned to us to follow him.

We arrived at an enormous bedroom, hovering somewhere between Louis XIV and Hollywood, where Marcel Deschamps sat propped up in a bed the size of a polo field, his emaciated, pale, hairless body looking all the more fragile in comparison. The strength of his voice as he tongue-lashed Lacombe, however, removed any fears that he'd die right in front of us. It even occurred to me that our visit might possibly be therapeutic, since the angrier he got, the pinker and more normal his face became—and reminiscent of his son's downstairs.

For his part, Lacombe chose to silently tour the large room like a tourist in a quiet museum. It was an odd scene—we and several search team members wandering around as if totally alone, being screamed at nonstop in a language I couldn't understand by a man who increasingly reminded me of a choleric chicken.

It didn't last, of course. As Lacombe had presumably calculated, Marcel's very real medical condition eventually caught up to him, and he collapsed against the small mountain of pillows behind him, gasping and wheezing, his body spent, his face shining with sweat, and his eyes—as at our first meeting—radiating with heat and frustrated purpose. If a candle really does burn brightest just prior to guttering, then all the energy this man had left resided in those eyes.

In the sudden calm, Lacombe gently sat on the edge of the bed, his hands in his lap like a doting nephew, and began to speak.

Paul translated: "Monsieur Deschamps, we have warrants both to search this house—and any other property you might own—and for your arrest for the murder of your father in 1947, in Stowe, Vermont."

Deschamps closed his eyes briefly, as if to summon additional strength, before reopening them and commenting in an exhausted whisper, "I have never been to Stowe and I did not kill my father."

With unexpected tenderness, Lacombe reached out and laid his hand on Marcel's. "Don't worry about that. We'll talk later. Preserve your health."

There was a knock at the door and a police officer gestured to Lacombe. Behind him we could see Gaston Picard, dressed as if ready for the races at Ascot. Lacombe exchanged a few words with the cop and then gestured to us to come over.

"I will now have to talk with these people. You may stay if you like, but you might also like to look at Marcel's office down the hall. I will be there soon in any case—it is where much evidence will be found, I think. At least I hope," he added with a smile.

We began taking his advice, filing past Picard, Guidry, Michel, and the others without comment, when suddenly Michel exploded, bursting from behind his elders and flying at Lacombe with his arms out. I saw the flash of those wide eyes, the glitter of saliva on his lips as he shoved me aside, and then saw Lacombe smoothly lean out of the way, grab one of Michel's wrists, and use his own momentum to hurl him up against the wall, where our police escort pinned him in place, mashing his cheek against the ornate wallpaper.

Picard began to say something to him, but it was a short command from the bedroom that instantly calmed things down. Like a trained Doberman, Michel dropped from attack mode, becoming silent and compliant. Lacombe nodded at the cop to let him go, and everyone resumed their demeanor of moments ago. It had been a jarring and odd display, and as Paul and I continued to move away, I began to seriously wonder about the mental health of this crooked clan.

Paul and I followed the officer down the hall to a room as English in appearance as the bedroom had seemed French. Here the walls were all dark wood paneling, the windows leaded glass, and the shelves filled with as many books as we'd seen in the library. There was an empty fireplace, lots of indirect lighting from heavily shaded lamps, and a scattering of rugs and overstuffed leather furniture that tinted the air with an essence of old wool and saddle soap. There was also a wall covered with stuffed animal heads and exotic ancient weaponry.

"Reminds me of some pictures I saw of the Playboy mansion once," Paul said as we entered. "Very hormonal—not unlike what we just witnessed."

The search team technicians were most earnestly at work here, and we ended up standing in the middle of the room, watching the equivalent of a three-dimensional training film as they slowly took the place and its contents apart. Lacombe had joined us by the time they'd reached the point of sounding the paneled walls for hollow spots, one of which they found among the animal heads and weaponry.

After some discussion and the use of some electronic sensing device, one of the search team worked her way back to the oversized desk across the room and located what looked like a television remote. She hit a button on it, and we all watched as one of the wall panels moved back slightly into a cavity, and then slid from sight to one side, revealing a trophy wall of a wholly different nature.

Before us, mounted on a felt-covered surface, was an artful array of modern pistols, rifles, and shotguns, knives, blunt objects, a single garrote, and even something that vaguely looked like a bear trap. Some of the items looked factory-fresh and never used, others like debris left behind by a war—stained, rusted, and ruined with use.

But the item that caught all our eyes almost as soon as it was revealed was modest, domestically practical, and curiously homely by comparison.

Carefully suspended against the dark green surface, surrounded by weapons designed to crush, maim, and mutilate, was a tool almost dainty in contrast, its fancy silver handle reminiscent of the butt end of an orchestra conductor's baton.

It was an ice pick.

CHAPTER FIFTEEN

I slowly slid my stockinged feet under Gail's bottom, careful not to spill the mug of soup cradled in my hands. We were sitting opposite one another on an overstuffed couch in her condo outside Montpelier, wrapped in heavy terry cloth robes, our legs entwined, our bodies tired and pampered from making love and sitting too long in a hot tub afterward. I'd taken a short break from the investigation to allow Lacombe and his bunch time to build a case against Marcel Deschamps, and to report our progress to Bill Allard in Waterbury, just a short drive from Gail's.

As usual, she was analyzing the recent past in practical political terms. "This must have made your various bosses happy," she said. "It's not every day you get handed a half-century-old homicide and solve it overnight. I heard the governor blowing VBI's horn on the news this afternoon—talking about how well a tactical approach can cut through the red tape."

I let the strong aroma of hot soup fill my nostrils before taking a cautious sip. "I hope he doesn't have to apologize later," I said after a pause.

Her eyebrows rose. "Is there a chance of that?"

I tried a vague approach. "It's up to the prosecutors now. It is an extradition case, after all—we can't have at him unless the Canadians think there's just cause. You know how that can go."

I should have known better. Her expression turned serious. "You sound like the case might be shaky."

"There are questions. We all think this came together pretty easily."

"Marcel Deschamps didn't do it?"

I made a face and shrugged. "The evidence said he did. Means, motive, and opportunity are in place. It even makes sense logically, sort of."

"But you're not convinced," she concluded.

"I've still got inquiries going," I admitted. "That's what I told Bill this afternoon. Despite the supposed straight line between Jean being murdered and his son killing him, there's a lot of messy, unexplained details and a couple of awfully convenient coincidences."

"Was Bill sympathetic?"

"More or less. He wanted assurances that (a) nothing I had going would unnecessarily upset the applecart, and that (b) Willy wasn't involved in any of it."

Gail laughed. "I can't blame him there. What did you tell him?"

"I lied on both counts. Willy's one of the best diggers I know, and how the hell do I know if we'll upset any apple-carts? We might. We might not."

She gave me a rueful smile. "Hardly the best start to a new career."

"You should know."

It was an unnecessarily pointed comment, which she absorbed thoughtfully, concentrating on the contents of her own mug. Just a few months earlier, she'd been a newly hired deputy state's attorney. Unfortunately, she'd quickly found it an awkward fit, given her penchant for championing the disadvantaged, and had locked horns with her boss during her first major case, winning in court and being all but fired in the process. Her advice on new careers, therefore, carried some cautionary baggage.

But I wasn't guiltless, either. I hadn't left a lifelong job as a municipal cop just because VBI suddenly came knocking. I'd been falsely accused of a theft a while back—a headline maker that a hungry deputy Attorney General had tried and failed to mold to his political advantage. During the mudslinging, he'd suggested that I'd committed the theft out of feelings of inadequacy—being a frustrated, aging flatfoot living with a rich, attractive, upwardly mobile younger woman.

Baloney, as the woman in question and I had rationally assured each other. But the portrait had stung, and when VBI became a reality, I joined as much out of pride as for its mission's altruism. That tainted motivation continued to nag me, especially now that we were living apart once more, and in distant towns for months at a time. In Brattleboro, whether under the same roof or not, we'd seen each other all the time. Ever since those opportunities had become more haphazard, they'd been laden with doubts and worries with no real basis in fact.

Which is why I'd asked Gail from my hospital bed how we were doing.

Apparently, my rudeness had now given

her pause. "I told you how I felt about us after they pulled you out of the snow," she began almost timidly. "But I didn't ask you the same question. Should I have?"

I shook my head, irritated with myself. "Only if you'd wanted the same answer. I'm sorry about that crack—not sure where it came from."

"I am," she said more confidently. "You've spent your entire professional life as an insider—the hometown cop. Now you're on the outside, trying to win the trust of everyone you meet, including your own bosses. You've got no base, no organization, a patchwork squad, and a seriously distracted girlfriend."

I wagged a finger at her. "Better not let your feminist friends hear you say that."

She poked me with her toe. "They're as sentimental as the next person. What do you think, though? Are we heading for a crash with all this career stuff, or can we make it work?"

I wanted to choose my words carefully this time. "We've gone through a lot worse. I'd like to think we can beat this, too. Might take some adjusting—now and then."

She smiled warmly and snuggled down more securely into the pillows behind her. "I can do that. Tell me about Willy and Sam."

I laughed at the abrupt shift. "I'm more of a wishful thinker there. It's tough to tell—they're so buttoned down about it. He's softened up a lot, though, so selfishly speaking, I hope they can pull it off. And they are fun to watch—hardheads in love. I guess time'll tell."

Along with everyone else I knew, Gail didn't like Willy Kunkle, but she also couldn't help looking pleased. "And the team in general?"

"I like Paul Spraiger. He doesn't talk unless he has something to say. Gary Smith and I knocked heads early on because of the VBI thing, but I think we've made up. And I don't know about Tom Shanklin, except that he's done nothing wrong and hasn't taken any potshots. He seems to be a nice guy. Just keeps his own counsel."

She appeared satisfied by all that, nodding ever so gently as she sipped her soup.

"Is Montpelier life living up to expectations?" I asked in turn.

Now that we'd addressed our mutual misgivings, the question was less loaded than it might have been ten minutes ago. Gail was relaxed enough now to show a real enthusiasm. "Even better. It's like everything I did before suddenly coming together. All those boards I used to be on, the selectman job, going back to law school, even selling real estate. They all make sense now—being put to use at the same time. I love making things happen that affect the whole state. The hassles are familiar, but the rewards make them more worthwhile."

"So, you're happily upwardly mobile," I said.

She didn't deny it, which made me feel just the smallest bit mournful. "Who knows?" she answered. "There's so much going on here, so many bright people... It's exciting to think of the possibilities."

It was that, and I knew I was sitting with a woman who had the smarts and drive necessary to be governor or a member of Congress. I therefore couldn't but wish her well in the pursuit of her dreams—while also casting backward to when things had been quieter and less ambitious. A farmer's son, I was more attuned to an evolutionary pace— and not so enamored of change for change's sake, which often seemed to rule in Gail's new environment. I had never undersold her sense of right and wrong, but it made me nervous to see her so avid about a lifestyle society was largely trained to mistrust. Politicians and lawyer/lobbyists weren't often credibly combined with integrity and idealism. As one-sided a view as any other prejudice, it still made me uneasy when it involved someone I loved.

Kathy Bartlett waited until I'd settled into one of the chairs in her temporary office on the second floor of the Sûreté building back in Sherbrooke. Paul Spraiger and Gary Smith were already there. I was newly returned from my trip to Vermont.

"The case against Marcel Deschamps is going soft," she announced.

I glanced at the other two, recalling how I'd told Gail that the governor's optimism might have been premature. From their neutral expressions, I guessed they'd already been briefed. "I can't say I'm surprised," I said. "What's been going on?"

"I think the crown prosecutor is starting to

190

buy Marcel's line that he wasn't in Vermont in '47, didn't kill his father, and honestly thought some rival had done him in."

"Based on what?"

"The video of Marcel's interrogation," she explained. "Canadian law demands that all police interrogations be videotaped. After Marcel's session, Lacombe and company began kicking around how credible he seemed. My counterpart, Boulle, decided he wanted an expert opinion, so he sent the tape to a behavioral science team in Montreal—apparently that's an option they use now and then. It would drive me nuts."

Guillaume Boulle was the Sherbrooke crown prosecutor Lacombe kept invoking, and the same man who'd accompanied us the night we'd raided Marcel's house. I'd heard his and Kathy's styles were beginning to clash, she being more type-A, and he having a barely veiled contempt for aggressive women. This latest glitch wasn't going to help.

"The report come back yet?" I asked.

She didn't look happy. "That's why you're here. They say he sounds truthful. That he has the right personality for a leader of a bunch of cutthroats, but that he didn't do this one."

"And you don't buy that," I guessed.

"It's too fine a line for me. How the hell can you tell if a guy *sounds* like he either killed or didn't kill his father half a century ago, especially if he's ordered hits in the meantime? I think it's a psycho-babble crock they've chosen over hard evidence. Why I don't know, unless somebody's playing footsie under the table."

In the silence following that comment, I could hear the hard drive of her portable computer humming on her desk.

"Kathy," I said cautiously, "are you blowing off steam, or do you really believe that? 'Cause if you do, you've got to act on it."

She gave me a rueful smile. "I'm a fish out of water here. It pisses me off."

I didn't say anything. I could feel the other two looking from one of us to the other, like spectators at a tennis match.

"All right," she relented. "I don't really believe there's any corruption going on. At least I don't have proof of it. But these guys are so mellow, I'd like to strangle them. I know god-damn well if I had Marcel in the U.S., I could find five shrinks to say those Canadian pro-filers are full of it. I don't understand why they're bending over backward to tank such a strong case."

I had my own doubts about that strength, which made me duck the debate entirely. "What're they going to do?" I asked instead.

"They've asked him to take a lie detector test."

Gary Smith laughed. "The head of a crime family? What the hell do they expect?"

"That he might accept," Kathy explained grimly. "Problem is, if he does—and passes—it means we're in shit up to our necks."

Smith's eyes widened. "You're kidding. I thought polygraphs weren't acceptable in court."

"We're not talking about court, Gary. We're talking about the crown prosecutor not pursuing the case because he doesn't believe the guy's guilty."

Gary thought back a moment. "What about all those weapons they found behind the wall—the murder museum? Can't they make a connection between any of those and Marcel?"

"They've been trying," she told him, "but they're mostly old hat. The bear trap's a perfect example—it had traces of human blood on it, but there's no record of a trap being used in an unsolved crime. The ice pick's a minor miracle as it is. Marcel's fingerprints would have decayed by now, but the handle was silver and became permanently etched by the skin oil—pure dumb luck, along with DNA matching being invented in the meantime to pin the blood to Jean Deschamps. Without that, we wouldn't have gotten this far."

"How 'bout the lawyer, Picard?" Gary continued. "He was in Stowe two days before they found Deschamps. What's he say about that?"

I could tell from Kathy's expression where that was headed. "Sorry," she said. "He claims he was taking in the sights. A little day trip. 'People do it all the time,' to quote him. And in case you were going to ask," she added, "it's a no-go putting Marcel in Stowe in 1947— or Picard or Guidry for that matter. They can't find anyone who'll admit to knowing where any of them were when Jean was killed."

I stood up to stop a discussion I knew had

no happy outcome, especially if my personal misgivings were going to be called into play. "Then it's wait and watch time. I take it Marcel's people haven't responded to the polygraph offer yet?"

"Right."

Gary was looking confused. "What *does* happen if he passes? Don't we get a crack at him? I thought this was an American case."

Kathy frowned. "It is, but only if we can extradite him, and that won't be easy. They're already muttering about the age of the crime, the lack of witnesses, the suspect's failing health, and their own lack of enthusiasm as legal stumbling blocks."

"So, what do we do?"

"We keep digging," I said from the door, "and hope we can turn things around."

I ran into André Rousseau of the RCMP outside in the hallway a few minutes later.

"You're back," he said smoothly. "Good trip?"

"Mostly just reporting to twitchy superiors. They're nervous about making a good impression."

"The debut of the VBI? There must be a lot of people hoping you'll fail."

I was getting tired of hearing that. "A few. I hear Marcel sounded credible to your behavioral scientists."

He shook his head. "Not mine—the SQ's. All very chummy."

I looked at him sharply. "Meaning?" I

asked, Kathy's similar implication still fresh in my mind.

"Nothing," Rousseau answered vaguely. "We have a file on Marcel Deschamps that goes back to when he took over—bribery, assault, intimidation, jury tampering, homicide—you name it. He's been connected to all of it one way or another, although never close enough to put him in jail. And yet he lives here comfortably in a big house, expecting to die of old age. It makes you wonder how that came to be, assuming the local police were on their toes."

"We have a lot of crooks living like that back home," I said carefully. "Doesn't necessarily mean the locals are on the take."

Rousseau looked at me with feigned shock. "Did I say that?"

He laughed and walked away, leaving me with an unpleasant taste in my mouth. As he'd demonstrated before, he was the foreign element here—the federal outsider from the big city. But I couldn't in all honesty entirely dismiss what he'd said. It had been known to happen.

The phone jarred me awake, filling me instantly with dread. I opened my eyes, focused on the motel room's dusky ceiling, and hesitated answering, knowing that midnight calls never bore good news, and that for someone to reach me this far from home boded twice as ill.

"Hello?"

"You are Gunther, of the United States?" The voice was male, low, and barely spoke English.

"Yes."

"You investigate the Deschamps?"

"Who wants to know?"

He ignored the question, as I thought he might. "Hell's Angels did not kill Tessier."

"Who did, then?"

"We meet."

"What good would that do? I'm just an observer in this country. You need to talk to the police."

He laughed scornfully. "Then I die. How you think Deschamps get rich in Sherbrooke without the police help?"

That was the third such statement I'd heard in two days. "What if I refuse to meet with you?"

"More people die. Tessier was number one. Now he gone, now the Deschamps bulldog is gone. People have protection no more. We want no more killing."

"Why don't you just tell me what's on your mind here and now and get it over with?"

"I have proof. Otherwise, this is talk only."

"Where?" I asked after a moment's hesitation.

"An old jail, abandoned. It is on Rue Cliff, near the gorge. You find this?"

"I have a map."

"It is near Rue Winter, at the corner. You will see steps to a porch and a door. Go in and we talk."

"Or go in and have my head blown off."

I could sense his exasperation as he cursed in French and then added, "Why? You can stop this. Lacombe is your friend. You will talk to him."

"Call him yourself," I suggested.

"He will not see me alone, and I do not trust them with him. Only you."

"I'll think about it," I finally said.

"One hour. You be alone, or people die."

The phone went dead.

I replaced the handset and lay in the dark, thinking. It sounded plausible. The Angels had been blamed for Tessier's death—maybe they had proof of their innocence and even of someone else's guilt. Given my suspicions about most of what had fallen into our laps up to now—from Christophe Bossard as Tessier's unlikely killer to Marcel's conveniently safeguarded ice pick—I found the nature of this phone call almost irresistible.

Which was probably the whole point.

At home, the solution would have been obvious—round up some backup, get to the site early, and proceed with caution. Here, with suspicions ballooning about the case and the people investigating it, I found myself uncomfortably at sea. I was an organization man, as attuned to teamwork as a fish to water, and since arriving in Canada I hadn't been shut out, information hadn't been withheld from me, I'd had no complaints.

So why this debate?

I got out of bed, conscious of the one-hour deadline, and turned on the light over the desk by the window. I opened a map and located the address I'd been given. It was north of the gorge, midway along its length, at the bottom of a three-sided, horseshoelike block of streets. Cliff Street paralleled the gorge.

Still unsure of my actions, I began to dress.

It wouldn't be the first time a generations-old crime family had found its way into a local police force, however discreetly. Some of the caller's reserve might have even stemmed from simple paranoia, rather than any knowledge of corruption. He was apparently sticking his neck out, indulging in covert diplomacy, hoping to keep the peace between two illegal organizations. It stood to reason he might be a little twitchy, with an old pro like Jean-Luc Tessier being knocked off with such ease.

Especially since Christophe Bossard—the unlikeliest of suspects—was being prosecuted for that crime.

I finished dressing and stood looking down at the map. I had no fear for myself, despite the concern I'd voiced to the caller. It didn't make sense that I should be anyone's target, and nothing suggested this whole thing wasn't as simple as it looked. Some guy from their side had something of value for someone neutral from our side. And I was that someone.

I scooped up the map and left.

Cliff Street was in the heart of the Vieux Nord neighborhood, which explained why most of the streets had Anglo names—Island, High, Court, William, even London. There was a shoved-together intimacy to the buildings, as if they'd moved imperceptibly closer to each other as the town had grown up around them.

I drove across Queen slowly onto de Montréal, looking for where High Street would take me one block south to Cliff. My headlights slid along dark, quiet walls and over empty, snow-covered lawns. Traffic was nonexistent at this hour.

The setting helped make me feel better about what I was doing. Had it been a warehouse district, or some industrial wasteland on the edge of town, I would have been more apprehensive. But this was as settled an area as Sherbrooke had to offer—something my anonymous caller had probably understood when he'd chosen it.

A row of trees loomed up ahead and High Street t-boned into Cliff. I turned left and parked. As I killed the engine, I could hear the dull rumble of water cascading through the gorge just beyond the screen of woods. It sounded cold and ominous, belying my efforts to feel good about being here.

I got out of the car. Across the narrow street, the old jail stretched up into the night sky. Four or five stories tall, built of featureless gray stone, it appeared to have a separate warden's quarters glued to its side—red-bricked and equipped with windows. But it, too, seemed abandoned and forlorn, despite the efforts to make it look homey.

I saw the steps the caller had mentioned leading up to the front door. Flashlight in hand, I tentatively climbed to the concrete porch and laid my hand on the doorknob. There were no lights and no sounds from within.

The door was unlocked and opened without

protest. Now thoroughly doubting my wisdom, I stepped into an empty, dusty room with a counter running across it. Playing the light around, I could tell where bars or metal meshing had once run from counter to ceiling, and guessed that the house had been remodeled from warden's home to front office before being abandoned altogether, presumably to linger in perpetuity on the local historical society's list of things to restore.

I'd done what I'd been told to do and was now suddenly at a loss, vaguely disappointed after all my misgivings to be merely standing alone in a cold and empty room.

"Hello?" I finally called out tentatively.

Nothing greeted me in return.

I walked through a gap in the counter and discovered a heavy iron door on the other side connecting the house to the jail itself. It was half open. I slipped into its dark embrace, hearing my footsteps echo off hard, unyielding surfaces all around, grit and debris crunching underfoot.

Before me was a long, high-ceiling stone hallway, lined with open doors. My flashlight revealed no colors whatsoever—just the sliding scale of a black-and-white photograph, looking a hundred years old.

"Hello?" I tried again.

I followed the reverberation of my own voice down the hall, pausing at each doorway to check where it led, mostly into narrow cells, each one fitted with an arched and shuttered metal-barred window.

At the far end of the corridor was a steel spiral

staircase. Though less apprehensive as my confidence grew that I was alone, I still wasn't inclined to head for the basement, so I climbed instead, making an unholy racket as shoe leather hit metal.

The second floor resembled the first, except for a wider area halfway down the corridor which might have once served as a dayroom. I approached it cautiously, still pausing at each doorway, but again only surrounded by sounds of my own making.

In that open, central area, however, my isolation finally ended—replaced by something far more tangibly grim. A man was sitting, legs sprawled before him, propped up against the wall, his eyes still open and his throat slit wide.

Although slowing down, his blood was still pumping all over the front of his denim Hell's Angels jacket.

He'd been killed while I'd been in the building.

I stood absolutely still, frozen as much by that sudden realization as by the overwhelming evidence that I'd committed a fundamental and potentially fatal mistake. Instead of wondering how and why this man might've died, I was seized by a double dose of anger and fear.

The clear sound of a shoe scraping the floor behind me snapped me out of it, and the anger won over, fueled by the guilt of having been so stupid. I turned, yelled, "Stop— police," and ran headlong down the cold, dark hallway, now in pursuit of clattering footsteps half falling down the metal staircase.

It was no more reasonable than having come here in the first place, of course. Alone, unarmed, and with no radio or backup, I should have stayed put, let whoever it was escape, and then found a phone to summon help. But impulse was driving me now—along with a furious need to take back control and make some sense of all these riddles. I knew I couldn't actually catch the man ahead of me, and that to succeed might earn me a knife in the chest, but I wanted to at least get a glimpse of him, if for no other reason than to partially offset my embarrassment.

I pounded down the first floor corridor, retracing my steps to the warden's quarters, and just caught the shadow of my quarry as he slammed through the metal door at the far end.

Bursting out onto the porch moments later, I finally spotted him, briefly and from afar— a dark shape in full flight—rounding the corner of Cliff onto Winter, his legs and arms pumping like a sprinter's. I chased after him still, but without the same drive, that brief glimpse having told me that I was no match for his youthful speed. When I then slipped and fell on an icy patch at the same corner, I didn't bother regaining my feet, but lay there instead, panting and stunned, slowly feeling the icy cold reassert itself until all that was left in the surrounding night sky was the ceaseless rumble of the water rushing through the gorge.

CHAPTER SIXTEEN

Gilles Lacombe entered the room on the first floor of the Sûreté building and looked at me sitting in a metal chair by the wall, a plastic cup of coffee on the table beside me. It was not an office, but a cross between an interrogation room and a storage closet, complete with no windows. A doghouse, in fact, I knew ruefully, despite the open door. I'd been brought here and debriefed by an SQ detective, who hadn't bothered hiding his contempt for my behavior.

But Lacombe didn't reflect the irritation I had for myself. He hitched a leg on the table's edge and thoughtfully asked instead, "You are not hurt, I hope?"

"A small bruise on the hip where I fell, richly deserved."

He nodded, as if to himself. "That is good. You are lucky." He then looked me straight in the eye and gently asked, "Why did you do this thing?"

His obvious disappointment hurt worse than I'd anticipated. This man had bent over backward to accommodate us, and his confusion now spoke more clearly of his generosity—and my betrayal of it—than any angry outburst could have. I couldn't bring myself to be honest and deepen the wound by admitting my paranoid suspicions of the night before. Better to just look as stupid as I felt.

"He told me to come alone—that he had

proof Bossard didn't kill Tessier—and not to bring anyone local. I thought it might help."

He was polite enough not to make any more of it. "Did the man tell you anything before he died?" he asked.

"No. I must've gotten there less than a minute after his throat was cut."

"He told you he had proof on the telephone. Did he carry anything?"

I shook my head. "I went back after I called for backup. He was clean. The other guy must've grabbed it."

"Or it was not real," Lacombe mused.

That possibility didn't make me feel any better. I hadn't thought the whole thing might have been a setup from the start.

"Was the dead man a Hell's Angel?"

"Oh, yes. And he might have called you," Lacombe said. "But it is possible the killer called him and you each one, so you could see the death of an Angel. It is good headlines, you as witness, as we have this morning, and it makes more tension between the Deschamps and the Hell's Angels."

"And it makes the cops look like idiots," I added. "I am sorry, Gilles. I really messed this up. I'd be madder than hell if I were you."

He smiled and patted my shoulder. "It is not so big a deal, Joe. Americans take this more personally than we do. You were not hurt. That is good. The rest is little. And they already call us idiots."

He took pity on me then. His voice warmed as he added, "And if somebody is making a war between the Deschamps and the Angels, it is not working very well. Both are still telling us they are innocent."

"How're things moving against Marcel?" I asked, mostly to shift the attention off me. "Bartlett was saying yesterday they think he might be innocent."

He shrugged philosophically. "We do what we do, they do the rest. If they will not prosecute, we have to return to..." he groped for the right expression.

"First base?" I finished to help him out.

"That is it. But I do not think it will be simple. Marcel fit as his father's killer. After all this time, I do not know where else we could go. Also, it will be difficult to keep the task force together."

"Marcel and his lawyers must know that."

He nodded. "It is an interesting time."

"Anything else come up from the search of his house?"

"The DNA found on the ice pick is the same as Jean Deschamps's, and Marcel had fingerprints on the handle, but the Deschamps can have the best lawyers in Canada."

"What about all the paperwork from Marcel's office?"

Lacombe thought back. "No," he said slowly. "They are still analyzing it, but it looks like mostly business affairs. It is clear they either have a second office we did not find or they do not write down what we would like to see. We also are running tests on all the other weapons we found in that closet. If not his father, maybe somebody else can be tied to Marcel."

He rose to his feet, preparing to go, and then stopped. "There is something interesting, speaking of killed people—a little history. We found documentation from the Second World War in the papers of Jean Deschamps that Marcel had stored. It looks like the father thought his older son Antoine had been murdered in Italy, and not killed in battle."

"By who?"

Lacombe resumed walking to the door. "They do not say. And it might not be true. What we found were copies of letters Jean wrote to the army. The replies all say that it did not happen that way—that Jean should be proud of his son's sacrifice, etcetera, etcetera."

He paused on the threshold. "I have to do some of my other work right now. I am very glad things worked out last night, Joe. I would feel badly if you got hurt."

"I know. And I really am sorry, Gilles. It was a spur-of-the-moment thing. It won't happen again."

He left then, but despite his kind words and gentle manner, I knew I'd crossed a line—and suspected I'd be seen as more hindrance than help from now on.

It was time to return home, not just to mend fences back there, since I knew I'd just made VBI look a little less than stellar, but because it was becoming clear that the case against Marcel—passed polygraph or not—wasn't panning out as we'd all hoped it might.

Despite the setbacks, though, I couldn't repress a paradoxical optimism, as if having just been deprived of the only prize I thought was available, I now could suddenly see others of equal—if less obvious—merit.

Lost in a flurry of new options, I slowly went upstairs in search of a phone.

Willy Kunkle came through my open door at the Commodore Inn back in Stowe and leaned up against the wall, watching me unpack.

"They throw you out or are you running for cover?"

I didn't look up at him. "Guess you heard."

"Hell, yeah. Didn't make the papers—not like if I'd screwed up—but no cop I know hasn't heard about it. Cowboy Joe, head of the Untouchables. They're all laughing their asses off."

I knew he was just rubbing it in—that was as natural as breathing to him. But it didn't make it any easier to take.

"Maybe it was a blessing in disguise," I said as a diversion.

He laughed. "God, I'm glad I never used that line on you."

I stopped what I was doing and straightened. "Where're Sam and Tom?"

"Sam's in her room doing homework. I dunno about Tom. We don't hang out."

I resisted suggesting why that might be. "Round them up. If I'm going to tell you what I'm thinking, they might as well hear it, too."

We convened in a small booth at the back of the inn's overdecorated bar. It was early evening, the TV set's volume was hovering at near murmur, and we had the place mostly to ourselves.

"I got Willy's version of the fallout," I told the other two. "What've you heard?"

I was looking at Tom Shanklin, on loan from the state police, curious about how he'd handle it.

"Not much," he said, his voice neutral. "Just that you had a meet with some informant that went sour. No big deal."

"Meaning everyone's having a field day."

He looked like he'd swallowed something distasteful. "A few people are blowing it out of proportion, but they've been filling my ear from the start."

"It's not like we don't meet with CIs all the time," Sammie complained more petulantly. "Things can go wrong. You get out with your butt intact, it's a success, right?"

Predictable responses all around, I thought, although I was pleased by Shanklin's. "Okay," I said. "I just wanted to know what to expect. For the record, though, this was more than a meet with a CI, Sam, as you well know. I was a guest. I should've let the locals handle it. Don't any of you downplay that if you're asked, okay?"

There was no response.

"Be that as it may," I continued, "I was telling Willy earlier that maybe it'll work out to our advantage anyhow, which is why I asked you here."

I paused to take a sip of my ginger ale. "The minute we found that letter from Marcel to his father—and were told by the SQ that if we hadn't, they had another way of pointing us to it—we all thought that was pretty convenient, right?"

"No shit," Willy muttered, poking through the small dish of pretzels in our midst.

"Still, the dead guy came from Canada, and so did his supposed killer. It looked likely he'd been whacked on our side of the border just to complicate things."

"Wasn't he?" Shanklin asked.

I waved that aside. "Probably. But what I'm saying is that we were happy to think that we were just the dumping ground."

"For good reason," Shanklin persisted. "There was no evidence to the contrary."

"Except that now the Canadians are having doubts about Marcel. They've offered him a lie detector test, which, if he takes it and passes, means the prosecutors at least will probably lose interest. That'll put us right back where we started. Whether we like it or not, we may have to either come up with an alternate bad guy, or find some new evidence to override the lie detector and profilers both. If we don't, Kathy'll have her hands full getting Marcel to our side of the border."

"How the hell're we going to do that?" Willy asked. "It was a goddamned miracle we found that letter."

"We found Arvin Brown," I argued, "and traced Jean Deschamps to where he spent his last night alive. The footprints are there, even if they are fifty years old. People are still around, documents are sitting on dusty shelves—they can tell us things if we find them and ask the right questions."

"It's a waste of time," Willy grumbled.

"You want us to look for someone besides Marcel?" Sammie asked, obviously intrigued.

"Not exactly," Tom answered for me. "He wants Marcel to be just one of several possibles."

"That's it," I agreed, struck again by Shanklin's objectivity. "Run through what might have happened here in 1947, but exclude Marcel as the killer."

"Meaning no letter," Sammie concluded.

"Right. No letter."

In the sudden lull that followed, I became aware of the bar's quiet vital sounds—the humming lights over the rows of bottles bracketing the cash register, the hiss of running water as the bartender washed glasses and set them into overhead racks. I wondered if I might be expecting more than these people were willing to offer, especially given how little we had after all this effort.

"Which begs the question—"Willy argued, "what got Jean down here if it *wasn't* a letter from his son?"

"What do we know about his trip?" I asked.

"That he left Sherbrooke without telling anyone," Tom said quickly.

"That when he was here," Sammie added, "he stayed at a swanky inn, ate high on the hog, and felt cocky enough to leave Arvin Brown a fat tip."

"He also packed a bag," Tom said.

"And registered under his own name," I remembered.

"Just as if he'd been invited down by his son," Willy concluded sorrowfully.

But Sammie wouldn't bite, "No letter and no son."

"Says you."

"Hardly sounds like he was flying under radar," Tom said.

"What does a typed letter imply?" I asked suddenly.

There was a silence reminiscent of a classroom full of stumped students. Willy finally volunteered, "Access to a typewriter."

"Anonymity," Sammie answered.

"Sure," Tom agreed, his surprise apparent. "The only handwriting was the word 'Marcel' in block letters."

"And we're talking about a time when few men used typewriters, much less had access to them on vacation," I added.

"Okay," Willy conceded grudgingly, "no letter, no son."

"So why did he come down here without telling anyone?" Tom asked. "Especially when he made no effort to be discreet once he arrived?"

I tried the trump card I'd been hoarding since Lacombe first gave it to me. "I don't know why he was alone, but he was chasing down a lead on who killed his son in Italy in World War Two."

Willy sat back in his chair. "You old bastard. What the hell's that all about?"

"Something they found in Marcel's office," I explained. "A bundle of Jean's old papers—including a few pieces of correspondence between him and Canadian armed forces types about Antoine's death. Jean seemed to think he'd been murdered and not killed in action. They weren't buying it."

I drained my glass and continued, "Remember the other flag we had that Marcel lured Jean down there?"

"The old secretary," Willy said.

"Right. She thought her boss had been whacked all along, so when she was given the heave-ho, she stole the receipt from the Snow Dancer Hotel—at least supposedly. One of Lacombe's people interviewed her using a soft approach. Didn't crowd her about the convenience of finding the receipt just when we needed it, but kept things conversational instead. From the report Paul and I read, when the interview eventually turned to Antoine, she got all enthusiastic. Antoine had been the fair-haired boy, as far as she was concerned, and Jean had taken his death hard, especially after hearing he might have been murdered. She said Jean went after the truth like someone in a 'Greek play,' quote-unquote. Claims he swore her to secrecy."

"But why?" Tom repeated. "What was the advantage to keeping it secret? He could've used his manpower to widen the search."

I had no answer for him, and Sammie was off on another tangent anyway. "How long before he died had he heard about Antoine?" she asked.

"Only a few months, which explains the small amount of correspondence. And she couldn't say—or wouldn't say—how he found out in the first place. One day he just asked her to start writing those letters—that's how she got in the know. And when we asked Lucien Pelletier what Jean was like just before he vanished, he said he was 'energized,' like he used to be before a big deal was going down."

"How do you go from that to getting him killed here?" Tom asked.

"Maybe we don't," I conceded. "But if we work on the theory that the Marcel letter is bogus, then a lead about Antoine's death is the next best way I know of encouraging Jean to cross the border."

"The guy who killed his son in Italy lives here?" Sammie sounded incredulous.

"Not necessarily. Jean was on a hunting expedition, from what the secretary said, chasing down old comrades in arms, superior officers, people who might've known the truth. He may have found someone living here that fit one of those categories, or he may have simply been lured across the border by someone who knew about his obsession. What we need to do is retrace his steps, not for who killed him, but for whoever he was looking for—a whole different trail."

"Or maybe not," Willy commented.

"Or maybe not," I agreed.

"Is the SQ going to help?" Tom wanted to know.

"Yeah. My screwup is a bigger deal around here than it is up there. Lacombe even said the whole thing might've been a setup by someone wanting a police witness to a Hell's Angels killing. And tensions *are* cranking up. The local press is all over this and the Angels have been quoted as saying they aren't going to be pushed around—that their pal will be avenged. The Canadians don't care much about Jean's ancient paperwork right now."

I half expected Willy to blurt out he had no intention of becoming an archive rat chasing down old army records, so I was surprised when he said instead, "If the letter was a frame, we could do more than just follow Jean's footprints. We could also go after whoever planted the letter."

"How?" Sammie asked. "It was buried in a suitcase covered with mildew—probably been there almost since Jean was killed."

But I understood where he was headed. "The Alvarez will," I murmured.

"Right. We found it through old-fashioned legwork, but that geezer secretary was ready if we hadn't. Why would there be a restriction on the barn behind the B-and-B, and a further one telling any new owners they couldn't mess with its contents? It had to be to preserve the suitcase and its smoking-gun contents."

Sammie understood now. "Trace the will's executor and maybe we find our bad guy."

"Okay," I concluded. "New attack plan. Since they're used to me up there, I'll go back to Sherbrooke and collect what I can on Antoine Deschamps, especially on when he was in Italy. Willy, you came up with the Alvarez angle; chase it down. Sam and Tom, we need to find out who was in Stowe and what it was like in 1947—the movers and shakers, the oddballs, the busybodies. Check the town hall, the newspaper files. Willy covered some of that ground already, so get ideas from him. Neither the state police nor the town cops were around back then, or just barely, so either the constable records or the sheriff's office might have something. Arvin Brown seemed on the ball—maybe he could tell you more, or give you names of people who might. Also, let's see if we can find out what Gaston Picard was doing here just before Jean's body popped up. He claims he was playing tourist. Maybe somebody saw him around town— sure as hell someone did business with him. Check all the local lawyers, Realtors, banks, anyone else you can think of."

We all rose to our feet as if summoned by a signal. "Any of you needs help, let out a shout. That's the whole idea behind this unit—we have the resources, the manpower, and the network. Let's put it to use and see if it works the way it's supposed to."

We filed out of the bar, Willy, I noticed, giving Sammie's shoulder a quick squeeze—the first outward sign of affection I'd witnessed so far. There was no telling how the Canadian prosecutor was going to fare with Marcel Deschamps and the pending lie detector test. But for the first time since this all began, I wasn't that concerned. We finally had something we could work on independently—and I could feel the longed-for adrenaline at last taking hold.

CHAPTER SEVENTEEN

Lacombe seemed bemused by my request. "You would like to see the papers on Jean's son's death in Italy? Why?"

We were sitting in his favorite restaurant for lunch, he eating seafood and drinking a beer, I nursing a Coke and a ham sandwich, wondering why they'd loused it up with some fancy bitter cheese.

"I wish I could tell you," I admitted. "Call it a hunch I can chase down while we wait for Marcel to decide about the polygraph. It'll probably be a waste of time, but it occurred to us we might've let a few details slide after we found that letter from Marcel to his father, like what the old man was doing in Stowe in the first place. I'm hoping those old papers might help."

I was purposefully downplaying my interest. This wasn't my turf. If Lacombe liked what he heard, I was fearful he'd take control of it, leaving me as empty-handed as before. I didn't ponder the irony that VBI had been created precisely to overcome such territorial self-interest—I was too busy both licking my wounds and hoping to earn my paycheck.

I should have known better than to play cute with him. He gave his trademark gentle smile and said, "They sound like the key to your lock."

Old-fashioned guilt got the better of me. I still couldn't shake the trouble I'd caused this man all too recently. "We're pretty interested in them. For the sake of argument, we're pretending the letter never existed."

"Because maybe it existed to make us happy only?" he suggested.

"Right."

He mulled that over a moment, chewing thoughtfully. "This is interesting. You are thinking the letter was not written by Marcel and that it wasn't sent to Jean—that it came to be after Jean was killed."

"Maybe," I stressed. "It's a little like deciphering a logic problem, because even if Marcel wasn't the author, it still might've been written to bait Jean, especially if Jean *thought* Marcel was in Stowe when he received it. We need to know for a fact that Jean knew Marcel's whereabouts when he left for Stowe. If we find a witness to Marcel being in Sherbrooke, for example, then we've also got proof that the letter was a complete fabrication, designed solely for us. Which is why the barn and its contents were preserved by the Spaniard's will—to create a credible time capsule fingering Marcel."

Lacombe smiled broadly. "*Incroyable*. This is very good."

"Only if you're interested in establishing an alibi for your prime suspect," I said. "Is there any chance we could find out which outfits Antoine was with in Italy, along with their rosters?"

He laughed softly. "You are a strange policeman."

I was tucked away in the Sûreté's property room in the basement, wedged into a corner at a small desk under dubious lighting, side by side with Paul Spraiger, a pile of yellowed correspondence spread out before us.

"Anything?" I asked him after he put the last sheet down.

"Same as the English stuff you read—pointed questions from Jean Deschamps, vague and meaningless gobbledygook from the bureaucrats: 'We've examined our records pertaining to the death of Antoine Deschamps and have found nothing to indicate anything at variance with the initial findings earlier forwarded to you,' blah, blah. Amazing how no matter the nationality, the bullshit smells the same."

"What about the private papers?"

He sighed and shook his head. Our research fit into two categories. Correspondence to and from various government agencies in both languages, and letters written between Jean and several of his son's co-combatants, all in French. "There's nothing here," Paul conceded. "Every one's a dead end. Either the writer didn't know Antoine Deschamps, except maybe slightly or by name, or he wasn't around when Antoine was killed and doesn't have any details."

I picked up the official report of that death and scanned it once more. Antoine Deschamps was killed in action in Italy on June 4, 1944, outside Rome during offensive maneuvers against an entrenched enemy force. His personal effects were collected and his body shipped home to his family. From what I could decipher from the bored euphemisms of such documents, he was shot during an assault, like so many others—plain and simple.

"We're missing something," I said.

"Could be Jean just couldn't accept the truth," Paul countered. "His whole life was based on an-eye-for-an-eye. An old-fashioned combat death was probably unacceptable."

I shook my head. "No. I mean literally. We're missing something. Even if he did go around the bend and invent a suspicious death, why aren't there any letters here from people who were with his son when he died?"

"He was just beginning to dig into it."

"I know," I argued, "but still, what do you do when you organize something like this? You make lists—who to contact, their addresses, their old unit affiliations. You start with letters from the son, picking up names of buddies who were with him. Any letters from Antoine?"

"Maybe he wasn't a writer."

I appreciated what Paul was doing. "Okay, let's say that's true. Who's the first person you contact if you're in Jean's shoes?"

Paul hesitated. "His commanding officer, friends he enlisted with, parents of friends who didn't make it back."

I waved my hand across the pile before us. "There's nothing like that here. What're the chances of writing letters to...how many do we have?...thirteen survivors in your own son's old outfit and not finding a single one who was at the right place at the right time?"

"What're you suggesting?" Paul asked cautiously.

I sensed what was behind the question.

"Not a military conspiracy. I'm not *that* paranoid. This has to have been picked over. I don't think Jean couldn't accept his son's death—from what we know, he wasn't the hysterical type. I think he either got a letter or a telegram or a phone call, or maybe met someone, and that's what got him going. I also think he found something tangible that kept him on track, and which isn't in this pile. How do you explain his actions otherwise?"

But Paul kept to his role of devil's advocate. "How do we know about those actions in the first place?"

I stared at him, and then repeated Willy's comment from the day before. "You mean the old secretary?"

He raised his eyebrows. "Maybe we should do our own interview."

Marie Chenin lived in a modern apartment building on the fringes of Sherbrooke, in a section I suspected had been farmland not long before. It was an expensive building, clean cut and tidily maintained, as neatly placed next to its neighbors as a brand-new domino. Approaching it from the parking lot with Paul, I couldn't help superimposing a sense of sterile imprisonment where only luxury and comfort had been intended.

We took a quiet, plastic-walled elevator to the fifth floor and walked down the hallway, striding through an invisible haze of new carpet odor and disinfectant.

Madame Chenin met us at the door, looking

old, bent, and frail, except for a pair of intelligent, calculating eyes.

Paul did the translating.

"Gentlemen, how nice to see you. Please come in. It's not often I get so many visitors in such a short time."

"That's kind of you to say," I answered. "I was afraid we might be imposing."

She led the way to a small, richly decorated living room with a sweeping view of distant mountains across miles of dazzling white, snow-covered countryside.

"Make yourselves comfortable. I prepared tea. Would you like some?"

She placed herself in an armchair facing a silver service matching the plush setting, if not the financial image, of a long-retired secretary. Paul and I had no choice but to sit like schoolboys on a small sofa opposite her. The windows ran the length of the wall across from us, their curtains wide open, and the snow-brightened light coming through them was enough to hurt our eyes. Despite her seemingly impeccable manners, Marie Chenin made no offer to ease our squinting at her.

For the moment, I decided to play along.

She smiled cheerfully as she passed us tiny cups and saucers. "I'm afraid the pleasure of your company will be all mine, since I can't imagine what I can add to what I told the other young man."

I took the time to sample my tea. "Actually, Madame Chenin, it's your helpfulness then that brings us back now. There aren't many people left from those days who have your sharp memory."

Her smile remained, but I could tell she was slightly irritated. "You haven't said if you like your tea."

I placed the cup on the low table between us. "Wonderful. We're not here to bother you about those papers you took from the Deschamps, by the way. That's ancient history."

She cut me a quick look and then offered us a small bowl. "I should have offered you sugar. I'm becoming forgetful."

We both passed. "We'd like to know more about Antoine," I explained.

She was visibly surprised. "Antoine? Why?"

"We think his death may have had something to do with Jean's disappearance. I understand you knew Antoine, before he went off to Italy?"

"Yes, of course I did." But she still seemed confused by my approach.

"Tell me about him—how he was, how he worked with his father, how he got along with his brother."

A change came over her then, and she settled back in her chair, abandoning the role of hostess. I sensed a burden slipping from her and remembered the intel report about her first interview—how merely mentioning Antoine had changed the tone of the conversation. I tested this theory by slowly rising, closing the curtains to quell the glare, and silently returning to my chair, all without protest from her.

She spoke softly. "Antoine was a wonderful

boy—strong, handsome, intelligent, and graceful. Very much like his father. I used to think they worked together more like brothers than as father and son, they joked together so."

"That must have been tough on Marcel."

Her face hardened slightly. "Who could tell? Marcel wasn't like Antoine at all. He was withdrawn, unathletic, given to moods. And he was devious, always working behind your back. I don't think Antoine's friendship with their father struck him as anything other than stupid."

"Did they fight?"

"The two brothers?" She shook her head. "They barely had anything to do with one another, and there was enough money so they could pursue different interests."

"Like what?" I asked, struck by this very different family portrait.

"I wouldn't know about Marcel. Probably money management. He always had the soul of a banker, even though Antoine was supposed to take over the business."

"We heard they both were, as a team."

She waved one hand dismissively. "That was the story later, after Antoine died. Marcel might have played a role in money matters, but the operational head was supposed to have been Antoine."

I was struck by her language—very business-oriented, as if she'd also been involved in the family's commercial affairs. I thought Lacombe might find it interesting to check the finances of this supposed retiree.

"Legend has it," I continued, "that Jean was

a bit of a pirate in the old days, building an empire out of nothing, hard on his enemies and loyal to his friends and family. Was Antoine like that, too?"

She smiled sadly. "He had many of those qualities."

"Why did he go to war?" I asked.

Her eyes widened. "Everyone did. Patriotism meant something back then. Our country called and we responded en masse. It was the right thing to do."

"Marcel stayed in Canada."

"Yes," she said sourly. "Still managing his affairs."

"With Jean's connections, he could've secured Antoine's safety, too. Fighting isn't the only useful thing that can be done in wartime."

But she was adamant. "Antoine wouldn't hear of it, and I doubt Jean even brought it up. Jean would have gone himself if he'd been accepted, but he was considered too important to the war effort." Her tone abruptly turned bitter. "Both he and Antoine thought the fighting would be a grand adventure, so it was up to the son to live vicariously for the father. And die."

I added fuel to the fire, suspecting that Marie Chenin's affection for Antoine—and perhaps his father, also—went beyond that of a loyal employee. "All to the benefit of the son who stayed behind."

"Yes," she admitted darkly. "He made out well."

"We've also been told Jean was so distressed after Antoine died that he made up the murder story to rationalize an otherwise senseless death."

She bristled at that. "Nonsense. Jean Deschamps was not some mental cripple. He had good reason for believing what he did."

"What was that?"

She stopped dead in her tracks, obviously at a loss. "I don't know. He never told me," she finally said.

"You must have had some idea, working with him so closely."

"He was told about it by someone he believed, but I don't know if it was by letter or in person."

"Was anyone else in the family aware of this?"

"No," she said emphatically. "I was certainly ordered not to breathe a word once he began his investigation."

"What about Picard and Guidry? They worked as a team with Jean, didn't they?"

"Of course they did." She looked at me nervously for the first time, and then glanced around the room, like an actor groping for a line. I was struck by the notion that she might have erred in some way. When she spoke again, it was slowly and with obvious caution. "There were many conversations I wasn't privy to... And they weren't *that* much of a team."

I sat forward and leaned my elbows on my knees, suddenly struck by a thought. "Madame Chenin, let's stop doing this. Things are going on here I'm sure you don't know about— things you never intended to be a part of. Do you know why you were told to give us that receipt?"

She stared at me, her mouth slightly open. "What do you...?"

"What did they say would happen?" I interrupted. "Do you realize the receipt was the primary piece of evidence used against Marcel for the murder of his own father?"

Her whole face contorted with confusion. "What?"

"Because it was known you so disliked Marcel, you were used to frame him for Jean's death. The receipt led us to the inn, which led us to Jean's old luggage, and that took us to a letter supposedly written by Marcel luring Jean down to Stowe so he could be killed. Did Marcel know how to use a typewriter back then?"

She rubbed her forehead as if fighting off a migraine. "No," she said vaguely. "I did all the typing... I don't understand. It's not what they said."

"Who said?" I pressed her. "Who told you to give us the receipt?"

Her hand dropped back down to her lap and she shook her head forcefully. "No one. I have committed no crime. I took the receipt and I gave it to the police because I thought it would be helpful."

I didn't speak for a few moments, letting the lie float in the air between us. Then, speaking very gently, I switched topics again. "Madame, after the police collected all the papers in Marcel's office, they found several concerning Jean's search for Antoine's killer. But they weren't complete—some were missing. Would you be able to help us find them?"

She looked at me, again caught off balance, her face suddenly drawn and tired as if exhausted by all the voices arguing in her head. "Why do you care?" she finally said, addressing us all, I thought. "They are both dead. No one has discussed this in over half a century."

"I would like to put things right," I said simply. "I'd like the truth to stand on its own, and for people to stop making the two men you loved into things they were not."

Her eyes focused on some midpoint between us. In the silence I could hear what sounded like an old grandfather clock ticking loudly in another room.

"And I think," I added, almost holding my breath, "that you did love them both very much—in every way a woman can."

She looked up at me, her eyes wet, the surprise revelation giving her some welcome relief. "Not many people know that."

"Nor will they—not from us."

She thought a moment, and then rose slowly to her feet. "I will be right back."

Paul Spraiger glanced at me as she left the room. "That was a gamble," he said quietly.

"What did I have to lose?"

Marie Chenin returned a few minutes later carrying an old accordion file laced shut with a black ribbon. She resumed her seat, the file on her lap, and began working the knot with her gnarled fingers. "When Marcel told me to go, after his father disappeared, I collected a few things to remember Jean and Antoine by. Marcel spoke of them so harshly after they'd gone, and changed so much of what they'd done. I'd thought Jean's passion to find an explanation for Antoine's death was like one of those tragedies I read in school, but Marcel's anger was even worse—I wanted some remnants of the days before Marcel."

I watched her fumbling with the knot, letting her focus on it as a way to settle her mind, and visualized her decades ago, in love with two men, both vibrant, creative, and dangerous, taking them both to her bed at different times to fulfill different needs, and then being abandoned almost overnight. It had to have been a life-altering experience, creating far more baggage than the thin file in her hands. Seeing this old, bent woman, I wondered at the reservoir of feelings within her, and at how she might have chosen to channel such abruptly thwarted passions.

I knew I'd surprised her, revealing how her dislike of Marcel had been so manipulated—so I also asked myself what she might do with her newfound knowledge, if anything.

She bent back the file's cover and peered into its depths. "What I took were not things of importance. I was so unhappy then, all I wanted were tokens of the life I was leaving, or which had left me."

She extracted a couple of sheets of paper—thin, flimsy, once creased—and held them in her hand. "Those are two letters Jean received. They're from men who were in Italy with Antoine. They meant a great deal to Jean—I remember when he got them, how happy he was when happiness came so rarely. I took them for that reason, even though they don't say much. Maybe they'll mean something to you."

Marie Chenin seemed spent by the simple act of handing them over, so despite my wanting to press her further, I rose to my feet, sensing I might have gotten all there was to get. As used as she'd been, both by others and by me just now, she was still no fool—and certainly not innocent of the ways of the criminal world. Her slightly doddering appearance notwithstanding, she struck me as a woman of strong will—who now that she was better informed wasn't going to be taken by surprise again.

I did ask one more question, however. "When Jean left for Stowe, do you remember where Marcel was?"

She seemed genuinely puzzled. "No."

"What about Guidry and Picard?"

She stared at me as if I'd just walked into the room, bringing her news she wasn't expecting. "I don't know," she finally murmured, sounding deeply lost in thought.

I reached out, took her hand in both of mine, and held it like a small, warm bird. "Madame Chenin, I am sorry to have brought all this back. Most of us try our best to let old ghosts sleep. I apologize for having woken yours up."

Recovering somewhat, she squeezed my fingers in return. "I don't think you need to," she said distractedly. "Sometimes the price is worth paying. Thank you for coming by."

It was graciously done, and maybe sincere. But the sudden hardness I heard in her voice made me wonder if her thanks was for what I'd said, or for something I'd unwittingly told her.

CHAPTER EIGHTEEN

Marie Chenin had been right about the contents of the two letters she'd given us. They were both bland, straightforward responses to inquiries by Jean Deschamps. But I understood why he'd been happy to receive them. Unlike the disappointments from the Canadian Army and others, these two were from men who'd apparently been with Antoine right up to the end. And they both expressed a willingness to meet with their late friend's father.

It took us a few days to trace the whereabouts of the two writers, one of whom turned out to have died ten years earlier, and more time still to secure the records I'd asked Lacombe to locate. The good news, though, was that by the end of all the digging, we had double confirmation that the surviving letter writer— Richard Kearley—was living outside Montreal.

Apparently, the unit they'd both served in was of some renown, as Paul Spraiger informed me. "Wow," he said, holding the paperwork in his hand. "The Special Service Force. I hadn't realized that before. Those guys were amazing—a joint Canadian-U.S. outfit. They were the forerunner of the Green Berets. The Germans in Italy called them the Devil's Brigade... This is incredible."

I looked at him without comment, causing him to flush slightly. "Sorry. I read a ton about World War Two when I was a kid. Still do, when I can."

I wasn't going to stop him now. "So?" I prompted.

We were back in the Sûreté basement, to which we'd both gravitated as our home away from home. It was quiet, private, and while keeping us in the building, also removed us from the bustle overhead.

Paul made himself more comfortable in his chair. "The Special Service Force was a small, elite group designed for guerrilla fighting in Norway. A civilian thought it up—an English guy named Pyke. He figured if a bunch of men with specially engineered snowmobile transports could be dropped into Norway, they could hassle the Germans enough with smash-and-run operations that the Germans would have to divert a disproportionate number of troops from the Russian front to go after them. The snow machines and special training would give the Force the edge over the bad guys—kind of like a mongoose and a snake, I suppose."

"Sounds suicidal."

"It was," he said brightly, "but it never happened, anyway. The whole Norway idea was scrubbed, the snow machines dumped, and the unit used as shock troops instead— still suicidal, but without the Commando glamour. They never used their parachuting skills, their skiing, or any of the sabotage, behind-the-lines techniques they'd been taught. Basically, Mark Clark in Italy—he was the head U.S. general over there—used them for ops no one thought they could win. And once, in something like twenty-five days in January 1944, they had fourteen hundred casualties out of a total of eighteen hundred men."

"Christ," I commented. "They had better odds in trench warfare."

Paul's eyes brightened. "Don't get me wrong. They weren't just cannon fodder. If it hadn't been for the fact they were considered a secret weapon, they would have been the most famous unit in the war. They were surreal— climbing sheer cliffs, carrying equipment on their backs up trails mules couldn't handle, fighting against amazing odds, and winning every engagement they were in. They were a total killing machine."

I heard that with mixed emotions. I'd been in combat a long time ago, and I remembered units like that. Every war had them. They were made up of people so well trained to do what they did, they almost became unfit for anything else. Very scary guys to be around.

"From what we know about the Deschamps

family," I said, "Antoine might've been perfect for this bunch."

Paul agreed, "If Marie Chenin was right about him and his father being gung-ho about the war effort, they couldn't have found a better outlet. Rumor had it that on the American side at least, a lot of the manpower came out of the stockades. The Canadians had entrance intelligence tests, but the killer instinct probably made them all more or less equals. From what I read, once they were in, their handlers were pretty careful not to let them mix too much with conventional units."

"You know a lot about them, even for a history buff," I finally said.

He laughed. "They were stationed in Burlington just before they shipped out— Fort Ethan Allen. My grandmother worked there on the janitorial staff during the war. She's the one who told me about them first. She thought they were great—full of spit and vinegar, as she said. Kind of made me wonder about her later, after I read up on them. Hard to think of your grandmother in that light."

I thought back to Marie Chenin and to the photograph of a dashing Jean Deschamps. I knew what he meant.

"You have a map of Montreal?" I asked. "Let's go talk to this guy."

Dick Kearley actually lived in the suburbs of Montreal, in a small community of one-story houses not far from the Saint Lawrence River, and closer still to a cluster of warehouses and factory buildings. If it hadn't been for an oddly European feel about some of the architecture and landscaping, I might have felt transposed into any industrial area in the United States, the only additional difference being, I was embarrassed to admit, the general cleanliness of the place. Whether it was the snow acting as a blanket or simply the truth, it seemed the whole neighborhood had just been given a thorough scrubbing.

Which still didn't make it in any way affluent. Though tidy, the houses were worn and tired, like a poor, hard-working man showing up brushed and polished to a child's graduation, proud to be there and eager to make a good impression.

The address we had was a clone of its neighbors—white-stucco, black shingled, and devoid of much character. Paul and I got out of our car, stretched in the cold afternoon air after the long and boring drive, and walked up the carefully shoveled path to the front door.

The man who answered the bell was of medium height and square build, with a strong, stubby, badly scarred hand that felt like wood when I shook it. His eyes were piercingly pale beneath a thick thatch of white hair, and his face, also scarred across one cheek, looked like that of a man who had truly seen the worst of what humanity had to offer.

"Are you Richard Kearley?" I asked him.

"I am," he answered in the clear, neutrally accented English common to many Anglo-Canadians.

"The same who fought with the so-called Devil's Brigade?"

His expression didn't change, but his tone hardened slightly. "The Germans called us that—and the press. We were the First Special Service Force."

"Nevertheless."

"Who's asking?"

I introduced us both, showing my credentials and explaining that we were part of an American-Canadian task force, hoping the reference might cast his mind back to his old unit's binational character and make our job easier.

It didn't seem to make much of an impression. "I figured you were the police, as soon as you drove up. You after one of the old Forcemen, or is it me?"

That caught me off guard. "Should it be you?" I asked.

He smiled tightly. "This where I break down and confess? Don't hold your breath."

I shook my head. "Mr. Kearley, we're here for a history lesson, not to bust your chops. We're looking into the death of one of your fellow combatants—Antoine Deschamps—back in '44."

He watched me carefully for a moment. "Why?"

I continued playing it straight. "It's been suggested that maybe he didn't die in battle."

"He wouldn't have been the first. Why do you care now? Especially Americans?"

We'd been standing in the open doorway all this time, we in our coats, he in a thin shirt,

235

and yet I was the one who began to shiver. "Could we come inside and do this?"

I wasn't sure he'd agree, but he shrugged and stepped back, ushering us into a neat, plain living room whose decorations seemed to have been extracted from a single inexpensive catalogue. Kearley closed the door but didn't invite us to sit.

"So?" he asked.

"It gets a little complicated," I admitted. "In a nutshell, we think Deschamps's father believed he'd been murdered over there, and that the paperwork was cooked to cover it up. We also think that belief got the old man killed as well—in the U.S.—which is how we come into it."

"Sounds like a movie," Kearley said. "I could see Antoine mixed up in something like that. Had a flair for the dramatic."

"So you knew him?" Paul asked, speaking for the first time.

"You wouldn't be here otherwise." He finally waved his hand toward the sofa. "Sit."

We both followed orders, still in our coats. "Do you remember a letter Antoine's father mailed you right after the war?" I asked. "He might have even mentioned his suspicions in it."

Kearley took an armchair opposite us. "Maybe I do. I couldn't've helped anyway. I didn't know about any murder, except that as we saw it, the Germans murdered every man they killed. I don't guess that's the same thing."

"You never met with the father?" I persisted.

"No."

Paul tried a different approach. "What was Antoine like?"

"Good man. Tough as nails. Could carry half his weight in supplies."

"When did you two first hook up? In Helena?" Paul continued.

I glanced at him, confused but assuming he was putting his history lessons to good use.

Kearley smiled thinly. "You know about Helena? Yeah. That's where it was. God, what a dump."

"Which was exactly the point, right? Colonel Frederick's grand plan—bury you guys in the boonies."

The smile spread. "I haven't talked about any of that in a long time."

"I guess that means you were one of the few who didn't marry a local girl."

This time, he actually laughed. "I came close. Those people were amazing. Why or how they took to us, I'll never understand. We were a bunch of loud, obnoxious bastards, and our training did its best to turn us into professional cutthroats. But they never seemed to mind, even when it cost 'em big." Dick Kearley shook his head. "I guess it was a time when people just did that. Couldn't happen nowadays."

"The Wild Bunch," I commented, "only magnified."

"It was that," he agreed. "We blew stuff up, destroyed bars and hotels, roughed up a few locals—almost got thrown in jail a few times—over the top." He pointed at Paul and added,

"Which was probably part of Old Man Frederick's plan, too. He knew it all, he did—what it would take to go to Hell and come back."

"You were at la Difensa?" Paul asked quietly.

"And Sammucro and Majo and Anzio later on. I was with them all the way to Rome before this pulled me out." He held up the blunted, scarred hand. "When Frederick was told to clear out the German rear guard so General Clark could get his picture taken in Rome, we did it, even though we hated the son-of-a-bitch, knew goddamn well the whole capture-Rome thing was a pile of crap, and that the whole Italian campaign should've stopped after they grabbed the airfields near Naples." He paused and added, "I gave this hand for a brass hat photo-op."

I followed Paul's lead, keeping the older man reminiscing, hoping it might lead us somewhere useful. "I heard you took a pounding."

"Always. I heard it said we had a six hundred percent turnover. But that's what we were designed for. We did what couldn't be done, and we did it fast 'cause we worked on the run. We knew if you stayed put for too long, they'd pin you down and squash you flat. That's what happened at Anzio, and that's why we broke out of there."

He'd undergone a total metamorphosis through this, from being the hostile, suspicious man we'd met at the door to the animated figure before us now, his eyes bright and his voice almost pleading, as if trying to make us believe that what he was saying wasn't just bravado. On the drive here, Spraiger had educated me further on the exploits of the Special Service Force, and on how their leader, Colonel Robert Frederick, had made it a point to turn them into the best fighters in the Italian campaign. The frustration of also being considered a quasi-secret weapon, and thus denied the publicity Mark Clark and others were garnering, must have been intense, especially after such sacrifice.

As if reading my thoughts, Dick Kearley suddenly rose to his feet and gestured to us to follow him down the hallway to the back of the house. Just shy of the kitchen, he cut through a door to his right, and led us into a room with a leather armchair, a few bookshelves, and along all four walls, row upon row of photographs, sketches, military insignia and memorabilia, including a red flag with a black dagger on a white shield. It was a shrine to a searing, brilliant, inescapable moment in a man's life, whose journey forever after had obviously suffered in comparison.

The nervous energy that had propelled him here seemed to quiet almost as soon as he turned on the overhead light. He stood in the midst of his recorded past history and gazed about himself in peaceful contemplation.

"This is Antoine right here," he said quietly, pointing to a shot of two men standing side by side, their uniform shirts open, their faces grimy, their bodies spare and muscular. They were laughing and holding bottles by their sides.

Paul and I studied the photo carefully.

"This was taken in Burlington," Paul finally said in surprise. "I recognize the buildings behind them."

"Yup. Summer of '43. We were dying for something to do by then. We'd been trained to an ant's eyelash, and we weren't doing the neighborhood any good. Good thing they got us going when they did."

"This Italy?" I asked, pointing out a scene of snow-covered rocks with mountains in the background. It was barren and hostile, like a picture of the moon.

"The doorway to Cassino," he said darkly. "Highway 6 down the middle, mountains on both sides. The Germans had it all so well covered they could bring down artillery on three and four men at a time."

He moved to a map. "Looks easy enough on paper. Highway 6 cuts between the western coastal mountains and the spine of Italy, up the Liri valley and straight to Rome. The Anzio landing just below Rome was supposed to draw the Krauts away from the mountains and give us a link-up force to aim for before taking the city. Didn't work worth a damn. The Germans didn't follow the plan. As it turned out, *we* were the ones applying pressure to save the Anzio bunch from being pushed back into the sea. And we had to do it mountain by mountain, sometimes boulder by boulder, and defend it against the Krauts who wanted it back."

He tapped another spot on the map. "That's where I sat in a foxhole all night being hammered by every explosive they had—airburst, armor-piercing, phosphorus, you name it. They used mortars like nobody I know. And it was cold. So cold your sweat turned to ice and your feet to frozen blocks. By the time dawn came around, I was the only one alive in that hole. The other five had been killed by shards of steel or rock. One poor bastard had just plain frozen to death. And that was just one night. There were dozens more like it."

"This Colonel Frederick?" Paul asked, standing before another picture.

Kearley looked at it with the fondness of a doting son. "Yeah. I was part of his personal guard for a while. So was Antoine. Almost the worst duty we ever had. The Old Man acted like he was bulletproof—always at the front, always moving from place to place. We came under mortar attack once and dove for cover. When we got back to him, he was still sitting on the same rock, like nothing had happened. Roger Scott caught it standing right next to him—a dud mortar round in the head. Felled him like an ox and the Old Man just worried about whether we could save him. He never even looked at the shell, which I thought would go off any second. More than once, he carried wounded men on his back to the aid station. He was one of those guys you only meet once in your life—if you're lucky. He was wounded nine times before we were disbanded, and half the unit cried when he was transferred after Rome."

"Did Antoine think as highly of him?" I asked, now hoping to gently turn the conversation to our advantage.

241

"Everyone did. Antoine told me once Frederick reminded him of his own father, which I didn't believe for a second."

"Antoine talk about his father a lot?" I'd already been struck by how this man, like Lucien Pelletier, referred to the dominant male figure in his life as the Old Man.

"Yeah, he did. Really proud of him. That was interesting to me, 'cause most of us thought our fathers were a waste of time, assuming we knew who they were. Forcemen generally didn't come from real solid families."

"He ever say what his father did for a living?"

"He was a businessman, if I remember right. I didn't think much of that. I thought businessmen mostly got rich from blood money—still do. But I kept that to myself. Antoine wasn't a man to piss off."

"Short-tempered?"

Kearley had been wandering around the room, speaking less to us than to the walls that held his most cherished memories. He now paused before a group shot of black-faced combatants clustered before a hay bale and listening intently to an officer whose back was to the camera.

"Let's put it this way," he said. "During the four months we were stuck in Anzio, we decided right from the get-go we weren't going to sit in holes and wait for a counter-attack. That first night, we sent out a bunch of patrols, infiltrated the Kraut lines, raised a little hell, and collected a few prisoners for the intel boys. It was the first time since

242

we'd seen combat we were able to try out some of our training—guerrilla warfare, search-and-destroy, sabotage. We got a reputation for wandering around at night, never making a sound, popping up where they least expected us, and cutting a few throats. That's where we got the Black Devils name, and later the Devil's Brigade. We drove the SOBs half out of their minds, and Antoine was one of the best at it. Not too pretty when he was working, but you couldn't knock his results. One time, we caught a German lieutenant who told us they thought we were division level—maybe sixteen thousand strong. I doubt we even had sixteen hundred then. You couldn't blame him, though—there were almost a hundred thousand Allies on that beach, and our pissant unit was assigned one quarter of the line."

I tried phrasing my next question delicately. "Mr. Kearley, I know you were all skilled in unarmed combat, silent killing, and the rest, so I don't mean any disrespect, but sometimes in those situations—given the backgrounds of some of the men—the opportunity must've popped up to be a little more thorough than was necessary."

He was totally unfazed. "Nut cases, you mean? We had a few. Almost none of them survived, though. Things had a way of catching up to them. Antoine wasn't one of those, anyway. He was just really good at his job."

"Actually," I continued, "I was thinking more about noncombat situations. You know—competitive, violent men, literally under the gun for days on end. I was wondering if any of them took it out on their fellows—like Antoine."

Dick Kearley thought a moment. "Charlie Webber and he had it out one night. It started normally enough—guys were always razzing each other—but I guess it got personal. Anyhow, we had to break them up, which we usually didn't bother doing—we'd take bets instead." Then he shook his head. "But it didn't last. Couple of weeks later, they were on patrol together, pulled off a good one, and that seemed to do the trick. If anything, it brought them closer together 'cause they were thick as thieves after that. That kind of thing occurred pretty often."

He rubbed his chin, thinking back. "It's really hard to say, though. There were so many people who would've been in jail if they hadn't joined the Force, and a few who ended up there anyway, for rape or murder or whatever. In fact, in every place we were stationed, including Burlington, at least one local business had its safe blown. They never pinned it on anyone, but we knew it had to be one of us. We weren't all that way, of course. We had college professors, too. But there was a rough element."

He looked up at me as if I'd just appeared. "Course, you were asking about Antoine. He wheeled and dealed with the best of them— made money stealing stuff and selling it to the troops, pimping for girls he conned to keep us company, especially at Anzio where we had time on our hands. But he wasn't one of the vicious ones."

244

"He might have pissed one of them off, though," I suggested.

Kearley didn't deny it. "Could be."

"When was the last time you saw Antoine?"

"The outskirts of Rome. We were the advance element, like always, ordered to secure all the bridges across the Tiber. The Krauts had declared it an open city, but I guess either word hadn't reached everybody, or they were jerking us around. Even after we'd cleared the bridges and had actually entered the town, there were enough snipers around that you had to watch your step. From what I heard, that's how Antoine bought it—probably chasing some skirt."

"But you didn't see it happen."

"No. We were in different parts of town." He paused and looked at the picture of Deschamps again. "I was sorry to lose him. There weren't many of us left by then—not who went all the way back to Helena."

"Do you know who might've been with him?" Paul asked.

"No idea. Things could get pretty fluid, 'specially if you combined something like the Forcemen with a city like Rome, ready for the plucking."

"How about the officer who signed off on the death papers?"

Kearley shook his head. "I doubt it. We had more active front line officers than any outfit I knew, so don't get me wrong—Frederick himself was a general by then, and still doing recon patrols behind the lines. But generally that kind of paperwork wasn't done with a whole lot of care. Someone would hand over a set of dog tags and tell the officer what happened and that would be it. And sometimes that 'what happened' part wouldn't be much more than, 'got hit by a sniper' or whatever. It could get a little vague, especially the way we were always way out front."

"What about Webber?" I asked. "You said they were close. Would he know?"

"He might've known," came the answer, "but he's dead, too. I think he caught one in France. The Champagne Campaign, they called it, except for the dumb turkeys that got killed in it. Anyway, I was homebound by then, so I don't really know." He paused and scratched his head, looking around at the bookcases. "But I might have it here somewhere. After it was all over, I went around collecting everything having to do with the Force—documents, books, articles, pictures. Kind of gave me something to do after all the excitement. It was a little hard adjusting..."

His voice trailed off as he began scrounging through the shelves, finally straightening up with what looked like a thick old log book.

"This might have it—a roster listing guys in, out, KIA, all the rest."

He spread it open on top of one of the bookcases and flipped through its contents—page after page of names in columns.

"Here we go," he finally said. "Webber, Charles." He ran his finger along the line and then grunted softly. "KIA—body not recovered. Might mean he went over the hill."

"Deserted?" Paul asked, sounding shocked.

246

Kearley looked up at him, obviously insulted. "Not that way. We never had a man run under fire—never. But you've got to understand the way we were. The Force wasn't standard military. It was all volunteer and it was made crystal clear from the start that no one expected us to survive. And that's how we were treated. Got an impossible job? Send in the Forcemen. Even if they get wiped out, it's no big loss—bunch of dumb crooks anyway. That was the attitude. We were there because we wanted to be, not because someone ordered us. And when it was all over, some of us left the same way—under our own steam. The assholes who kept trying to get us killed called that desertion, but to us, it was just leaving after a job well done, no muss, no fuss. I read an article by an old Force officer who went back to the battlefields after the war, and he said he met dozens of supposed MIA Forcemen or KIAs 'without bodies' who were living in France and Italy, married with kids, who'd just decided to set down roots where they were. Made more sense than going back home to jail or poverty or a life they'd run out on in the first place."

He closed the book. "I don't know what happened to Charlie Webber. He was probably blown to bits and never found. But he might be living over there right now, happy as a clam. I think he's dead, though, 'cause if he'd made it, he'd be living where you come from—Vermont."

"Why's that?" I asked, startled. "He have family there?"

"Hell, no. That would defeat the purpose. It's just that when we were in Burlington, he never missed a chance to leave base and explore the state. Used to say it was Heaven on earth and a bunch of other crap—made it sound like a woman. We used to kid him about it."

The old man's shoulders slumped at the thought and he lowered himself into the room's one chair, as if conceding defeat. "I wish I'd had someplace like that. Instead, I came back here and spent the rest of my life in a brewery, going through wives till I finally gave it up."

I sat on the bookcase next to the roster, my legs stretched out before me. "Civilian life takes some getting used to afterward, doesn't it?"

He looked up at me tiredly. "You been there, too?"

I didn't go into detail. "Oh, yeah."

He sighed. "It was like living a dream—the action, the friendships, the strain of staying alive. Adrenaline was like breathing back then. Didn't matter if you were fighting the enemy or stealing a general's jeep. We were always on the go, walking the edge, looking for a challenge. We hated it when they'd pull us back from the line, and sometimes we'd creep back up on our own just to raise a little hell."

He examined his damaged hand, flexing it on his lap. "After that, life can get pretty empty."

I picked up the book beside me. "Mr. Kearley, can I borrow this for a while? I promise I won't let it out of my hands."

He didn't bother looking up. "Hell, yeah. It's not doing me any good."

CHAPTER NINETEEN

Gilles Lacombe was driving out of the Sûreté parking lot as Paul and I got out of our car. He rolled his window down and called us over.

"Where have you been? I have not seen you in days. Are you okay?"

I leaned on the windowsill, feeling slightly guilty. "To be honest, I've been staying out of your way. I'm still trying to live down what happened in the old jail."

He looked almost horrified. "Joe, are you always this way? I would think that anyone who lives with you would like to strangle you. You are not married, correct?"

I laughed. "Correct."

"As I thought." He called out past me to Paul. "Paul, get your boss into this car. We are going to dinner right now. Very nice place. We will have some wine, talk a little. Okay? Right now. Come on."

"What about your own family?" I chided.

He pulled out a cell phone as we climbed into the vehicle. "I call my wife. She knows the value of rest and relaxation."

We drove downtown to a dark, quiet, and possibly expensive restaurant on North Wellington, although neither Paul nor I ever saw a bill.

"*Alors,*" Lacombe said once we'd settled into a discreet rear booth with a feel of executive privacy. "Is this all right?"

"Wonderful, and much appreciated," I told him.

He flagged down a waiter and took our drink orders. He and Paul both had wine. I held out for a glass of Coke, much to our host's disgust. "You are not also going to order a hamburger, do you understand? It is not that kind of restaurant. But you will have to order meat—it is the only thing that will stand up to that awful stuff."

I conceded the point, even though we hadn't been offered menus yet.

"So," Lacombe asked after the drinks had arrived, "what have you been doing?"

"Digging into the past, trying to find out what happened to Antoine."

"You have proof now Marcel did not stab his father?"

"God, no—we're a long way from there."

"It does not matter any more," Lacombe said. "That is why I was looking for you."

"He took the polygraph?" Paul blurted out.

"Yes, and passed like a sweet child. It was this morning. His lawyer called in a surprise, said they would do it, and it was done—bim, bam—just like that." He snapped his fingers.

"Jesus," I murmured. "Does that kill your investigation?"

Lacombe was all smiles, no doubt practicing what he'd been preaching to me to do in the parking lot. "Yes, it is gone into smoke. *Fini.* The *procureur* told me not an hour ago that he sees no reason to go on with what we have."

"But where's that leave you?" Paul asked.

Lacombe shrugged and distributed the newly delivered menus. "Only in a different place. Another thing that happened this morning was the discovery of another Deschamps worker, dead in an alley behind a bar not far from here."

"Any leads?" I asked.

"A button from a denim jacket, like what the Angels wear. Very convenient. It was even found in the dead man's hand, just like in a mystery story. Not," he added carefully, "that we and the Sherbrooke police won't make sure the Angels did not do this thing."

I looked at him for a moment, sensing much more behind his words. "What do you think's going on, Gilles?"

He'd already begun scanning the menu, but now put it flat on the table, suddenly solemn. "I know no more than I did, my friend, but I do think something has changed. A house of cards has fallen into pieces, and it was built to make us put Marcel Deschamps into jail."

"Until he passed the polygraph," I suggested.

"That is it. Now we can see two things: Marcel was probably set up with the ice pick and all the rest, and a carefully laid plan is now in chaos. That means to me two more things: at this moment, Marcel is mad as hell, and the person who laid the plan is desperate. This is a very bad situation, I think."

There was dead silence around the table. Lacombe then smiled, sat back, retrieved his menu, and brightly asked, "And so what will you have with your Coca-Cola?"

As advertised, the dinner was a nice break from routine, but the conversation leading up to it continued to rattle around my head, even though all three of us worked hard to avoid shop talk while we ate.

Over coffee and dessert, however, I felt free to relax. "What's Plan B, Gilles?"

"Now is when the rules begin to work for us," he explained. "In the old days, when we wanted to get a wiretap, it was very easy, and the federal people from the U.S. would look at us with envy. Nowadays, we are much in the same boat as you, except," he held up a finger, "in a situation like this. If the judge can be persuaded that all other options have been exhausted, then we can get a tap. It is an irony that with the polygraph, the case against Marcel Deschamps is over, which also means I can tell the judge that the case against the Deschamps family is finally without other options. That will therefore be the first thing I will do—put not Marcel but his organization under surveillance for twenty-four hours a day, including his phones. As for the rest, I am less sure."

"You don't have any candidates for who's trying to screw Marcel?"

He waved his hand equivocally from side to side. "Many choices. It could be someone inside, like Picard or Guidry or one of the lower people. It could also be an outsider, like the Rock Machine, which has been very silent through all this. We may also be making assumptions we should not, in thinking the Angels are not involved."

"If we're playing Machiavelli," Paul added, "we could also throw in Marcel himself, who's now been proven innocent by the prosecution, which is a great place for a guilty man to be."

Lacombe raised his eyebrows at me. "So you see. It is that way. The one good thing—assuming Paul is not right about Marcel, however—is that a great plan has been thrown off the rails, which means anything can happen. I think somebody is very frustrated right now."

He took a sip from his coffee and then added, "It could get interesting."

I was up late that night, fiddling with my notes, calling Sammie in Vermont for an update, watching television inattentively, feeling like I was sifting through the remains of a shattered mosaic covering an acre of floorspace. There was the prominently mounted ice pick, complete with incriminating trace evidence, an ancient and elaborate trail connecting it to Marcel, a growing pile of bodies implying a gang war between two Sherbrooke factions, and several old-timers with intriguing tales of internecine rivalry. I'd also heard the Sûreté might be corrupt, that Marcel and Antoine had either been a great team or the equivalent of Cain and Abel, and how Antoine was either murdered or died a hero in combat. My brain was teeming with voices in contradiction, in support of one another, or just saying things I simply couldn't understand. I was racked by the conviction that at some point in all this, I'd stared the truth in the face and had simply kept moving.

The knock on the motel room door, therefore, brought me back with a start, making me drop the pen I was holding and causing my reading glasses to slip off my nose. I glanced up at the TV screen, now filled with two people standing silent and transfixed in what looked like a gloomy cellar, and realized I must have dozed off. The bedside clock read three-ten in the morning.

Still dazed, I climbed off the bed, my back stiff and my butt sore, and walked to the door, discovering I was still wearing my shoes. I also noticed I'd dropped the door key upon entering after dinner.

Shaking my head, I bent down for the key and simultaneously opened the door, expecting to see Paul Spraiger, whose room was next door.

Instead, out of the corner of my eye, I saw a dark pair of high-heeled cowboy boots—still damp from the snow outside—and heard the distinct and chilling pop of a silencer just inches above my head. As something shattered behind me, I instinctively kept tucked over and charged like a linebacker at the pair of legs before me.

I heard the air go out of the shooter's lungs as we smashed into the wall across from my door, and felt a halfhearted blow of a gun butt glancing off my shoulder as we slid to the floor.

My life-saving position now did me a disservice, folding me under the other man's collapsed body, an advantage he used not to fire another shot but to push me aside and scramble to his feet, obviously so surprised at the turn of events that he could only think of running.

But I did not feel so accommodating. Perhaps due to the frustration I'd been wrestling with moments earlier, I lashed out at his ankles as he regained his footing, tripping him up and making him sprawl on his face, his long-barreled gun bouncing away on the rug ahead of him.

The sight of the weapon brought my vulnerability sharply to mind, and I made a flat dive up and over his squirming body in an attempt to get hold of it. But he was younger than I, faster, and more desperate, and he managed to catch the side of my head with his elbow just as I went over him, throwing me off balance and giving him the chance to get back on his feet.

Fortunately, even my last-minute meddling didn't alter his eagerness to escape. Ignoring the gun, he took off down the long hallway as I untangled myself, picked up the weapon, and gave chase.

So far, not a word had been said.

My room was on the third floor, with the stairs and an elevator at one end of the hall, and an interior fire escape at the other. My assailant had chosen the latter, no doubt hoping for the fastest way out, which, considering my chances of catching him, was a smart move—and made me all the angrier I hadn't yelled for Paul before taking off in pursuit.

The shooter took the stairs in leaping bounds, bouncing off the stairwell walls like a careening bowling ball. Much as I wished I could do the same, however, my older anatomy wouldn't stand for it. I moved as fast as I could, but he was putting some serious distance between us.

He reached the bottom with a crash and slammed through the door to the parking lot like a bull leaving a chute, smashing the plate glass window in the process. By the time I reached the same spot, he was halfway across the lot, heading toward a small, rust-splotched sedan.

Which is where his luck took another downward turn.

Apparently, this presumed hitman had pocketed his car keys as he might have on a trip to the supermarket, and now—extracting them from his pocket at a dead run—he dropped them in the snow. He slid to a scrambling stop, dropped to his knees, and flailed around in the slush for a few seconds as I stopped also, grasped the gun in both hands, and tried to draw a bead on his leg to slow him down without killing him. But he was still too far off, I was breathing too hard to be steady, and my opportunity disappeared almost as fast as it had cropped up. With a frustrated punch at thin air, he regained his feet and ran for the embankment overlooking King Street, vaulting the guardrail and vanishing from sight.

I didn't know what options I had. By all appearances, the car was his, and would lead us to him if I gave up the chase. But chances were just as good it had been stolen, or that this guy would end up as dead as the man I'd found in the old jail. I didn't want to risk losing another piece to our puzzle.

Despite the obvious arguments, therefore, not to mention that I was wearing only a shirt and slacks, I climbed over the guardrail after him.

The bank was steep, covered with deep snow, and stopped right at the edge of the road below. By the time I reached it, I was wet, my hands were numb and nearly useless, and my face and ears were stinging with cold. Ahead of me, across a trickle of predawn traffic, the shooter was cutting across the sidewalk, heading for a dead-end road leading down toward the river. I couldn't figure out what the hell he was doing.

The side street he'd taken turned out to run between a darkened office building and an abandoned business lot, and ended at a metal barricade, beyond which were some smaller buildings and a few trees. In their midst, his bobbing shape receded, still aiming for the ghostly pale expanse of the river ahead.

I was breathing hard by now, my lungs aching from the frigid air. My feet had become as senseless as my hands, making me feel I was running like Frankenstein's monster, stumbling and lurching in wooden clogs. I began to wonder how much longer I could keep this up.

My quarry's intentions, however, finally became clear, and their simplicity—for no reason at all—gave me the incentive to continue. He was going to cross the frozen river to the south side of town. There was no reason to think this man wouldn't outpace me there as he had so far, but the appearance of that huge, pan-flat, almost shimmering expanse as I emerged from the trees inspired me with visions of ice skaters at full tilt, and for some reason I believed, as perhaps did he, that once on its surface, I would move like an arrow in flight.

I didn't, of course. Surprisingly, the river's surface wasn't crusty with frozen snow, as I'd expected, but smooth as a hockey rink, which put me flat on my butt almost as soon as I touched it. Thankfully, the target of this hypothermic exercise wasn't faring much better. Although he was better dressed than I, his cowboy boots were serving him poorly.

As a result, the distance between us remained roughly the same as we staggered and slid our way toward the river's midpoint, two small silhouettes caught in the translucence of the city's night lighting.

Then things began turning in my favor.

Accompanying a small but growing chorus

of distant sirens, a twinkling of emergency lights began appearing out of the darkness like otherwordly fireflies being drawn to an open field. Also, announcing himself with a yell in my direction, Paul Spraiger stepped out onto the ice, moving with far more grace and speed than either I or the man we were after.

I stopped and waited for him to catch up.

"You okay?" he asked, panting as he drew abreast.

"Yeah—just cold. How'd you know where I was?"

"I thought a bomb had gone off when you two hit the hallway. The walls shook. But by the time I got out of bed and to the door, all I saw was you heading downstairs. I watched from the window, figured out what was going on, and called for backup." He held up a cell phone he was holding in his gloved hand. "I've been keeping them up to date on this."

We could see ahead of us how the winking, colored lights had concentrated on the far shore, making the man ahead pause, look back, and begin to consider an alternate plan, his body language making plain his confusion. Behind us on the north shore, additional shadows were stepping onto the ice.

"Won't be long before the snowmobiles arrive," Paul muttered, and then spoke into the phone, "He's stopped heading south. Now he's going for the bridge."

True enough, the shooter had cut east down the river's center toward the Montcalm Bridge and the gorge beyond.

"Why's he doing that?" I asked, beginning

an angled course to shorten the distance between us.

Paul, though capable of more speed than I, chose to slide along beside me, apparently not as ready as I'd been to act as though this were our jurisdiction. "Damned if I know. Terrain's wilder on the other side of the bridge— maybe he's hoping to escape into the woods along the shore."

He put the phone to his ear and updated whoever was on the other end. Within minutes, we saw the festive police lights rearranging themselves, moving like a herd toward the bridge. Simultaneously, we heard the distinctive whine of several snowmobiles firing up behind us, and saw their jittery headlights spring forth from the dark shoreline as they headed onto the ice. Slowly but surely, the cordon was tightening around the eastern end of the river.

Abandoning our short-lived detachment, we both began jogging toward the bridge as well. The urban cowboy had almost reached it by now, and two strings of uniformed cops, advancing from either abutment, had just set foot on the frozen water. With high-pitched screams, a couple of snowmobiles sped by, hoping to grab him before he vanished under the bridge's archways.

But it wasn't to be. As suddenly as they'd come to life, the machines slid to a halt a few hundred yards from their target.

Paul had the phone to his ear again. "They're holding off because of thin ice," he told me. "The water moves so fast from the bridge to the first dam, they don't want to risk their men."

We came abreast of the frustrated snowmobile riders glaring into the gloom under the arches. To the right and left, the people who'd gained the river's surface from opposite sides of the bridge were very slowly feeling their way toward the middle, roped together like mountain climbers. Paul and I, lighter than the machines, continued cautiously up the middle.

Suddenly, the darkness before us vanished as in a lightning strike. The police had rigged portable lamps along the railing overhead, facing downriver, illuminating the entire scene as if it were an enormous barren stage—and the man in its glaring midst a trapped intruder.

A loudspeaker crackled. In contrast to its bellowing metallic voice, bouncing off the hard surfaces around us, Paul's quiet translation sounded like the whispers of a prompter.

"This is the police. Move back toward the bridge. You are on thin ice and could break through at any moment. Do not go any farther."

For a moment, it seemed the man might follow orders. He twisted around jerkily, his body slightly bent as if both fearful and spring-loaded, but then he obviously saw what looked like a better option. His feet slipping initially, he began running toward the darkness and the faint but ominous rumble of falling water, heading for the quasi-wilderness Paul had mentioned earlier.

But things didn't work out for him. It looked like he stumbled at first—he seemed to go down on one knee. But as he struggled to rise, we saw his pants clinging wetly to his leg, and realized he'd broken through. He took a couple of more steps, went down as before—but deeper this time—and tried to push himself back up with his arms. Then the other leg vanished from sight. Momentarily, almost playfully, his dark-clad torso stayed level with the ice's hard, even plane, and we suddenly saw the pallor of his face as he plaintively looked back over his shoulder at us all before disappearing from sight as if through a trapdoor. Instantly, the river's surface became as bland as before—pale, cold, and impassive—with no trace or memory of the man it had just swallowed whole.

"So much for finding out what that was all about," Paul said softly.

CHAPTER TWENTY

I'm sorry about this," I told Gilles Lacombe. "I couldn't wait around for a bunch of medical types to do this the official way. And I'm getting pretty good at thawing myself out anyway."

I was lying in my tub back at the motel, immersed in water so hot it limited visibility. Lacombe was sitting on the toilet seat beside me, slowly removing layer after layer of clothes, hoping to get comfortable.

"It is not a problem," he said politely, pulling off a sweater. "Is it working?"

"I can move my hands and feet again, but I can't say I'm toasty yet."

He laughed weakly. "You are lucky."

Paul was leaning against the doorjamb. "I read somewhere warming yourself up like that can cause a heart attack—all the cold blood from the extremities rushes back to the core and drops its temperature further down than it is."

"I guess this is your chance to see if they were right," I said testily, having no intention of getting out. "I take it the cowboy didn't survive his midnight dip."

Down to his shirt now, Lacombe shook his head. "We have not found the body. If it went over the dam, it will be under the ice now. We will not find it until the spring. This has happened with fishermen and skaters. We know he did not make it to the shore."

"What about his car?" I asked.

"We are looking at it. In the computer, the registration says the man is a muscle-for-hire. He worked for several of the bars and clubs on Wellington Sud."

"Any affiliation to either the Angels or Deschamps?" Paul asked.

"The two of them," Lacombe told him, squinting through the steam. "And people who have nothing to do with them."

"Great," I said. "Maybe he has a note in his pocket, signed by whoever hired him."

"Better be in waterproof ink," Paul said.

"I am afraid I have some questions about

this," Lacombe added. "I do not understand how this man knew where you lived in this motel."

"Take your pick," Paul suggested. "It's not like we've been undercover."

Lacombe nodded. "Oh, that is true, of course. But how he knows the room number becomes a little problem. Also, why try to kill you, and why try to kill you right now? What have you done that causes worry?"

The next day, Willy looked at me from across the conference table back at the Stowe police department and seconded the question. "I don't get it," he said. "What the hell do *you* know that deserves a bullet?"

The whole team had been pulled out of Canada, except for Kathy Bartlett, who was still fighting with her Canadian opposites to get Marcel extradited.

"We were rattling a few offbeat cages," I told him. "We must've hit the right one."

Tom Shanklin looked unconvinced. "The World War Two angle? How's that make sense?"

Paul Spraiger had been sitting back in his chair, seemingly half asleep, and now stirred himself to say, "It doesn't, necessarily, but this attack followed right on the heels of our digging into Antoine's death."

Gary Smith sounded doubtful, too. "You don't kill a cop because he's getting close to something—another just takes his place and everyone's a whole lot more pissed off."

"That's if you're thinking," Paul persisted, speaking on my behalf, since I had no more to contribute than anyone else.

"If you're feeling cornered and you tend to lash out by nature," he continued, "shooting a cop might seem like a no-brainer."

"So we pick out the suspect who's an idiot with a short fuse?" Willy asked.

"More realistic would be to keep on the pressure," I suggested. "If it hadn't been for that literal thin ice last night, we might've had a pathway back to this creep—there's no reason to think he won't try again, especially if he feels I'm after him personally."

Sammie could see what I was driving at. "You think the grand plan is to knock off the top cop and throw the troops into confusion?"

"That's crazy."

"Makes sense to me," Smith disagreed. "Look at the IQ's of most of the jerks we go after. Plus, opening the World War Two can of worms wasn't the only sudden change here. Assuming Marcel was framed for his father's death, that plan just went down the tubes, too."

"All right, all right, but so what?" Willy persisted. "It's not like we can tie the boss like a goat to a tree." He suddenly laughed. "Not that it's a *terrible* idea."

Amid the scattered laughter, I suggested, "We could hold a press conference to make it look like I'm the right target."

There was a telling hesitation in the room. "What do we do with you afterward?" Paul asked.

"Nothing," I answered him. "We don't

know for a fact any of this is true. It'll just be another iron in the fire. Besides, the governor and Bill Allard have been breathing down my neck—a press conference could be a good way to throw them a little meat and test our theory at the same time. Can't hurt, right?"

No one bothered answering that.

I glanced at the notes before me. "Anyhow, the World War Two connection is the only soft spot we've found so far—I don't see that we have a choice. Willy, what did you find out chasing down Federico Alvarez's last will and testament?"

"It's on file at the courthouse, and it reads like what the innkeeper told us. The good news–bad news is that the paper trail had too many legal firewalls for me to track it back to any source besides a lawyer who won't talk."

"What's good about that?" Smith asked.

"Shows they got something to hide. Cuts down on the chance we're just dealing with some crazy, compulsive bastard who liked old luggage."

Smith looked unconvinced. I couldn't argue with him. "That's one possibility. I've known a lot of nuts who've hired attorneys. What would it take to crack the lawyer open?"

"Won't need to," Willy answered. "He figured we might waste his time, and he thinks it's bullshit anyhow, so he told me off the record all he's got is more documentation leading nowhere. He used some legal babble that didn't mean squat to me, but the gist of it was that Alvarez was secretive enough—and the whole thing old enough—that we're not going to find out what was behind it. All the major players are long dead."

"All right," I conceded. "We'll have to drop it. Speaking of lawyers, did we ever find out what Gaston Picard was doing down here just before Jean Deschamps showed up on Mount Mansfield?"

"I checked that out, too," Willy answered. " 'Nother dead end. I talked to lawyers, bankers, Realtors—like you said. Also the town clerk, since we were already over there digging through files, and even a couple of travel agents. I tried the airport manager and crew, just for what-the-hell. I asked Gary here what ideas he had, and he put me onto a few more people. Total waste of time. Picard might as well've not even been here."

I thought about that for a moment. "Seems unlikely, doesn't it? Drive all the way down and not meet with anybody? Where was his car parked when it was ticketed?"

Gary Smith spoke up. "Main Street, opposite Shaw's."

"Why the ticket?"

He hesitated. "Overdue meter, I think."

"When?"

"Around noon, more or less. I could look it up."

"That's close enough," I said. "High roller hits town, parks for a long time on the main drag at midday. Why's he here?"

Willy sounded disgusted. "Meet someone for lunch. Shit."

267

I tried easing the pain. "You thought of everything else."

" 'Cept the obvious."

"What good restaurant's near there?" I asked Gary.

"There's more'n one."

"We'll need a list, starting with the most expensive. If Picard did the choosing, he probably went five star. We can divvy it up and get it done under an hour." I glanced back at my notes. "Sammie, you and Tom were going to see what you could find out about Stowe in the late forties."

"It was more upscale than Arvin Brown said," she said, fishing a sheet of paper from her pocket to consult. "A thousand-foot rope tow was put on the mountain in '37. By 1940, a sixty-three-hundred-foot chairlift went in—first in Vermont—which had carried a million skiers to the top by '53—"

"Sounds like ripe pickings," I interrupted, "for a sharp-eyed investor."

"Or a crook," Willy added.

"Which goes to what we're after," I agreed. "We need less history and more about the people back then, especially anyone who might've been handy with an ice pick."

Sammie gave me a hapless gesture. "If you mean old rap sheets, that part's turned out to be almost impossible. What cops they had are gone and buried. We couldn't find any police files anywhere. We got names of some of the old movers and shakers, just by talking to any geezer we could find, and some of them spilled a little gossip, but what do you do with that?"

I pulled the Special Service Force roster book we'd borrowed from Dick Kearley from under the papers before me and slid it across to her. "That's a list of the people Antoine served with in the war. Inside is a printout of known surviving Canadian taxpayers from the RCMP. But it was an American/Canadian brigade, and the Mounties admitted their records might be iffy. Still, it'll give you something to compare against anyone you might find in the town clerk's archives. Later, we can try the Pentagon for what they have, too."

I looked around the room and saw her disappointment reflected in most of the faces there. "I know this isn't fun—geriatrics, ancient history, and dusty files—but somebody on the other side thinks we're getting close, which means the ball's back in motion. We've got to do the homework."

I placed my hands on the table and rose. "Okay. While you and Tom are doing that, the rest of us will find out who Picard had lunch with—assuming that's what happened. Maybe one will help the other. We're looking for a missing link here, and we know it exists 'cause I wouldn't've been shot at otherwise, right?"

It was midafternoon by the time I entered the Deeryard Restaurant. A couple of people were sitting by the stained-glass windows drinking coffee over shimmering tablecloths, but otherwise the place was in the dark and peaceful chasm between lunch and dinner, its staff either prepping the bar for the evening onslaught, discreetly vacuuming the carpet far away from the clientele, or creating muted chaos from beyond the leather-padded kitchen doors.

I stood stock still in the middle of the room, adjusting to the tasteful gloom, when an artificially cultured voice asked, "May I help you, sir?"

I discerned the emerging form of a man in a jacket and tie, looking much like a television anchorman in his perfection.

"I hope so." I pulled out my badge. "I'm Joe Gunther, Vermont Bureau of Investigation."

The man's tone changed from fake cultured to instant nasty, which made me think he might be as unpleasant a colleague as he was obsequious a host. "We passed inspection two months ago with flying colors. What son-of-a-bitch complained this time?"

I pocketed the badge with a sigh, wondering if I shouldn't drop the whole VBI intro. "I'm not a restaurant inspector. I'm a cop working a homicide. What's your name?"

The man at least paid me the compliment of looking astonished. "Oh. I'm sorry. I thought... Johnny Philbin."

He seemed torn over whether a handshake was appropriate. I let him dangle his wrist in the air uncertainly.

"You work lunches or are you dinner only?" I asked him.

The hand dropped. "Both."

I mentioned the date Gaston Picard had received his parking ticket. "How 'bout then?"

"Yeah, I think so... I mean, yeah, I was here."

"You take reservations for lunch?"

"We take them. They aren't necessary. Dinner only."

I pulled a photograph of Picard from my pocket, provided earlier by the Sûreté, and repeated a question I'd tried unsuccessfully at two other places on the block. "This is important. Take your time. Tell me if you remember seeing this man that day."

He barely glanced at it. I prepared myself to be disappointed. "Sure."

"You saw him?"

"Yeah. He had lunch with Mike Sawyer," he said without expression, as if sharing common knowledge.

"Who is...?" I asked nevertheless.

"He's a famous guy around here. Ran the first really classy restaurant in the valley—Michael Sawyer's it was called. Old guy, but nice, and knows his food business. Gives you hell if you mess up, overtips if you do it right."

I waggled the photograph I was still holding in my hand. "This one a regular, too?"

Philbin shook his head. "Never saw him before. I just recognized him because of Sawyer. When Mike comes to eat, I pay attention." He smiled with an oily self-satisfaction. "Makes it worth my while."

My earlier dislike of the man returned. "During your hovering to be of service, did you hear what they were talking about?"

He slid both hands into his trouser pockets

and shrugged his shoulders. "I don't know if I'm supposed to talk about that. Isn't there some kind of right to privacy thing there?"

I stared at him a moment, wondering if he was trying to be cute, angling for some money, or just plain stupid. "There's your right to remain silent when I arrest you for impeding an investigation."

The hands came back out. "Jesus Christ. You don't have to get so touchy. They talked about a lot of bullshit—the old days, their health. The same kind of crap all these old farts talk about."

"How about their waiter? Who was he?"

He surprised me by suddenly looking uncomfortable. "I was."

I understood immediately. "Screwed the real waiter for the tip. Where's Sawyer live?"

Philbin was anxious to get this over. "Edson Hill area." He gave me the precise address. "It's where a lot of bigwigs live."

"He get there just because of the restaurant?"

"Why don't you ask him?"

I went to Edson Hill with Gary Smith. He called the homes there "starter castles," and shared a few past tales of their owners' eccentric behavior. His take on them was like that of an indulgent father who didn't mind a little mischief from his children. It was one of the interesting things about Stowe that I'd already noticed—that the simmering anger some towns felt for the occasional wealthy resident had been diluted by compromise here, either because there were so many millionaires, or perhaps because Stowe had made its peace with what it had become.

That thought prompted me to test Gary on a topic closer to home. "What do you think about VBI, now that we've been working together awhile?"

He was still looking out the passenger window at the parade of huge houses, most of them new, many of them reflecting in their architecture the stone and woods that defined the entire region.

"I'm still not sure why they dreamed you up, what with VSP already in place, but it hasn't bugged me any."

"We haven't been too pushy?"

"Our PD wouldn't have ended up with this case anyhow, and you guys have been good to work with, 'cept maybe Kunkle. He's a little much."

"But if you were asked, we'd get a passing grade?" I persisted, knowing such a conversation would be taking place at higher levels, if it hadn't already.

"Nobody gives a shit what I think, and we're probably stuck with you people anyhow, so who cares?"

He relented after I made no comment and turned toward me. "Look, I know you didn't create this thing, and I don't much care why you joined up, although it's obviously working for you. But maybe that's what does bug me about it. I've done okay in this department. I got a good chief, we get our fair share of action, and I've had some pretty interesting assignments. With VBI coming on, that'll probably all change. We won't need detectives in-house, and I'll be back to pulling over speeders."

"Not necessarily," I argued. "We only handle major crimes—cases you'd hand over anyhow, just like you said. Your department will still need plainclothes officers. The only difference'll be that if you ever want to move up, you won't have to wait for the chief to leave—you can apply to join us and get career options you can't even dream of now unless you join the state police and virtually start all over again."

He shrugged, unconvinced. "If that's true, then every hotshot in the state'll be lining up to join and I won't have a chance." He pointed to a log-built home on our right—well appointed but low-key. "That's it."

I swung up the driveway, distressed if not surprised by his answer. Cops were often bureaucratic fatalists, resigned to any and all change doing them dirt in the long run— and convinced that there was nothing they could do about it. The Gary Smiths of this world would have to be led to any new realities, not pep-talked to them—prior disappointments and a natural conservatism dictated that.

Mike Sawyer stepped out onto his home's wraparound porch before we got out of the car. He was as bald as an egg, thin, small, and straight-backed, immaculately dressed in very expensive slacks and a thick cardigan sweater. Had he been wearing a white cap, I would have thought myself about to board a yacht.

274

"Mr. Sawyer?" I called out from where I'd parked.

"Who are you?" he asked without preamble.

"We're police officers," I said, keeping it simple. "We were wondering if we could ask you some questions."

He didn't move from looking down at us, his hands on the wooden railing before him. "About what?"

I made a gesture of slapping my sides with my arms. "Kind of cold out here. Mind if we come in?"

He obviously did, but luckily was old and well mannered enough not to say so. He indicated a set of broad steps to his right and motioned us to join him. We shook hands formally, exchanged names, and he ushered us stiffly across the threshold.

We entered a heavy-beamed living room with a pile of brightly burning logs in the fireplace and some classical music playing in the background.

"This is very nice," I said.

"It's functional. What do you want?"

I faced him, noticing for the first time just how old he was. Sawyer's clothes were so luxuriously thick and well tailored that from a distance they'd given him a youthful, fashionable flair. But up close, I saw how his neck and head protruded from them like a turtle's from its shell—bare, wrinkled, withered, and frail.

"Would you like to sit down?" I asked.

"No. I'd like an answer."

275

I remember how the unpleasant maître d' had described Sawyer as a tough guy with demanding expectations.

"We'd like to ask you about Gaston Picard."

His expression remained the same. "What about him?"

"You met him several days ago over lunch. We were wondering what you talked about."

"I doubt that's any of your business."

I began to reassess the turtle analogy. "It is, actually. We're conducting a murder investigation."

"Good for you. Do you have a warrant?"

"Do we need one?"

He smiled thinly. "My question comes first, and yours just gave me the answer. If at some point you feel you do need a warrant—and can get it—then maybe we'll continue this little chat."

That was our exit line, except for my unwillingness to take it. "I get your point, and you're perfectly within your rights, but can I ask you a couple of general things? They're more history questions than anything else."

He looked at me curiously for the first time. "History questions?"

I moved into that small opening. "Yeah. I heard you used to run the best restaurant in town—Michael Sawyer's."

"That's common knowledge."

"So I just found out. When was that in operation?"

"Sixty-four to eighty-nine."

That was a letdown. "What did you do before then?"

"I ran other restaurants."

"In Stowe?"

"Yes, and elsewhere."

"When did you open your first one in Stowe?" I asked, sensing I was slowly getting where I wanted to go.

Sawyer moved over to the front door and opened it. The sudden cold air matched the change in his tone. "I don't recall—old-timer's disease," he said, tapping his very sound head with his fingertip. "Make sure you bring some paperwork next time you come."

"That was useful," Gary said once we were heading back down the hillside.

"I thought so," I admitted.

He gave me a scornful look. "How?"

"Because he threw us out just as I was getting to when Jean Deschamps was killed. We'll have to hassle the town clerk some more to get the records, but I'll bet money that man was around Stowe in the mid-forties, which makes him the first solid connection we've got between the whole Sherbrooke bunch and Stowe besides Jean's frozen body."

Gary Smith smiled. "You think he's the one who kept the body on ice?"

"He's a good candidate. They didn't build home freezers then like they do today. You're too young to know that, but when I was a kid, I remember the wonder of step-in freezers the size of bedrooms. The first one I ever saw was in a restaurant."

CHAPTER TWENTY-ONE

We'd all but taken over the Stowe town clerk's office, much to her distress, and exacerbated matters by staying on past closing, an affront to procedure that had taken several phone calls to make acceptable.

Now we were sitting around a large wooden table—Tom and Sammie still comparing the Special Service Force roster with Stowe residents of the time, and Gary Smith and I poring over unwieldy bound volumes of voting, tax, and real estate records that had gradually spread across every available flat surface. Working the computer data banks in Waterbury, Paul Spraiger was trying to find out what he could about Michael Sawyer before he'd come to Stowe. Willy, as usual, was off doing something he hadn't deigned to share with the rest of us.

Gary finally leaned back in his chair, reached toward the ceiling with both hands in a stretch, and laconically announced, "Think I got it."

"What?" I asked as the other two glanced up.

He tapped the book before him with his finger. "Says here Sawyer bought a residence on the edge of town in '46, turned it into a restaurant the same year—something called the Snow Bank—and held it until..." he paused while he pulled another open book toward him and consulted its pages, "1951. That's when he sold out and opened another place nearer downtown named Mike's, which he held onto till Michael Sawyer's opened in '64, like he told us."

"Fancier and fancier each time," Sammie commented.

"I guess," Gary agreed. "Doesn't go into those kinds of details here."

"He must've been doing pretty well to create the first restaurant out of a remodeled house and then go upwardly mobile just five years later, especially since Stowe hadn't hit the big time yet," I said.

"Could be Sawyer was as good as they say he was and just caught the wave of the future," Sammie suggested.

I chewed that over for a few seconds. "Maybe. I just can't shake the feeling of a whole lot of birds suddenly landing in the same tree. Picard, Sawyer, Deschamps—"

"Guidry," Willy added from the doorway, where he'd typically appeared without making a sound.

"Meaning?" I asked him.

He strolled over to a chair, taking his time to settle down. "I been bugged by a couple of things, so I decided to check 'em out. Remember what that note said? The one that Marcel was supposed to have written to his old man, inviting him down?"

"Yeah."

"He said 'we're' having a good time down here. And 'come down and join us,' as if he wasn't alone. Always made me wonder."

"You figure it out?" Gary asked.

Willy made a face. "Not really. It's weirder than that. I didn't have anywhere to start with Marcel, since the letter was the only thing we had connecting him to Stowe. So I went back to the Alvarez register at the old Snow Dancer Hotel and looked at it closer up, thinking that if Jean checked in, maybe the son did, too, under another name—or somebody else we'd recognize."

He shifted in his seat as we waited. "There was nothin'. I checked it three times."

"Willy," Sammie barely muttered in a warning tone.

"Okay, okay," he answered. "I guess Alvarez was a pretty snotty guy. Turns out he had a coding system for when anyone arrived with hired help. The guest would be registered like normal, but the slave—maid, butler, chauffeur, whatever—was just marked down by a symbol next to the guest's name. Deschamps had one of those marks."

"No shit," Tom said.

"That's what I thought, so I drove back to Richford to talk to Arvin Brown again. We never asked if anyone was with Deschamps when he walked into Brown's place. Turns out he had a chauffeur. He didn't come in, but Brown delivered him some grub in the car. The description pretty much fits Pierre Guidry. I asked how he could still remember that, and he said the whole night was burned into his brain—plus he thought the chauffeur was as much an asshole as his boss was like a movie star."

"I'll be damned," I said.

"That's not all," Willy continued. "Since we're hot after Mike Sawyer, I asked Brown about him, too. He knew Sawyer—asked him for a job once. Said the guy was a prick and that everyone hated him except the customers, since he brown-nosed them and they didn't give a shit anyhow. I drew a blank trying to connect the dots between Sawyer and any of the other players, but Brown did tell me the rumor mill was running hot and heavy when Sawyer set up his first restaurant..."

"The Snow Bank," Gary added.

Willy looked at him dismissively, which made me think of Gary's comment about Kunkle earlier. "Whatever. The thing is he paid cash on the barrel head for the place and paid the same way to fix it up."

"They speculate where he'd come from?" Tom asked.

Willy smiled. "Yup. You'll love this—Canada. He said 'out' and 'about' like a Canuck. But he never owned up when he was asked—just told people to piss off."

"Your kind of guy," Gary said.

Willy laughed. "Yeah—probably right."

"But what's that tell you about the 'we' reference in Marcel's supposed letter?" Sammie asked.

Willy tilted his head to one side. "Nothin'. That part's still got me goin'. I did ask Brown if we might be able to get some more dirt on Sawyer, though, and he coughed up a woman named Amy Butynski. Used to be one of his waitresses. Brown said she was smart, had done okay for herself, and still lived in town. Sounded like he once had the hots for her, but I don't think he ever scored."

"That's relevant," Sammie commented peevishly.

Willy laughed again. "I think so," and he raised his eyebrows at her. She stared at her paperwork, her face reddening.

"Sammie," I said. "Why don't you call Lacombe and ask him to run a check on Sawyer? And tell Paul what we've got—maybe it'll help him in his digging." I checked my watch and then looked at Willy. "It's still not too late. You want to go visit Ms. Butynski?"

The address Willy had took us north of town on Route 100. As we drove slowly through traffic, I seized the same opportunity I'd taken with Gary earlier. "How're you liking this detail so far?"

"Why?" he asked. "Want to fire me?"

I shook my head. "Nope—straightforward question."

"I doubt that. How many have asked you to can me so far?"

"Nobody. One of them said you were a little over the top. I thought that was pretty mild given the shit you've handed me over the years. That was a nice piece of work, by the way, chasing down Guidry."

After a moment's silence, he answered my question, "It's okay. I didn't think I'd like being out of Bratt."

"Having Sammie around must help."

He didn't answer, but he didn't deny it, either.

"I have an idea about who 'we' and 'us' were

in Marcel's fake letter," I said. "When Paul and I interviewed Marie Chenin, I asked her as we were leaving where Marcel had been when his father disappeared. She didn't know. But when I asked the same thing about Picard and Guidry, she looked like I'd just told her about some favorite relative dying."

Willy looked at me but remained silent.

"Let's say," I continued, "that this whole let's-keep-the-trip-to-Stowe-a-secret routine was a crock—cooked up so everyone could claim ignorance at the time and stop any police investigation dead in its tracks."

"Meaning everyone knew Guidry was along in his chauffeur mode. That would explain Jean keeping a high profile while he was in Stowe."

"Right," I agreed. "But then why would Chenin look so surprised by my question?"

Willy smiled. "'Cause it wasn't Guidry that got her thinking. It was Picard."

"And two makes for 'we,'" I said.

"So the two of them killed Jean together?"

I equivocated there. "I think they rigged the letter framing Marcel. It still doesn't make sense to me why they would've killed Jean."

Amy Butynski lived in a handsome, three-story brick house with white trim and a slate roof. There were two bright lanterns mounted to either side of the front door and a neatly shoveled path connecting the driveway to the walk. As Arvin Brown had told Willy, it looked like life had been good to his old flame.

A striking woman answered the door—tall, slim, white-haired, and yet remarkably youthful in appearance. Her face and hands looked twenty years younger than I knew they were— assuming I was right about her identity.

"Are you Amy Butynski?" I asked.

She smiled broadly, displaying a row of perfect white teeth. "I was. It's been quite a while since anyone called me that. It's Sommers now."

We fished out our shields and told her who we were. To my relief, she didn't take us for health inspectors. Instead, she merely drew back and invited us in, calling out to her husband as she did so.

We were ushered into a pleasant living room by both of them, he being a stocky man with an open face and an easy demeanor, unintimidated by our appearance at his door.

After disposing of the usual chatter about whether we wanted coffee or something to eat, Amy asked us, "Why was it you wanted to see me?"

I smiled apologetically. "It's a little off the wall, to be honest, and as you guessed, it deals with ancient history. We heard you once worked as a waitress for Mike Sawyer at the Snow Bank."

She laughed and rolled her eyes. "Oh, my gosh. That *was* a long time ago. I haven't thought of those days in ages. What could you possibly want to know about?"

"We need all the help we can get, actually," I told her. "So maybe the best thing would be to start with some general questions, like how long you worked there?"

She was sitting beside her husband on the couch, and now casually took his hand in her own—a long-standing habit, it appeared, born of easy companionship. My sympathy with Arvin Brown's sense of loss was tempered by the guess that his intended had found her own perfect mate.

"Let's see," she began. "I was about sixteen when I started. That would make it 1946."

"Just after Sawyer opened the place," I said.

"That's right. I'd forgotten that. Anyhow, I stayed on until about 1949. It was all I could take of the man."

"Difficult?"

She laughed. "A perfect monster—treated everyone terribly, except the guests, of course. They all thought he was heaven."

"Why'd you stay on so long if he was that bad?" Willy asked.

She looked a little sad as she explained, "I needed the money. My family wasn't very lucky in that area, and the tips were some of the best in town."

"She wouldn't tell you," her husband said, "but she was supporting the whole family back then. Her father had been crippled in a logging accident, her mother was sickly, and she was the oldest of five kids."

She squeezed his hand harder. "They don't need to hear all that."

I moved on. "Still, it must have been tough working there."

"It wasn't so bad. You had to get used to

him, is all, and a lot of people couldn't. His bark was worse than his bite by far."

"Had Mike been in the restaurant business long? Seems an odd thing to choose if you're short-tempered."

"I'm not sure he had been, now that you mention it. For one thing, he wasn't that old—in his twenties somewhere. But I also remember thinking he was learning the ropes as he went. He made some mistakes a real professional probably wouldn't have—things like underordering supplies and not having enough food on hand for a Friday night. He was smart, though, so that happened pretty rarely, and in no time flat, he was right in his element. Went on to become quite famous, around here at least. I suppose you already know that."

"We'd heard rumors," I conceded. "Did you have any idea of his background? Had he fought in the war, for example?"

"Or did he even come from this country?" Willy added.

She laughed again. "Which one do I answer first? Actually, it's no to both. I don't think he was in the war, and I'm pretty sure he'd come from Canada."

"How did you come to those conclusions?" I asked.

She looked thoughtful. "On the war thing, it was more of a feeling I had. It was definitely something you didn't talk about—unless you wanted Mike in one of his rages. I guess that could have been due to a traumatic combat experience, too, but I always sensed it was because he'd never had the chance to fight. People forget it now, especially since Vietnam, but the whole world was wrapped up in that war, and unless you had an arm or leg missing—I'm talking about the men, of course—you were made to feel like you had to explain yourself. The war had finished by then, obviously, but I still felt a leftover sense of shame in him."

"What about the Canada connection?"

"That's easier. He spoke like they do, and he had some pictures he'd pinned to the wall over his desk."

"Could you recognize the places?"

"I remember one was Sherbrooke, all lit up at night. I asked him about it and he told me they once called it the Electric City in an effort to attract more tourists. This was during the Depression, when all they had going for them was hydro-power. The whole town looked like a Christmas tree. It was a wonderful postcard."

I glanced at Willy and asked, "Did he ever say he was from Sherbrooke?"

"If he wasn't, he knew a lot about it, and he spoke perfect French, too. Nowadays, half of Stowe is filled with Canadians—it wasn't that way back then, but there were still a fair number that came down to ski or visit, and he'd chat with them whenever they came in to eat."

"You got those pictures on you?" I muttered to Willy, who dug into his inside pocket.

"When these French-Canadians came to visit," I asked Amy Butynski, "did they *just* come to eat, or were they friends of Sawyer's?"

She thought back a moment. "Most of them were customers, but Mike had a small office, and I remember him taking a couple of men back there once. I walked in on them by accident. I thought the office was empty and I was getting some more order pads. Mike got really mad at me—it stuck in my mind because there was no reason for it, not even for him. They were speaking French."

I handed her the pictures Willy was dangling from his one hand. "I know it's been a long time, but do you recognize any of these faces?"

She looked at them all carefully—of Jean, his son Marcel, Guidry, and Picard—but finally shook her head and gave them back. "I'm sorry—it's been too many years."

"That's okay," I told her. "It was a long shot. How did the restaurant do in the beginning, before Sawyer got the hang of things?"

She shrugged. "It seemed to do fine. I mean, the customers were few and far between at first, but that's pretty normal."

"Sawyer paid cash for the restaurant," Willy explained in his own shorthand style, "and to fix it up after."

She stared at him wide-eyed. "Really? Wow. No wonder we didn't have any problems early on."

"What do you mean?"

She shifted her gaze to me. "Those beginner glitches I mentioned—Mike would yell at us and have a fit, but it was never any trouble to buy our way out of a jam. Once, when he underordered filet mignon on a Friday night, he didn't just admit it to the customers and

288

push another item. He went across town and bought what he needed from a competitor. It must have cost him a fortune, but he didn't seem to care."

"Did he live high on the hog?" Willy asked.

"I didn't think so. He was better off than I was, but then almost everyone was. He didn't drive a fancy car or anything."

"Probably being discreet," I said softly, mostly to myself.

Amy's husband spoke up at that. "I don't suppose we could ask why you want to know all this?"

"You could," I told him, "but we wouldn't be able to tell you much. It's a very old story, with quite a few holes in it. And we're not actually singling out Mike Sawyer—he's just one of many leads."

"Did the restaurant have a freezer?" Willy asked abruptly.

Butynski's face lit up. "Yes. Actually, that's another example. Right after we had the problem with the meat shortage, Mike had one put in. It was quite a big deal—I'm not sure anyone else had one then. They were quite rare in those days. In fact, the government had started a program of building community freezers here and there so that people could use them the way municipal swimming pools are used now—for the benefit of all. But typically, Mike wasn't interested in anything like that. It was always first class for him. It made the newspaper, if I recall correctly, and the freezer was enormous—as big as a room. In the summer, some of us would go in there to cool off—when Mike was away, of course."

Unconsciously, both Willy and I leaned slightly forward in our seats.

He spoke first. "What time of year did he put it in?"

"Easy—late winter, before the ground thawed. That was part of what made it news—that he didn't wait till summer, or spring at least. It must have cost him much more to have it done then, but he was insistent, even though it caused a big mess and lost him business."

"Ms. Butynski... I mean Sommers," I asked, "was there anything unusual about the freezer? Maybe a locker that Sawyer kept locked or even a separate room he might have used for storage?"

She was silent for a moment, and then shook her head. "It was just a room. It had shelves running along both long walls, of course, but they were open, and it had hooks for the bigger pieces of meat, but that was it."

That was disappointing. I was so sure we'd found where Jean Deschamps had spent at least the first few years of his afterlife.

"You said you used to go in there to cool off during the summer," Willy asked. "Where did you sit?"

"On the box," she answered pleasantly, "at the back."

"How big was that?" I asked, as impressed by our luck as I was by Willy's inspiration. "Maybe seven feet long by three or four wide?"

She smiled broadly. "Exactly. How did you know?"

CHAPTER TWENTY-TWO

The mood in the air was refreshingly upbeat, especially after so many setbacks. We were sitting around our quasi-official table at the Commodore's bar, Willy and I updating Paul, Gary, and Tom about our conversation with Amy Butynski.

"Assuming the box had Jean's body in it," Tom was asking, "who's the connection between Mike Sawyer and Sherbrooke—Picard, Guidry, or Marcel?"

"Rule Marcel out," I said. "He may be a crook and he may've benefited from his father's death, but I think he was clueless here."

"Joe thinks the 'we' in the letter was Picard and Guidry both," Willy explained. "Could've been, too, with Guidry as the pig sticker and Picard the mastermind."

"They set up Mike Sawyer in a fancy restaurant just so they could put a body in the freezer?" Tom asked incredulously. "Give me a break."

Willy didn't take offense, his optimism holding the upper hand for once. "Sawyer was probably only a money launderer at first. But the freezer was installed in late winter, just before a body in the snow would begin to thaw. It was luck of the draw. Jean Deschamps was indulging in chasing down his son's supposed killer. He came to Stowe, perfect for Guidry because it was not only across the border, but where Sawyer had already been put in place. Guidry knocks the boss off and sticks him in the snow, while Picard pays Sawyer to order the freezer and—probably a few years after everything's calmed down—lays the trail that eventually nails Marcel by salting Alvarez's records, setting up that weird will, and planting the letter that led us to Marcel. A nice, neat, lawyerly approach."

"But why bother?" Tom complained. "Why not just knock off both father and son and take over the business?"

Willy was beginning to lose patience. "Because it was a *family* business, duh, and to destroy that means to destroy the works. Besides, now Guidry moves up from chauffeur to right-hand man, and Picard becomes the consigliere, all because snotnose Marcel turns into this smoking son-of-a-bitch who transforms Pop's outfit into a multimillion-dollar hotrod. Everyone comes up roses, with the extra advantage that the first two have this rabbit in their hat they can use against Marcel whenever they want—which is when he comes down with galloping cancer and talks about handing everything over to *his* son, Michel, who is guaranteed to piss it all away."

Tom was silent, considering Willy's version of reality. Gary Smith, however, seemed won over. "I'll be damned. That would explain why things have gone to hell since Marcel passed the polygraph, and why they tried to hit Joe for poking around beyond the trail they laid out."

"I think it's been more Guidry than Picard," I said. "He's the one with the street-brawler past. Could be the two of them are falling out, which would explain the stupidity of trying to shoot a cop."

Gary Smith reached for his silent pager and looked at the display. "Be back in a sec," he said, and left the table.

Tom Shanklin didn't look totally convinced, but obviously had no counterarguments. "What's the next move? See what the Canadians can make fit?"

"After meeting Butynski, Willy and I did just that—we called Lacombe to try some of this out. He already had a little on Sawyer, from Sammie's call earlier, and confirmed that Sawyer was a bad boy up there before leaving for the U.S. during the war, which is why he didn't get into the fighting, apparently. The kicker, though, is that he may've been here illegally all this time, which means we'll have something to squeeze him with. I doubt he'll want to go back to Canada to do time at his age, even with their soft sentencing."

I took a swallow of my Coke and then asked Willy, "Where is Sammie, anyway?"

He curled his lip. "Obsessing, surprise, surprise. She's still running that World War Two roster against the Stowe records."

I saw Smith returning from the phone out in the hallway, and could tell from his expression he wasn't bearing good news.

He didn't sit down. "I hope you didn't plan to talk to Mike Sawyer again."

No one said a word.

"He's been found dead at home. Shot three times, with a frozen hot dog shoved down his throat."

We drove to Sawyer's house in a caravan, to find the Stowe PD had already cordoned off the area, laid out a narrow path into the building, and made sure that whatever evidence there was would be preserved. I'd already called the mobile crime lab, and since Waterbury was just down the road a few miles, their response time promised to be mercifully short.

In the meantime, donning white coveralls, a cap, and booties, I followed the access path into the house to see Mike Sawyer one last time.

He was still in the tastefully appointed living room, now oddly silent and somehow not smelling quite right. He was sitting in an armchair, his head thrown back grotesquely. The bullet wounds were to his chest, the dark stippling around the holes indicating the shooter had stood very close. The now thawed hot dog was there as advertised, protruding from between his lips, probably placed there posthumously as a statement to us—this was a man who was not going to speak. Ironically, I'd figured that would have been the case anyhow, despite my high hopes around the table at the Commodore. The one time I'd met Mike Sawyer, I hadn't thought him easily susceptible to pressure. Killing him had therefore been totally gratuitous, which gave me a glimpse into the character of the shooter.

Three hours later, we were back at the Stowe police department, with nothing much to work with. The neighbors hadn't heard or seen anything. Sawyer had lived alone and had apparently let his killer in. There were no signs of a struggle or of anything being disturbed in the house, and while the forensics team had collected a fair amount, including an open package of frozen hot dogs in a sink, they'd found nothing immediately revealing except a large empty freezer in the basement—presumably Jean Deschamps's Arctic condo for the last few decades. Basically, we were left hoping that either the surveillance Lacombe had ordered on Marcel's gang would reveal Guidry's having left for Stowe, or that the Customs and Border Patrol people we'd alerted would get lucky and give us a call.

But we still hadn't heard from either one.

It was therefore in a relative state of despondency that Sammie Martens found us, having at long last extricated herself from the town clerk's office.

"No luck on the Sawyer shooting?" she surmised.

"Sure," Willy came back. "We won't have to worry about how to make him talk."

She put a single Xeroxed sheet on the table before me. "Then maybe we should try this guy."

I studied the document as she explained to the others, "Roger Scott. He's lived in Stowe since the war, bought big early, held on till the land rush of the 1970s, and has been selling here and there for a bundle ever since. He's also on the roster you gave me of the Special Service Force—the only one, so far as I can tell."

She looked exhausted, her hair unwashed and lank, her eyes ringed with dark, puffy skin.

"Nice work, Sam. He must've been the man Jean Deschamps came down to visit," I said.

She sat heavily in one of the chairs surrounding the conference table. "Wonder if they ever met?"

"We'll find out tomorrow," I told her, "after you get a good night's sleep and I give that press conference announcing I have a secret."

Tom Shanklin looked at me dubiously. "You still doing that—after Sawyer?"

"All the more reason. Sawyer's death proves we're on the right track. Someone—presumably Pierre Guidry—is running around trying to plug as many holes as he can. What better time to present him with another and force him into the open? Besides, I already told Lacombe I would."

"How did the shooter know we were hot on Sawyer's heels?" Willy asked.

"Sawyer probably called to report after our first visit," Sammie proposed.

"Maybe," Willy grumbled.

"What're you thinking?" I asked him.

"That things are a little leaky in your pal Lacombe's outfit. Seems like a lot of bad happens right after you tell 'em what's doin'."

I hated the idea of that.

He held up his one hand and began folding down his fingers, one by one. "The press tumbled to Jean Deschamps's identity right after you hit Sherbrooke. The old gangster Lucien Pelletier was conveniently recommended to fill your ear about how Marcel was a son-of-a-bitch who hated his father, while swearing Jean didn't have Guidry along as chauffeur the day he vanished. The secretary—what's her name, Marie Chenin—spilled the beans about Jean being lured down here by his son just before we could report the same news back to Sherbrooke. That guy in the motel knew exactly what door to knock on before he took a shot at you. And now Sawyer gets whacked before we get a chance to squeeze him. You can explain all that a bunch of different ways, but they make for a pretty interesting bundle, if you ask me, and most of them trace back to the Sûreté."

"And to Jacques Chauvin," Paul said in his typically quiet voice.

We all stared at him, while my private gloominess was suddenly given a reprieve.

"The old Sherbrooke cop we talked to almost as soon as we got there," he reminded us. "He put us onto Pelletier. The first domino, if Willy's right," he added. "It looked to me like he had free run of the building."

I saw Willy give Paul an appraising glance—a ringing endorsement from a hard-core independent like Kunkle, and one I was happy to second.

"Could be," I conceded. "I'll give Lacombe

a heads up. It doesn't alter the value of putting more heat under Guidry's feet."

"Sure," Willy finally agreed. "What the hell? Worst that can happen is you die with your boots on."

"By the way," Paul added in the silence following that crack. "When you meet Roger Scott, you might want to ask him why Dick Kearley thinks he died from a dud mortar round while he was standing next to Colonel Frederick. Remember?"

The press conference setting me up as a target went off the next morning as planned, ostensibly to update the media on the Sawyer murder, and also to appease the governor, the commissioner, and my boss, Bill Allard.

I tried to do the latter first, explaining VBI's role yet again, and handing the mike to Frank Auerbach so he could say how happy he was with the teamwork. I also downplayed the attempt on my life in Sherbrooke, which had taken its time to filter down to the U.S., and highlighted the effectiveness of our working with the Sûreté, stating with confidence that the mystery of the "frozen man of the mountain," as Jean was being called, would soon be solved.

The real point of the exercise, though, was brought up at the end, when the inevitable question was asked about how we were planning to arrive at that goal.

"At this time," I answered in practiced bureau-speak, "we are following a number of solid leads, any one of which could give us the break we need."

"Is there one you like better than the others?"

"You could say that," I said coyly. "It's pretty vague right now—more of a theory. I haven't even shared it with my team."

"Why not? Isn't that a little unusual?"

"We all have ideas we chase down now and then on our own—saves on informational clutter. If this works out, though," I added with a laugh, "you might end up with some interesting headlines."

Afterward, Bill Allard was not amused. He called me on my cell phone five minutes after the story aired on the radio. "What the hell's this private theory crap? You sounded like Sherlock Holmes, for Christ's sake. The point of this unit is to support the locals, not hold out on them."

"I'm not. Auerbach's in on it. I wanted the opposition to think I know something I don't. We're hoping it'll flush them out. I'm sending you my report by fax within the hour."

The edge left his voice as he asked, "You're sure you know what you're doing?"

"Absolutely," I lied. "It's all under control."

Even by Stowe standards, the house Sammie and I drove up to east of town later in the day was a standout. Most of the mansions—Gary Smith's "starter castles"—were built of wood, designed ostentatiously but with a nod toward

the surrounding countryside. This one was a
pile of gray rock, complete with turrets,
leaded stained-glass windows, and a front
door big enough for a rider atop a horse.
Castle it was, with nothing of the beginner
about it.

We rolled to a stop in the front courtyard
and admired a full view of Mount Mansfield
across the Stowe valley, its recumbent profile
clearly etched on the horizon. Cold, white, and
distant, it brought to mind Jean Deschamps's
masklike face staring up from the autopsy table.

"Geez," Sammie commented, gazing at the
house, "what the hell did he do to buy this?"

I swung out of the car into the crisp, freezing
air. "Let's see if we can find out."

The front door opened almost as soon as I
pushed the bell, revealing a starchy, round man
in a dark three-piece suit. "You are the police?"
he asked in a stiff, formal voice.

"Yes," I answered, as we both showed him
credentials that he scrutinized carefully.

"Follow me."

We did that, down a long, dark-paneled hallway lined with heavily framed oil paintings, to
a pair of double doors that, once thrown open,
led into a towering library with twenty-foot-
high windows overlooking the valley below. I
felt transported back either to the England of
centuries ago, or to the Hollywood set of *My
Fair Lady*. Sammie merely stared, her mouth
unashamedly open. Sprinkled among the bookcases were inset curved display cabinets, softly
lighted and closed off behind glass doors, holding a variety of precious objects from women's

ancient baubles to jeweled snuff boxes and ornate ivory calling card cases. Perched above the carved mantelpiece, in an obvious place of honor, was a hideous-looking carved mask of what looked like a gargoyle, complete with devilish eyebrows and a snarling mouth. To my untrained eye, the entire collection seemed of museum-grade material, and there was a lot of it.

"How may I help you?" came a voice hidden beneath the glare from the windows.

I spoke to the light, waiting for my eyes to adjust. "I'm Joe Gunther. This is Special Agent Samantha Martens—Vermont Bureau of Investigation. We were wondering if we could ask you a few questions."

"You said that on the phone. Do you like objets d'art?"

I was beginning to make out a huge desk beneath the windows, and behind it the outline of a small, wispy-haired man. "Less the value and more how it looks."

"Meaning you don't like the mask."

"What is it?"

"Very old, for one thing, and as you guessed, very valuable. An homage to Greek mythology. It's a faun. Feel free to look more closely."

I did so, moving from case to case as I might have at an exhibition. Special lighting made each object glow as if from within. I imagined that at night, with the room dark aside from these bright, shimmering pools, this library took on the feel of a magnificent tomb buried far beneath a pyramid.

"You been collecting long?" I asked.

301

"Most of my adult life."

"What made you start?"

There was a pause, suggesting I might have overstepped some boundary.

"Surely, this is not why you asked to see me."

"Right. Actually, we're investigating the death of a man found frozen on the mountain."

"The fifty-year-old corpse," said the shadowy outline.

I walked up to the desk, trailed by Sammie and the butler. The voice emerged as a thin, pale invalid, sitting in a wheelchair, vaguely reminiscent of Marcel Deschamps. "You heard about that?"

"I subscribe to the local paper, Mr. Gunther."

Uninvited, I sat in one of the large armchairs facing the desk, enjoying the slight squeak and smell of leather that accompanied the move.

Roger Scott waved a hand at the man behind us. "Go, Robert."

We all patiently waited until Robert had closed the doors behind him.

"He the only one working here?" I asked.

"I have others. He's the only one that lives with me. Why do you ask?"

I looked around. "Big house, a lot to run. I just wondered."

"Because I'm in a wheelchair? The house was built to accommodate that. It's much more efficient than it looks."

There was a hint of pride there I decided to exploit a little. "It is amazing, and filled with beautiful things. How long have you lived here?"

"I moved in forty-one years ago, although I've added on as my income allowed."

"But you were in Stowe before then, right?"

The pale face smiled. "I have a feeling you already know the answer to that. I came here right after the war and built a house nearby—on the same acreage, in fact."

"You've done very well for yourself."

"Meaning, where did I get my money? I inherited it, Mr. Gunther, and then built on it through some fortunate real estate deals. What does any of this have to do with the frozen man?"

"We think you knew his son," I said. "Antoine Deschamps. You fought together in Italy."

I wasn't sure what I'd been anticipating, but I didn't expect the burst of laughter I received.

"We *all* fought together—in Montana, in Burlington, in the Aleutians, *and* in Italy. That was one of the hallmarks of our unit."

"The First Special Service Force."

"Yes. Back then, people used to confuse the name with the Special Services branch of the Army—basically the music bands. That was on purpose, to help keep us under wraps. But it wasn't a mistake anyone made twice."

"Rough outfit."

"Energetic, yes. We were a throwaway group—a suicide battalion, if you want to get melodramatic. We felt we had nothing to lose by enjoying ourselves while we were still alive."

"And your Colonel Frederick encouraged that attitude?"

"Ah, you've been doing your homework.

303

Probably rented that movie, *The Devil's Brigade*."

"No."

"Just as well. Typical mythology, although it captured our reputation for doing the impossible."

"How was Antoine Deschamps at that?"

Roger Scott shook his head slowly for a moment. "Not yet. I want to ask you a couple of things first, given the courtesy I've just paid you. Why is any of this relevant to the investigation of a man found frozen to death out there, even if his son and I did fight in the same unit?"

"We think Jean Deschamps came to Stowe to meet you. Did he?"

"No. What did he want? Details about his boy's death?"

"You know about that?"

"Not really. I have to admit, I may have been leading you on a bit. I didn't actually know Antoine Deschamps—not well, at least. We were in different regiments. I heard he was killed outside of Rome. I didn't see it, though. I wouldn't have been of much use to his father."

"How do you know that's why he came here?" I asked.

"It's what a parent would want to know. Did he suffer? Was he a hero? Did he have any last words? I was ignorant of all that. I could have told him his son was an abusive, foul-mouthed, skirt-chasing, self-serving thief and a liar, but then so was I and every other Forceman. It's what Robert Frederick trained us to be."

"Actually," I tried again, "I haven't been totally candid. Jean Deschamps thought Antoine was murdered in Italy, not killed in combat."

Scott absorbed that thoughtfully. "Could be. It was known to happen."

"Was there anyone who springs to mind in that context? Someone who hated Antoine enough to want him dead?"

"Not that I knew of. Passions could run high, of course, and every one of us had been taught to kill a dozen different ways. Rumors were that about half of us had been pulled out of prison to quote-unquote volunteer, although I suspected that's part of the mythology again. Still, there were some fierce fights, and I always suspected not all our casualties were combat-related."

I waved my hand at the room around us. "You don't seem cut from that kind of cloth."

"I had a wild streak, but you're right. I wasn't alone, though. There were a lot of pretty regular people mixed in—teachers, musicians, cowboys, you name it."

"How 'bout someone named Charlie Webber?" I asked.

Scott's face hardened. "He was no poet. Why do you mention him?"

"How do you know about him?" I asked instead. "He was in the same regiment as Antoine."

"Some were better known than others. You have to understand—the Force hovered between fifteen hundred and two thousand men. That's small by Army standards, but it's still a large number. And the turnover was impressive." He paused, thinking back. "After a while, getting to know people proved to be counterproductive."

"But you knew Webber."

He refocused on us. "Yes. Charlie Webber. Few people didn't. He died, too. Should've been from a bullet in the back, delivered by one of us, but instead it was from natural causes, as we used to refer to combat deaths back then. The man was a psychopath, in my opinion. Is he the one you think killed Antoine?"

"We heard they'd had a falling out at Anzio, but then later became best buddies, glued at the hip."

Scott shook his head. "I can't imagine anything worse."

"What did Webber do to you?" Sammie asked.

There was a long pause. "I hold him responsible for putting me in this chair."

We didn't say anything, prompting him to add, "In your research, did you ever hear mention of the Champagne Campaign?"

We both shook our heads, although Dick Kearley had spoken of it.

"I thought not. Not a Hollywood-style story. After Italy was all but over—at least after the generals got their pictures taken in Rome—we were reassigned to southern France, first to take the Iles d'Hyères, and then to sweep along the French Riviera to Cannes, Nice, and the rest. The first part was tough, but then it got easy, and people like

Webber became bored and restless. He'd been promoted, and the regiments had been mixed up enough that I was now serving under him. In any case, he was so focused on getting laid and drunk by then, he ordered us into a small hilltop village without reconnaissance. We were ambushed and shot up. I caught one in the spine, several others were killed. Useless casualties, all. Webber was supposed to be leading us, but of course, he was sacked out with some girl instead."

"He didn't get court-martialed?" Sammie asked, her sense of propriety offended.

"He was about to be, but then he was killed," came the answer. "I think it was suicide, really. He didn't want to go back to prison. Life was never going to improve beyond that point, where he could break every rule in the book in the name of patriotism, so he rushed a machine gun nest single-handed and was blown up by his own grenade. A hero's death for a homicidal maniac. Another of war's ironies."

I caught the bitterness in his voice and reflected back on my own experience of combat and war—and to the men and women I'd known whose wounds, though less visible than Scott's, had been far more crippling.

"You seem to have done well, nevertheless," I said, giving vent to those thoughts.

He'd been staring at the marble mask over the mantel while he spoke, and now shifted his gaze to me. "Of course. Police officers. You probably both have military backgrounds. Someone like me must be like an alien from a distant planet, and not deserving of much sympathy—rich, pampered by servants, surrounded by beautiful things. It never occurs to you that can be as arrogant an outlook as any snobbery from a rich person."

He pulled away from the desk and rolled around its edge, heading toward the double doors as he spoke. Hesitantly, we both rose and fell in behind him, realizing the interview had ended.

"It doesn't matter," he continued. "That's the price of a democracy. Majority rules. If the little people decide the rich are useless assholes, regardless of what we may have done for their country or the welfare of its economy, then they're right and we're wrong. That's all there is to it."

He grabbed one of the doorknobs and retreated slightly, pulling the door open. "I'm assuming you have what you came for."

Sammie stepped into the hallway, where Robert was waiting for us. I paused on the library's threshold. "You were right that we did some homework before coming here," I said. "Including interviewing a man who saw you killed by a dud mortar round as you sat next to Colonel Frederick."

Scott merely tilted his head forward and tapped it with his fingertips. "Another combat death that wasn't. Makes you wonder how many people died inside of coffins, simply because no one bothered checking for a pulse. It was a dud, and it knocked me out cold, but, as you can see, I survived."

I couldn't argue with the physical evidence,

but as we drove back down the long, winding driveway past the wrought-iron gates, I wondered about the definition of the word "survival."

CHAPTER TWENTY-THREE

Gilles Lacombe called that afternoon, just as the sunlight was yielding to the gloom of another winter's night.

"Joe?" he said. "I have unfortunate news. Pierre Guidry has just been found dead—strangled with a wire."

I stared at the phone for a moment. "You know who did it?"

He let out a hapless laugh. "I am not sure I know anything anymore. Was it not Guidry that you thought killed Jean Deschamps?"

"Once upon a time. Who knows, now? Wasn't Guidry under surveillance?"

Lacombe was obviously embarrassed. "His phones were tapped and we were watching him. But we did not have a full surveillance team for him. There has been much going on up here since you left. We have been very much stretched out."

"The sharks gathering?"

"It is known the Deschamps are weak. Almost all the criminals we know have tried something by now. There has been much violence. The phone taps have told us that Michel is fighting for control."

"Michel?" I asked, recalling how out of control he'd been the last time I'd seen him. "What about his father?"

"Marcel is almost gone," Lacombe reported. "He is still at home, but it is clear he will not live for much longer."

"What's Picard doing?"

"We are guessing he is being the loyal family servant, as always."

"Why guessing? Don't you know?"

"We have not seen him in two days, but he is the one with the low profile."

Given Guidry's condition, I wondered how low that might be.

"Joe," Lacombe added, "there is one extra thing, maybe small. Marie Chenin did a meeting with Michel. It happened outside and we could not hear it."

I felt like a curtain had been drawn wide open. "Before Guidry was killed?"

"Yes."

"Was Picard in on it?"

"No. She was very strong that she meet Michel alone."

"And Picard hasn't been seen since?"

Lacombe was silent for a few moments. "You are thinking Picard is dead, also?"

"Could be. Did you get pictures of Michel's meeting with Chenin?"

"Videotape, with a telephoto lens. He is very excited by what she says. We have talked with her, but she tells us nothing."

"What's his attitude generally? Is he doing a good job rallying his forces?"

"I would say not. Michel is a young man I don't think well equipped for this. His emotions are very strong."

I chewed on that a bit, thinking it at best an understatement. From what little I knew of Michel, his "emotions" were cranked up enough to make him certifiable. But that was just a gut feeling. "Okay, Gilles," I said, "thanks for the update. Let me know if Picard resurfaces."

I rounded up what members of the team I could find. The Sawyer homicide had pulled away Paul Spraiger and Gary Smith, but Willy, Tom, and Sam were available.

I told them about Guidry.

"Great," Tom said. "What's that do to all your theories?"

"What's Lacombe say?" Sammie asked more precisely.

"No clue," I reported, not wanting to influence their thinking prematurely. "Apparently, the power vacuum in the Deschamps camp's causing all hell to break loose. Marcel's dying, Michel's running around in a panic, and Picard's nowhere to be seen."

"There's your bad guy," Willy said. "Clearest scenario is that Guidry and Picard had a falling out over who would end up top man. Picard snuffed Guidry, and now he's tucked away somewhere waiting for the boss to croak so he can run up a new flag, which'll probably include a treaty with the Angels and maybe the Rock Machine, too."

"What about Michel?" Sammie asked.

Willy shrugged. "Who cares? He's a pimple. Once the dust settles, he'll either fall into line or have a tragic accident. One thing for sure, though, the trap you set with that press conference just went south."

It was a workable theory—one I hadn't considered. We'd certainly witnessed similar ham-handed power plays before. But there were subtleties here that had dogged me from the start—ancient alliances that resisted fitting the brutal picture Willy had painted.

Like between Marie Chenin and Michel, whose playboy past, I thought, had helped camouflage a far more complicated and dangerous personality.

"Guidry was garroted with a wire," I said. "Why not shoot him or blow him up? Did Picard strike any one of you as a man who'd order that kind of death?"

"It's not like he did it himself," Willy argued. "He probably told one of his psychos to do the dirty work and the guy put a little of his own into it."

But Sammie wasn't buying it, either. "There's a way this all fits together, and it's not Picard suddenly getting pissed at Guidry. This guy's waited half a century for his plan to play out, for Christ's sake. He's going to get impulsive now?"

"I'm wondering about Marie Chenin," I finally admitted. "Lacombe just told me she and Michel had a very emotional private meeting shortly before Guidry was found dead and Picard disappeared. I think it was so she could tell him she'd been used by those two to frame Marcel. When Paul and I met with her, it was pretty clear she didn't know why she'd been asked to produce the receipt to the Snow Dancer Hotel. She hated Marcel for the disrespect he'd shown Jean and Antoine, not because she thought he'd killed one of them. And when I asked her where Guidry and Picard had been when Jean went missing, it looked like a light lit up in her head, which I'm sure had everything to do with Picard. I think she squealed to Michel to atone for fingering Marcel, inadvertently adding to the mayhem in the process."

Tom returned to a problem he'd had from the start. "She was also the one who claimed Jean's investigation into his son's death was a secret, and backed up Pelletier by saying Jean went to Stowe alone as a result. That was probably a setup by Picard and Guidry to keep themselves out of the picture, especially after they discovered Marcel really did think his father had traveled solo."

"But why would she have allied herself with those two?" Sam asked. "We know Guidry at least was buddy-buddy with Marcel, and she hated Marcel. What was the angle there?"

"Money," Willy said shortly.

"Partly," I agreed. "Also, it must have been tough for her, losing two lovers, one right after the other, both murdered. She was young, impressionable, attracted to strong men. It makes sense she'd form an alternate alliance with somebody in that situation."

"Picard?" Tom asked.

"That's what I think," I said. "He's a patient planner. It probably meant nothing to him to tuck her into his pocket for future use—or just to have her available. Pretty much what he was doing with a lot of people behind Marcel's back."

Sammie scowled. "But Guidry killed Jean. If you're saying she knew they were together down here, you're undermining your own theory."

"I think she was given compelling proof of Guidry's innocence," I said.

Willy was becoming irritable. "What the hell's that mean?"

But Tom had seen where I was headed. "He's saying someone else killed Jean."

It was eleven o'clock at night when the phone rang. Normally still up at that hour, I'd called it quits early to catch up on some sleep, and so had to grope around a few seconds, both for the phone and the wits with which to answer it.

"Yeah?"

"Is this Joe Gunther?" The voice was hesitant, no doubt surprised by my gruffness.

"Yeah. Sorry. What's up?"

"No, *I'm* sorry. I didn't mean to wake you up. I was told this would be okay."

"It is, it is. Who're you?"

"Oh, right. Patrolman Jim Patton of the Stowe police. We haven't actually met, but the Chief asked me to call. He's got something to show you and wanted to know if you could drop by the PD to take a look at it."

"Now?"

Patton paused, obviously in a spot. "I, uh... I guess it could wait. He's actually coming in from another direction. I could get him on the radio, maybe, and tell him tomorrow morning would be better."

I sighed. "Don't worry about it. I'll be there in fifteen minutes."

"You sure?"

"Yeah." I hung up and lay in the dark staring at the ceiling for a couple of minutes, finishing the process of waking up. As he said he would, Frank Auerbach had largely stayed out of the picture until the Sawyer killing. But now his department was looking at two unsolved homicides, and even with Bill Allard's having opened up the spigots to deliver more VBI agents, Auerbach still had his hands full—putting out political wildfires, if nothing else.

I had no idea what he had to show me, or why it was so urgent.

Ten minutes later, I'd washed my face, put my clothes back on, and was heading out the door for the short drive to the PD. The hallway outside was quiet and dark. I heard the muted rumble of an ice machine somewhere in the distance. I pocketed my key and headed toward the lobby.

"*Joe.*"

It was a loud whisper from my right. I stopped and saw a door partway open, only darkness beyond it.

"In here—*quick.*"

I hesitated, took an automatic step in the door's direction, and began to say, "Who is—?" when two arms reached out, grabbed me by the shoulders, and pulled me across the threshold in a neck-snapping jerk. Before I could shout out, a knee came up and caught me in the stomach, knocking the wind out of me and sending me sprawling to the floor.

Gasping for air, writhing in pain, I felt hands all over me, pinning me in place, stuffing something soft into my mouth, and wrapping what felt like thin wire around my hands and feet. Outside of a single "Don't hurt him," there were no words spoken, the lights stayed off, and the men around me acted like a well-rehearsed team. Finally, one of them lay on top of me, making all movement impossible, and several hands gripped one of my arms with viselike ferocity. Still struggling as much as I could, I heard the slight click of plastic hitting plastic, and then felt a sharp needle jab in my shoulder.

I heaved up convulsively, but too late. Almost instantly, I felt a numbness spreading out from the injection site, and in under a minute, my body began relaxing despite my best efforts. The last thing I remembered was feeling as I had just a half hour before, when I'd turned off the light to drift off to sleep.

The only distraction being that this time I was going under in the middle of a panic.

It was dark when I woke up with a headache so blistering, I thought I saw small planets circling my head. I closed my eyes, concentrated on trying to dislodge the cloth wad in my mouth, got nowhere, and ended up sitting motionless, trying to figure out what the hell was happening.

That was when I heard the sound—a pulsing, rhythmic thunder I could feel throughout my body—and realized how cold I was. I thought back to when I was on Mount Mansfield, again in the cold, the dark, and all alone, surrounded by the howling wind.

Except this was not wind.

I steadied the fear rising within me, breathing through my nose in slow, steady repetitions, and concentrated.

I was riding a train.

I opened my eyes again. The planets were still there—dim, perfect circles, in front of me but not extending to either side, and illuminated like gentle nightlights in a child's room. I blinked several times, trying to adjust my focus against the aftereffects of the drug I'd been given.

They were breathing holes. I was in a box.

The fear subsided. It almost made sense, although why I'd been kidnapped instead of killed I didn't know. But I knew I was heading north into Canada, that I was a guest of one of the Deschamps factions, and that given the effort put into my packaging, I was in no immediate lethal danger—assuming the gag in my mouth didn't swell any bigger with my own saliva.

I tried wiggling my feet and hands. Circulation was good, although the hands were half numb from the cold, but I could feel I'd been strapped to a chair of some kind, which in turn, I supposed, had been mounted to the inside of my box. I'd been as carefully encased as an egg in a carton.

One of the planets darkened on the right, then another beside it, then a third as the first reappeared. Someone was moving in front of my refuge, slowly and without sound.

I heard a slight scratching about waist high, then a loud snap, and finally the breathing holes were replaced by an enormous rectangle as the front of the box swung back to reveal the shadow of a man standing before me.

A man with a withered right arm.

Willy Kunkle reached forward, pulled the duct tape from my mouth, causing no small amount of pain, and plucked the wadding from my mouth.

"You okay?" he asked quietly.

I couldn't speak at first, my mouth was so dry. I nodded.

He took a penlight from his coat pocket, held it between his teeth, and began loosening my bonds. As he freed one hand and then the other, I bent forward to finish the job myself, at last finding my voice.

"We heading to Canada?"

"Already there," he said. "I think to Sherbrooke. You been out for a couple of hours."

"How'd you find me?"

He stepped away from the box's entrance so I could try to stand up—easier said than done given how long I'd been cooped up. "I saw the grab. I wasn't so sure Guidry's death meant they still wouldn't try to nail you. They're in such a mess right now, who knows who's following whose orders? So I've been keeping an eye on you. I'm right across the hall, so I heard your phone ring and was up when you left. Saw three guys mug you and followed you here."

"Does anyone else know?"

I could just make out his rueful expression in the dim light. "Caught me by surprise. I didn't have time to let anyone know. They hustled you out pretty fast. I thought about doin' a John Wayne—maybe shoot one and bust the others, but then I heard one of them say not to hurt you, so I figured it might be better to see where they led me. Besides, I might've got you killed." He smiled suddenly. "And you're kind of my meal ticket right now."

I stood up at last and started moving around, flexing my limbs as much to get them warm as to check their condition. "We in a boxcar now?"

"Yeah. Bonded so it didn't get checked at the border. Trust a bunch of smugglers to have a few customs people in their pocket."

"How'd you get in?"

Willy shook his head. "Jesus Christ. What's with all the questions? I slipped in while they were wrestling the box on board."

I could sense his own self-doubts, which, given the man, would never find voice. A less bull-headed, more reasonable course of action would have been to identify the car I was in, locate a phone, and get the authorities to stop the train.

Not Willy's style at all, and not that I was about to complain.

"You find a way out of here yet?" I asked instead.

The real reason for his testiness became clear. "No."

I borrowed the penlight and began exploring our prison. It was much larger inside than it might've looked speeding by at a railroad crossing, and aside from a few small ventilation portals letting in the dim light, as tightly sealed as the crate I'd been in minutes earlier. As far as I could tell, there was but one way in or out, and that was the car's huge, central sliding door, which was locked.

I returned Willy's pen to him and asked, "Got a plan?"

In reply, he squatted down, reached up under his pants leg, extracted a small semi-automatic, and handed it to me.

I peered at it in the gloom—a very nasty, compact piece. "I suppose now's not the time to tell you this is a violation."

He smiled benignly. "I'm handicapped. We're exempt."

He handed me an extra clip from an inside pocket, shoved a smaller wooden box over to one side of the large entrance to hide behind, and motioned to me to do the same opposite him. It wasn't original or flashy, but it was a plan, and it had a hopeful element of surprise factored in. All things considered, it made me feel almost confident.

CHAPTER TWENTY-FOUR

We stayed hidden on either side of the boxcar door for another hour. I got up periodically to move around, do some jumping jacks, and otherwise fight the cold. Willy sat as still as a stone sentry. By the time I felt the train slowing down, I half suspected that even given the uncertainty we faced, he'd fallen fast asleep.

The steady rhythm of wheels hitting track joints became jumbled as we entered a train yard, crossing junctions and switches, the train finally creeping as it searched out its berth. By the muffled sounds of bells, street traffic, and other trains passing by, I imagined we were enmeshed in the tangle of tracks on the south shore of the Magog River that I'd seen from Lacombe's office window the first day I'd visited him.

At last, we came to a shuddering, clanking stop, the sudden silence feeling louder than the noise just preceding it. Across from me, Willy briefly laid his gun down before him and gave me a thumbs up.

I quietly checked to make sure I had a round chambered, slipped off the safety, and waited.

When it finally came, that first sound made me think of a rodent—slight, stealthy, and evasive. There was a delicate scratching at the hasp, followed by a small click, and then a low moaning as someone pushed gently against the heavy door. A fresh current of cold air swirled into our dark enclave as a pale slit appeared in the wall between us, gradually growing to about five feet wide, or a little larger than the width of my erstwhile box.

We'd resealed that earlier, and left it parked front and center. Now, the dark shape of a man crossed from the opening to the crate and lit up the corner of one of its sides with a flashlight.

After a moment's scrutiny, he let out a low command in *Joual,* prompting another shadow with a dolly to join him from outside.

This was our moment, since as soon as these two tilted the crate on its side, they'd realize it was too light for its presumed contents. Looking across at Willy, I pointed first to him and then at the door, at me and then at the two near the box. He nodded once and we moved as a single unit.

I took five fast steps to the man closest to me, pushed the back of his head so he fell forward with both hands braced against the box, shoved my gun against his temple so his buddy could see what I was doing, and said, "Don't move—police."

Simultaneously, Willy had swung around to the open door, stuck his head out quickly, found a third man standing guard, and silently gestured to him with his gun barrel to join us.

We stripped them of their weapons, had them lie on their stomachs, and used the wire and duct tape that had once bound me to tie their hands and feet. Their mouths I left free.

"Who's in charge here?" I asked them.

One of them said something fast in French, presumably not a compliment.

"No one going to fess up?" I turned to Willy and winked at him as I spoke. "Drag the big one over to the far side of the car, interrogate him any way you want. I'll work on these two. We'll see who comes up with the best story."

Willy laughed. "All right. This ought to be fun."

He holstered his gun, grabbed the man in question by the scruff of the neck, and hauled him away into the shadows.

I squatted down between the remaining two and rolled them both onto their backs so they could see me. "I hope the guy Willy's talking to has a low pain threshold—might speed things up."

Behind us, the sounds of Willy's retreat faded into the distance, accompanied by several dull thumps and a few guttural outbursts from his guest.

"Okay," I resumed. "I don't speak French and you're pretending not to speak English, but let me tell you how this plays out just in case one of you is a quick learner. I'm a kidnapped American police officer, in mortal fear for his life, rescued in the nick of time by a heroic fellow officer. Through a trick of fate I haven't invented yet, we managed to get hold of at least one of your guns." I held up the largest of the confiscated weapons. The more intelligent-looking of the two narrowed his eyes slightly, obviously confused about where I was headed.

"All the Sûreté'll know is that we had to fight it out, killing you one by one. It'll be a hell of a story—make me look like a hero. And the local cops'll eat it up 'cause that's the way they wish a lot of these things would turn out."

I slowly pulled back the gun's hammer.

"You're full of shit," the one I'd focused on said, his words straight from some American action movie and his accent sounding as if the dialogue had been dubbed into French and back again.

"You think so?"

We were interrupted by a loud noise and a sharp cry from far down the boxcar.

I leaned into the man's face. "What's your name?"

"Didier."

"Well, let me tell you, Didier, I've been shot at, punched, drugged, and half frozen to death by you flamers, all of which has given birth to a giant case of the give-a-shits. I'm home free here—the helpless victim fighting to save his life. Even if the Sûreté does smell a rat, they'll cut me some slack because we're all brothers and you're not. Face it—you're out of luck."

There was another yell from the gloom. Didier tried to raise his head. "What's he doin'?"

"Willy doesn't talk as much as I do," I explained. "Gets right down to business. Guarantees him more fun that way."

"This is a crock. I watch TV. I know the 'good cop–bad cop' routine."

I believed him about the TV. "You want to risk your friend's health on that?" I asked.

He closed his eyes briefly. The man next to him said something, which Didier answered tiredly.

He then looked at me again. "We got you pegged. Your sidekick ain't much, but he's no torturer. Besides, the guy he grabbed don't speak English."

"So you say." But I was as impressed by his insight as I'd been by his John Wayne imitation. This was a step above the average thug.

Didier sighed heavily. "It don't matter anyway. You already won without knowin' it. I'll talk, but not because of this little comedy."

"Why, then?"

He hesitated, as if taking one last measure of a final step forward. "Marcel Deschamps is in a car near here, waiting for us."

That caught me unawares. "I thought he was almost dead."

"He is—this deal was a gamble, to buy his son time."

"Michel?"

Didier made a sour expression. "It's complicated. He better tell you himself."

"Who says he'll want to talk to me?"

"I do. The three of us are about all he has left."

"What about the three who grabbed me?"

"Goons—bought and paid for. They had no idea."

I looked at him suspiciously. "We've been studying the Deschamps organization pretty closely," I said. "I don't remember anyone high up named Didier."

His voice sounded tired. "We're not on the

inside. We're hired guns—worked for Marcel for years, and now Michel. Marcel didn't trust his own people no more, so he used us behind the scenes."

I thought about that for a moment. Marcel's having private operatives didn't surprise me, but given Michel's reputation, I hadn't expected him in the same context. Then again, little of anything we'd guessed about this bunch had turned out to be true. "You kill Guidry?"

That brought a defensive reaction. "No way. We get things done, find things out. But we're not triggermen. That was Michel all by his lonesome."

"The way we heard it, Michel can barely wipe his own ass."

"Old news. He's a snot nose, and Picard and Guidry helped keep him in the dark so they could make the grab after his father croaked. But Marcel tumbled and faked being sicker than he was. He's the one who put Michel and us together and then trained Michel so their power play would blow up in their face." He paused and then added, "Of course, that was Plan A, before Michel turned into a magic act and came out of the top hat as full-fledged wacko."

My headache had faded over time. It now caught its second wind. "Did he kill Sawyer?"

"Guidry did that, and put a contract on you before. He was paranoid you'd pin Jean's death on him."

"We already had."

Didier smiled and shook his head, by now

totally free of any inhibitions about talking. "In your dreams. You've been wrong from the start. Guidry didn't kill Jean Deschamps. He was just in the right place at the right time."

"What do you mean?"

But this time he didn't play along. "Enough. We got to get back to Marcel. The motor's off—he'll start getting cold. You want to take me to him and leave the other two with the gimp, fine, but I'm done talking till I make sure Marcel's okay."

"Willy?" I shouted over my shoulder. "Bring the other guy back."

He did so, still dragging his prize like a sack along the floor. The man's mouth had been taped shut, and there wasn't a mark on him. Willy was looking satisfied with his play-acting as a torturer. "You get what you wanted?" he asked.

I pointed at Didier. "He nailed you from the start, not that it matters. He's spilling his guts anyhow. Marcel Deschamps is in a car near here, waiting for these three. I'm going to have a talk with him, if you don't mind babysitting the other two."

"I don't mind," he said, "but I'd like to scope the scene before you stick your head into another trap."

I conceded the point. We bundled Didier's companions together, back-to-back, left them temporarily in the boxcar, and escorted Didier, still bound and now gagged, out of the rail yard, across a service road, and to a row of trees lining a parking lot behind a dark, empty-looking warehouse. Alone in the lot was a white delivery van. Didier pointed his chin toward it.

"He in there?" I asked.

He nodded.

Willy left our side and disappeared into the shadows hemming us in, as quietly as the gentle breeze that occasionally wafted in off the ice-solid water beyond the tracks.

Fifteen minutes later, Willy reappeared. "It's clear. I'll keep watch for a while after you get in, then go back to the others. How long's the train staying put?"

I removed the duct tape from Didier's mouth. He gasped with the pain, compressed his lips several times, and finally said, "Seven tomorrow morning."

He and I crossed the parking lot. I walked up to the sliding side door of the van, placed Didier before me as a shield, and pulled it open. Before us in the feeble light from the overhead dome lay Marcel Deschamps, propped up on a camp cot, swathed like a baby in layers of blankets. He didn't look startled at the sudden intrusion. I even half wondered if he was still alive.

Until his eyes moved.

"Deschamps?" I asked. "You okay?"

He said something in French to Didier.

"English," I ordered.

Didier answered first in French and then turned to me. "I only told him we'd screwed up, and that I'd been shooting straight with you. Can I start the engine and get the heater going?"

I unwrapped the wire from around his hands and let him climb up between the front seats to get behind the steering wheel. "You touch the gear lever and I'll blow your head off," I cautioned him, as I quickly patted down Marcel's blankets for weapons.

I needn't have been so cautious. Didier kept his word, clambering back to Deschamps to tuck him in more comfortably. Throughout, Marcel's gloved hands lay still on his lap and his eyes remained at half mast.

"You feel well enough to speak?" I asked him, at last climbing in myself and slamming the door shut behind me.

"A little," was the whispered reply.

I decided not to waste time. "I need to know about your father's death."

If possible, the face before me paled even further, and Marcel moved the fingers of one hand in Didier's direction. "Tell him."

"Jean Deschamps was sort of nutty about finding Antoine's killer," Didier began. "He tracked down Roger Scott because he thought Scott and his son had been tight during the war. According to what Jean had been told, Scott was a schoolteacher before the war, and maybe a good judge of human character. Jean wanted to pick his brains about Antoine. Turns out Scott was actually Charlie Webber, and that him and Antoine had found a treasure just outside Rome—a buried trunk in a fancy villa, jammed with jewelry, rare art, and gold. But one of 'em got greedy, Webber killed Antoine, making it look like a combat death, and then changed his name after he got shot and paralyzed later. I have no clue how Jean knew Antoine had been whacked in the first place, but he sure didn't know Scott and Webber were the same. What happened when Jean and Webber met is a mystery—Guidry was the only other one there and being the swift bodyguard he was, he was outside the room. But for some reason Webber ended up sticking Jean with an ice pick. Didn't do him much good, 'course. He might've been strong enough to knock somebody off, but he still couldn't get out of that wheelchair. Guidry came running in, put two and two together, and saw the chance of a lifetime."

"He's not that clever," I said flatly.

Marcel gave a pale imitation of a laugh.

"Picard sure is," Didier answered for him. "Guidry called him that night in a panic. Picard drove down and they set it up together."

It was like hearing a tune that had lingered too long just outside memory's grasp. In that single moment, all the disconnected bits and pieces of this case began falling together.

"How did Sawyer fit in?"

"He was a money launderer Jean had authorized the year before. Stowe was nothin' then, but it was a coming thing and it was nearby. The U.S. dollar was lookin' good. Picard being the legal eagle sent Sawyer down from Canada to open a restaurant, which is a great way to wash money. Picard came up with the angle of keeping Jean's body on ice—typical lawyer move—but he needed a freezer. Enter Sawyer."

"And they had to move fast," I suggested. "Before the snow melted and Jean's body thawed."

"Right on. After that, all they had to do was con Marcel with fake loyalty, be rewarded with top jobs, and cruise through the years on what Jean had created by busting his ass—knowing all the time they had a big-time secret tucked away for future use."

"But Marcel's fingerprints were on the ice pick," I protested.

Marcel looked disgusted.

"Piece of cake," Didier explained. "Ice picks were used all the time back then. All Guidry had to do was hand Marcel this one a couple of times to chop ice. The only joke was that DNA came out of nowhere to help 'em out even more. That was pure dumb luck. Anyhow, once the ice pick was squared away, they planted the other clues you found and made sure they had a small gang in their pocket to back them if things got tough, which of course they were hoping would be never."

"Like Marie Chenin and Lucien Pelletier," I guessed.

"And their inside man, Jacques Chauvin," Didier agreed. "Not counting some hired muscle. All of 'em either pointed you where they wanted you to go, or told Picard and Guidry what you were telling the Sûreté. Like when they leaked Jean's name to the U.S. papers as the frozen stiff, just so Chenin could pretend the publicity reminded her that she had that old hotel bill."

"And the trigger for all this was Marcel getting sick and Michel being tapped to replace him?" I asked.

"Right."

"Hadn't they anticipated that possibility? No offense, but none of them is any spring chicken."

Marcel's whole body quivered slightly and he raised a hand to point at me. "I knew. I knew."

Didier leaned forward and adjusted the sick man's blankets again after he fell back against the pillows, exhausted.

"Marcel had been smelling a rat for years," he said over his shoulder, "at the same time that the other two were getting suspicious about how much Marcel knew, which really wasn't that much. So each side was making plans and building up private manpower while they were all pretending to be a big happy family. Picard and Guidry found out they weren't going to be able to use Michel like they'd used Marcel after Jean's death, so they sprang their trap."

"By pulling their fifty-year-old frozen rabbit out of the closet," I concluded.

Didier smiled. "Yeah—too much, huh? Dumping him out of a plane? You gotta give 'em points for style."

"Who flew the plane?" I asked.

He shrugged. "Beats me. Lot of guys might do that for the right amount. But that was just the beginning, anyway. They also had to fake a war with the Angels. They knocked off Tessier, since they knew he was in Marcel's pocket—not knowing Tessier had the three of us as backup—and then they killed the guy who supposedly called you that night at the old jail. You were a big help. And then they sliced one of their own and put an Angel's button in his hand. Very Hollywood."

"And very useless after Marcel passed the polygraph," I said.

"Yeah. That's when the shit hit the fan," Didier agreed.

I looked directly at Marcel. "But you still didn't know who'd killed your father."

Marcel merely tapped the side of his head.

"He had a pretty good idea. It just happened to be wrong. We only figured it out after Guidry lost his nerve, tried to knock you off, and did kill Sawyer."

That still didn't make sense to me. "How? Those dots don't connect to Roger Scott."

There was an awkward silence. Marcel's glance fell to his idle hands.

"Michel did that," Didier said. "He got tired of screwing around, grabbed Guidry, and got it out of him."

I shook my head. "He tortured him. I knew he was shy a full load. You guys are too much."

Again Marcel jerked to life, waving a hand at me and croaking, "They are the killers. We were just businessmen."

I didn't argue with him. "I'm guessing Picard suffered the same fate. Where's he stored?"

There was no comment from either one of them.

"Why grab me, then?" I persisted. "What

was that going to do for you? You told me you were buying time for Michel. Am I the diversion while he heads out of the country?"

Again, there was only silence. I looked from one of them to the other, wondering at this sudden reticence, reviewing all I'd learned. As far as the Deschamps lineage was concerned, the three relevant intertwining threads were ego, pride, and revenge. Jean had set out to redress his son's murder in Italy. Marcel had conspired with his son to right the wrong of Jean's death. So what of Michel in this parody of a Greek tragedy? He'd killed in turn, ignorant of ever having known either Jean or Antoine, but inflamed by passions he'd inherited in psychopathic proportions from a father only reputed to be as cold as a calculator—but who'd proved to have been willing to sacrifice his final legacy for the sake of family honor.

Michel had to be the remaining loose missile in all this, and the silence I was getting now implied that his destiny was as yet unfulfilled.

A coldness crept into me as I finally understood.

I swung around, opened the door, and stepped outside, looking back at Marcel one last time. "I may have been behind the ball on most of this, but I am goddamned if I'm going to let this play out the way you want it to. You can go to your death knowing your vanity destroyed your own son."

Marcel's eyes widened and he opened his mouth to speak, but I slammed the door to cut him off. I'd already heard more than I wanted to.

CHAPTER TWENTY-FIVE

I ran back to the railroad yard as fast as I could, slipping on the snow, calling Willy's name before I even reached our boxcar.

He stuck his head out the door, his gun in hand. "What the hell's goin' on?"

"We gotta find a phone. Fast," I said, already heading back out toward the street.

"What about these two?" He shouted after me.

"Take their wallets for the IDs and cut them loose. We can round them up later."

Willy caught up to me as I was slowing down before a public phone booth mounted to the side of a darkened building.

"What happened?"

I picked up the receiver and began dialing the Stowe police department. "If we're lucky, nothing yet. The reason I was grabbed was to stall us."

The dispatcher picked up on the other end.

"This is Joe Gunther. Is the Chief there? It's an emergency."

"Nobody's here. The patrol's out and everyone else is in bed."

"Roust them out, then. Send a unit to the Roger Scott residence. Somebody's on the way to kill him, if he hasn't already. You know the address?"

"Yes, sir."

"Okay, move on it. I'm in Sherbrooke with Kunkle and heading your way as fast as I can."

"Who's trying to knock him off?" Willy asked as I stepped from the booth to the curbside, having just noticed a patrol car in the far distance beginning to turn down a side street.

"Fire your gun a couple of times at that pile of pallets," I told him.

He did so immediately, filling the night air with noise and two blinding flashes. The car stopped, straightened out, and its strobe lights came to life.

"I think we just got a ride," I said.

Thirty minutes later, we were in a helicopter heading for the American border like a darkened rocket in the night—Willy, Gilles Lacombe, myself, and the flight crew.

Lacombe was on a cell phone, as he had been virtually from the moment we'd left the ground, exchanging information with his people back at headquarters.

Willy and I were wearing headsets, connected to the onboard communications.

"Why in Christ's name is Michel going after Scott?" Willy asked over the engine's din.

"To satisfy family honor," I told him. "The

real Scott was killed in battle—something I was told days ago but didn't follow up on. Another man named Webber—a certified weasel—stole his dog tags, probably for a rainy day, and then later relieved some Italian villa of a zillion dollars' worth of jewels, art, and gold, killing Antoine Deschamps at the same time."

"You're kidding me. A heist?"

"Not surprising, given the people involved. Anyway, my guess is Webber shipped it home somehow—easy if you knew the right people—but then got shot and crippled in southern France. He also was reported killed—probably by himself—which is when I think he put those stolen dog tags to good use. Roger Scott was reborn as a wounded vet, shipped home to meet up with his loot and a future as a rich Stowe eccentric."

"Did Jean Deschamps know that?"

"No, which is why he was so relaxed when he came to Stowe to interview Scott—eating out on the town and staying at a fancy inn."

"So Scott killed father and son both," Willy said.

"Right. The way Marcel's been polluting his brain, Michel doesn't think he has anything left to lose. His own father's all but dead of cancer, he's killed both Picard and Guidry, the organization's about to be eaten by jackals, so all that remains is family pride. The final debt must be paid, regardless of the cost."

Lacombe shut his phone down and put on a pair of headsets. "They have just located Marcel Deschamps in a van in his own driveway.

337

The preliminary evidence is telling us he is dead of an overdose."

"Suicide?" I asked.

"That I do not know. Was he strong enough to do it?"

I considered that, along with the dexterity it would have taken. It was clear to me Didier had followed orders one last time. But I wasn't sure—had I been in his shoes—that I wouldn't have done the same thing.

"He might have been—yes," I told Lacombe. "Did they find the others? Didier and his two pals?"

"Not yet, but they did find Gaston Picard in the basement of the Deschamps home."

"Tortured to death?"

Lacombe merely nodded as the pilot broke in, speaking English out of courtesy. "You might want to take a look out the port window," he said. "I'm also switching you over to the police frequency below, by their request."

We all three craned toward a flickering glow in the left window. I clearly recognized the outline of Roger Scott's castlelike mansion below us, engulfed in flames like a vision of Hell.

"Joe, you there?"

I recognized Frank Auerbach's voice.

"We're right overhead, Frank. Is Scott still alive?"

"We got complications there. We set up an LZ for you upwind to the northwest. I'll see you after you land."

• • •

From the ground, the fire looked like it was spewing from a volcano, spiraling upward as if propelled from deep below the surface. It roared and crackled with cyclonic energy, pulling oxygen toward it with enough force to make our clothes flap.

Frank Auerbach came running toward the helicopter with Paul Spraiger in tow.

"What complications?" I yelled at him over the rotor noise and fire combined.

He pointed to a small stone building precariously near the inferno. "They're in that garden house—Scott and the guy you warned us about. Sammie's with them."

"We were told there was another guy, too."

But Willy Kunkle grabbed Frank's lapel in his fist before he could answer me, shaking him as he shouted, "What the hell do you mean, Sammie's with them? That place is about to go up, you stupid bastard."

I laid my hand on his and shook my head. "What's going on, Frank?"

Auerbach had freed himself and was already walking toward the building, circling around to keep it between the flames and us, since the heat was almost unbearable.

He spoke over his shoulder. "Our first units got here just as Scott was being dragged out of the house by what's-his-name. The other guy got away—he was seen running off and we haven't been able to find him."

"So it is Michel Deschamps in there?"

"Right. He had a gun, held them off, and barricaded himself in the garden house. Sammie went in to negotiate before I could stop her, and she won't come out."

"God damn her," Willy snarled. "Typical."

We were about thirty yards away from the building's front door, shielding our faces with our hands to avoid being burned by the towering flames beyond it. Frank spoke into his portable radio, and one of the deck guns mounted to a distant fire truck swung over and doused us with a cooling, drenching shower—an incongruous sensation in an otherwise sub-zero night.

"Okay," he yelled, "let's go. I talked to the fire chief just before you landed. We'll be lucky if we have ten minutes before that place ignites."

Doubled over in our watery cocoon, we began walking toward the cottage's door, straight toward the searing, howling, air-sucking maelstrom overarching it, straining to see what was happening beyond the doorway. A hundred feet shy of the cottage, however, there was a sudden low rumble, like the sound of a truck entering a tunnel at high speed, followed by a huge, round, boiling bubble of fire that burst from the open door and the two windows on either side of it.

We stopped dead in our tracks, stunned by what we'd seen, utterly and instantly convinced that no human could have survived it.

Willy began running toward the heat, screaming.

Frank and I only hesitated a second before

following. Although that one fireball had come and gone in an instant, there was little doubting its effect. We were giving chase to save Willy's life, and no more.

Inside, the light was red and yellow and orange in a dancing demonic medley, throwing shadows against the walls like a slide projector gone wild, making visibility difficult and confusing. Also, now free of the water's protective mantle, my skin instantly began to sting in the oven-hot heat.

Willy was on his knees, his back to us, before an upended slate potting table, his one arm flailing as he threw what looked like gunny sacks over his shoulder, finally revealing a startled Sammie Martens lying dazed beneath them.

"Cut it out," she yelled at him, struggling to sit up. "I need those to protect my face."

"I thought you were dead," he said in a half sob, frozen in mid-motion.

After a split-second pause, she reached up and gently touched his cheek with a grimy hand. "It went overhead. I'm okay." She pulled herself up by the table edge, trying to see beyond it into the room. "What about Michel?"

The rest of us then followed her gaze, suddenly reminded of what had brought us here.

There, against the far stone wall, leaned a wide-eyed Michel Deschamps—his hair gone, his face blotched red and peeling—crouching behind a wheelchair-bound and slumped-over Roger Scott. He had a gun jammed against the crippled man's temple, although it wasn't clear the latter was even alive.

We dropped down immediately as Michel screamed in English, "Back off or I'll shoot him. I swear I will."

We shuffled up next to Sammie, who, barely glancing at us, shouted, "Relax, Michel. This is a no-win situation. There're dozens of cops outside and you're badly hurt. Just put down the gun so we can get you out. You did what you came to do—the house is toast and the treasure along with it. Scott's a pauper now. Your family's avenged. Come on, Michel. There's not much time left. It's a miracle we're all still alive."

"I don't need time," he answered above the freight train rumbling of the fire behind the wall. "I need this man dead."

"Then shoot the son-of-a-bitch and get it over with," Willy shouted.

Sammie broke her concentration to stare at him.

"I want you out of here," he told her.

"Michel," I called out. "It's Joe Gunther. I just came from Sherbrooke. It's all over. Your father's dead. Let's end this. You put your gun down and we'll bring that man to justice—hold him accountable for killing your uncle and grandfather both. It'll be clear to the world what he did. You die in here, nobody'll know. You'll just go down as being a madman."

I could barely breathe because of the heat by now, and had stripped off most of my upper clothing despite my burning skin. In the shifting, crimson light, the rafters and window casings were beginning to smoke, building up to a second, perhaps permanent blowout.

"We got to get out of here," Auerbach warned. "That's not a request."

"I can get them out alive," Sammie said barely audibly, her arm still balanced on the table's edge, her weapon pointing directly at the two before us.

But it was no longer her call to make. In a gesture as fatalistic as it was born of a survivor's instinct, Roger Scott suddenly came alive, swept back with one arm and caught Michel on the side of the head, throwing him off balance.

Michel staggered out from behind his human shield just long enough for Sammie to say, "Shit," and shoot him between the eyes.

As Michel slumped to the floor next to the wheelchair, however, Scott leaned over and snatched the pistol from his dying hand. A hellish smile on his parboiled face, he then pointed the gun at us, yelled, "Get it done!" and began firing.

Willy and Sam both emptied their magazines into him.

Auerbach didn't hesitate. As the first rafters overhead suddenly burst into flames, he shouted, "Out, out, out!" and started grabbing shoulders and arms, pushing us toward the open door.

As we ran toward the welcoming cool darkness, a muffled roar told us the entire garden shed had burst into flame.

We stood in a circle outside the Stowe PD command post a few hundred feet from the flames—a large truck equipped with radios, cell phones, and things to eat and drink—being tended to by EMS people who were trying to cover us with blankets and treat our burned faces and hands, although we weren't being too cooperative. Everywhere I looked, I could see flashing red and blue lights—all of them made paltry by the towering pyre before us.

"What a way to go," Sammie said, still shaken by the ordeal.

"Scott chose his," Willy said simply, pausing to drink from a Styrofoam coffee cup, either recovered from his emotional outburst or working hard to pretend it hadn't happened. "Took a little trip back to the good-ol'-days and died like a Forceman should. I don't know about Michel."

"I doubt Michel knew either," I admitted. "He had so many devils dancing in his head, I don't think he had a clue anymore. He just plain ran out of options." I gave Sammie a look. "Nothing you could've said would've changed that."

"I suppose," she murmured, looking both defeated and exhausted.

"That wasn't true for Scott, though," Auerbach argued. "We had nothing on him that would've stuck."

Paul Spraiger had been standing on the edge, staring at the blaze, seemingly lost in thought. He turned at Frank's comment and pointed to the fire. "We weren't part of his thinking. He'd already died with that... His whole life is in those flames—the life he created from scratch, probably from the day he

344

stole Roger Scott's dog tags from his corpse, not even knowing why."

He turned to face me directly. "Sammie told me about the mask you saw when you visited him."

I nodded vaguely. "Yeah—ugly thing."

"Ugly maybe, but pretty important."

I glanced at him. "How?"

"I found a picture of it and showed it to her. If she's right, it was called *Mask of a Faun*—believed to have been sculpted by Michelangelo when he was fifteen. A priceless work of art—unique."

"You think it was the same one?"

"It vanished in 1944, from a hiding place outside Rome."

We all fell silent for a while, contemplating the wreckage we'd witnessed.

"You think the mask could survive a fire like that?" I finally asked.

Paul thought a moment. "If they don't find it in the ashes—which isn't likely—we may never know. Real or fake, it's probably been pulverized by the heat and debris... Unless it vanished just before this was set."

I glanced at him and he shrugged. "Along with Michel's mysterious companion."

CHAPTER TWENTY-SIX

I'd just shut my suitcase when Willy Kunkle knocked on the open door and entered my motel room. Our blistered faces made us look like we'd spent too much time on the beach.

"Headin' home?" he asked.

"Eventually. I've got to wrap up a few things with the brass in Waterbury, and I want to say hi to Gail in Montpelier. Feel like I haven't seen her in months. But then I'll head home. Be nice to take a few days off, turn something out in the woodworking shop. What're you up to?"

He was wandering around the room, brushing his fingers along whatever surface was near. "I don't know. Maybe goof around a little. Go over to New York State. Whatever."

I straightened and looked at him. "I didn't know you went in for sightseeing trips."

He didn't return my gaze. "Yeah, well... It's Sammie's deal."

I smiled and turned away, pretending to fidget with the suitcase some more. "Sure—should be fun. I ought to get Gail off for a weekend soon. Give her a break."

There was a long, awkward silence.

"I'm really glad she made it out alive," I said softly.

He sighed and finally settled down on the edge of the window sill. "God, I was so scared..."

I didn't speak, startled by an emotion I'd

never before witnessed in Willy, and continued my fiddling.

He cleared his throat. "So...about this VBI job..."

"You want to stick with it?" I asked, looking up at last.

He gave a half shrug. "I doubt it's up to me, and they strike me as a pretty snotty bunch."

I picked up my bag and headed for the door. "You know how I feel about it, and you're looking good in my report. You might be surprised—we may catch 'em at a weak moment."

I paused on the threshold to look back at his silhouette, framed against the window's white gauze curtains. His head was bowed as he stared at the floor, his one good arm stretched out, his palm resting on the sill. A complicated, difficult man, fighting more internal battles than any of us could know, except—maybe, eventually—for Sammie, if she could stick it out. I was suddenly tempted to ask him what he was thinking about—to gain access to some of that turmoil. But I guessed what his reaction would be, so I resisted, closing the door instead to leave him with his thoughts.